MOMS' NIGHT OUT

Written by
TRICIA GOYER

Based on the Screenplay written
by Andrea Nasfell and Jon Erwin

B&H
PUBLISHING GROUP
Nashville, Tennessee

978-1-4336-8482-1

Published by B&H Publishing Group

Nashville, Tennessee

Dewey Decimal Classification: F

Subject Heading: MOTHERS—FICTION \ PARENTING—
FICTION \ FAMILY LIFE—FICTION

Representation by WTA Services, LLC,
Smyrna, TN.

2 3 4 5 6 7 • 17 16 15 14

[Blessing] Noun. a beneficial thing for which one is grateful; something that brings well-being.

CHAPTER ONE

Allyson sat down at her notebook computer, splaying her fingers over the keyboard. She listened closely, and a soft smile lifted her lips. The room echoed quiet, peaceful. Crickets chirped outside, doing what they were designed by God to do best. If only she could have the same feeling of rightness. Of purpose.

The blank computer screen before her was white, clean. The only thing in her home that was. Her fingers clicked on the keys, getting down her thoughts for her blog. Ragged fingernails, desperately in need of polish tried to distract her. So did the Legos scattered on her chevron sculpted rug, but Allyson told herself to focus, focus on her post. She'd promised her husband Sean that she wouldn't give up in dispensing wisdom to the world. A mommy blogger she was not . . . not yet at least. But couldn't a girl dream?

> It's 5 a.m. And do you know where your children are? Mine are in bed. I should be in bed. It's Mother's Day. But I'm not. Wanna know why? Because I'm a clean freak! I'm talking Freaky Deaky Dutch.

> If you were to lock me away in a white room
> in a straitjacket it would actually feel comforting,
> as long as the walls were spotless and nobody
> wore shoes.
>
> I can actually feel the house getting dirty.
> Like I have nerve endings in the carpet. And
> it affects me. Wanna know how? First, I feel
> distracted.

"Dis . . . tr . . ." Allyson typed out the word as she wrote it. She glanced at the Legos again, and the hair clip lying next to it. And the cleaning supplies . . . she'd left them out, hadn't she?

She shook her head, telling herself not to worry about that now. *What was I typing?*

"Focus, focus," she mumbled to herself, and then began typing again.

> Even as I try to write this, I'm thinking of
> the cleaning supplies I left out, and how one of
> the kids is going to get up and drink Clorox.
> Warning labels stream through my mind.
> DANGER
> KEEP OUT OF THE REACH OF CHILDREN
> HARMFUL IF SWALLOWED
> DO NOT INGEST
> CAN CAUSE BLINDNESS
> AVOID CONTACT WITH MUCAS
> MEMBRANES
> PARALYSIS IS A POSSIBILITY
> CAN CAUSE PREMATURE AGING IN THE
> FACIAL REGION

YOUR CHILDREN WILL NEVER BE THE
SAME

POISON CONTROL CAN'T HELP YOU
ANYMORE

YOU HAVE FAILED AGAIN

DHR IS ON THE WAY TO TAKE YOUR
CHILDREN AWAY

YOU ARE A FAILURE

My imagination then takes the wheel from
there. I can picture it now. I'll end up having to
call poison control, and they'll say, "Sorry, Mrs.
Field, too many times this month." And take my
kids away.

I can honestly picture two men in pressed
white shirts, black suits, and ties. The first man
looks serious in his black-rimmed glasses. The
man standing behind him appears like a retired
WWF fighter who isn't too happy about retiring
and is actually looking forward to wrangling
my children. I shudder as he lifts a pair of
handcuffs.

I've played it all out in my mind, which is
kind of ~~funny~~, ~~scary~~, morbid. But that is only
the beginning. After I feel distracted—from my
messy house that taunts me—I feel stressed.

STRESSED!!!

Then I have a "moment."

Picture with me those 1950s black-and-white
reels of atomic bombs exploding, mushroom
clouds, and the nuclear holocaust that happens
in its wake. Not that I'm comparing myself to
that—well, sort of.

At least that's what it feels like on the inside. Like just last week.

It was a simple outing, and I was trying to have a simple conversation, with my husband, Sean. If you're one of my 3.7 blog readers (no, not 3.7K, just 3.7), then you will know how utterly sweet and handsome Sean is.

I was trying to have a normal, nothing-earth-shattering conversation with Sean when I felt the hairs on the back of my neck standing on end. The noise in the van was getting to me.

It started with our two-year-old Beck hitting his pinwheel against the minivan window, over and over and over. (Mommy friends, we know that just because something doesn't have an on/off switch or a volume button doesn't mean it's a quiet toy!)

And just when the tapping of aluminum on glass had caused my heart to go into palpitations our four-year-old Bailey's voice overshadowed the tapping.

"Mom. Mommy!" Her voice rose to an ear-piercing level, filling the cavern of our van, and echoing in my ears.

Tension tightened in my gut, and then it released—liquid frustration (anger?!), pushing out into my chest, my arms, gaining in speed.

My head whipped around to look to the passenger seat behind Sean, hair flopping around faster than Willow Smith's.

Eyes wide. Mouth snarled. "I am talking to Dad-dy!" My words exited out of my mouth like a spout of hot lava.

Yes, this was me having a "moment" with my daughter. Stress anyone? And the root of it had been those dang carpet fibers crying out with voices of injustice over the mud clots I've yet to vacuum from their masses.

There is no such thing as, "Not thinking about the house, the mess, the chores until I get home." We know, don't we? We know how we left the house—cleaned-up or not—and it taunts us no matter where we travel or where our journey takes us.

I tried to picture the wild-eyed, red-haired mommy-monster from my children's eyes, and she wasn't pretty. Still, she was unleashed, unwilling to be reined in. It felt good to release some steam in a bad sort of way.

Out of the corner of my eye I spotted Sean's hands tightening on the steering wheel. I glared at him, almost as if I was daring him to say something. You'd think after eight years of marriage that he'd have learned to *not. say.a.word*, but obviously Sean hasn't learned, for these words proceeded out of his mouth:

"Hey, hon, about the stress level. It's a little high, and you know that psycho thing you just did . . ."

"Did you just call me psycho?" I huffed. "PSYCHO!" I repeated. My response was brilliant, I know. And my response *was* kind of psycho. But it was just beginning.

If that little mad mommy manifestation wasn't bad enough it wasn't five minutes later when

I had another "moment" with some helpless newlyweds.

I couldn't help myself. I saw them in their cute convertible, pulled up so innocently waiting at the stoplight. Maybe it was the fact that I once had a cute convertible just like that. A convertible that we had to sell to buy a "family car" after Brandon, our first child, was born. Could that really be six years ago?

Their convertible was spotless. No ketchup stains on the seats. No smashed juice pouches under the floor mats. "Just married," was written in washable paint on the side of the immaculate car.

With hearts. HEARTS!

Sean's window was rolled down, and I felt myself lunging toward it as if another entity had entered my body. I leaned over Sean, nearly propelling myself on his lap, stretching as close to the open window as I could.

"We just wanted to say congratulations!" I called out, noting the syrupy sweet smiles on their faces. "And savor this moment in your life!"

The couple looked at each other with puppy-dog gazes. Gazes of contentment and trust. I told myself to stop there. Stop with the congratulations . . . but I didn't listen.

When I first started speaking I thought it would help me. But then the words continued faster, like a runaway horse. Clearly my emotions were doing the talking.

"Enjoy the moment," I began again. "Because you're just going to blink, seriously going to blink, and soon it's going to be over and replaced with just volumes of voices!"

"Mom!" Brandon called trying to get my attention, emphasizing my words.

"Mommy! Mommy!" the other two voices called out.

"Amazing, amazing beautiful volume!" My hands trembled as I called to the newlyweds and looks of horror crossed their faces. *Who is this woman?* their wide eyes seemed to proclaim.

I glanced to the kids in the backseat who were strangely quiet for the first time that day. Maybe because they were enjoying the show of the crazy lady in the front seat was putting on for them.

My words didn't stop there. Although now I wish they would have.

I cleared my throat and a trembling voice emerged. "You can only take so much before you crack!"

The young bride wrinkled her nose and looked up at me as if I'd grown a second head. I could almost read her thoughts. *Crazy woman in a minivan.* But then her shock turned to horror. Horror *is* the best word for it.

The woman in the car looked at me again, only this time it wasn't me she was seeing. The shock there was new, fresh . . . as if she were peering into her own future. A waking nightmare I supposed.

I bit my lower lip over the look on her face. It was the look of a girl whose fairy tale just ended. I murdered it. I am a fairy tale murderer.

It's then, friends, that I realized the truth. The daily-stuff affects the attitude-stuff more than I'd like to admit. Like Tetris blocks, I think I have everything sorted, shuffled, and tucked in its place until I can't move fast enough, and the blocks don't fit as I planned, and the emotions pile up higher and higher until *Bam*!

I am like the Bruce Banner of stay-at-home moms. He doesn't want to turn into the Hulk. It just happens. Which is exactly how I feel.

One minute I'm a normal person. The next minute the large, green monster grows inside me, bursting out in every direction. I grow and transform into something unrecognizable, scary even. Maybe psycho, until I'm so big that not even the ceiling can hold me down. Hold me in.

And even though I've figured out the reason for my hunky, junky alter ego I'm not exactly sure what to do about it. How can I feel okay about my house that I clean but never STAYS clean? Or my kids who take pleasure in seeing their crazy-eyed, hair-pulling mama's antics over their littlest mess-ups and misdirections? Can I change? Can I ever fix the thing that seems to be unfixed the most, **namely myself**?

I love my kids. I love my husband, my
minivan. My minivan is awesome. I have this
incredible life, so why do I feel this way?
Anyone? Anyone?

Allyson read her words over again, fixed a few typos, and then
hit "publish" before she could change her mind. Most of the wise
and witty blog posts she read had answers, not questions, but she
was at a loss. At least she had a few things to look forward to.
Today was Mother's Day, and today Sean would be home after
taking a trip for work. His absence often made it harder for her to
cope. She smiled thinking of him striding through the front door
. . . his arms opened wide for her. Did he realize how much she
needed him to hold her up?

She glanced again at the number of page views on her blog
from last month: 18. Three for every post she'd written. Sean, her
mother, and Izzy (her best friend), no doubt. Although Allyson
wasn't sure if Izzy had read the last post, and her mother had commented that she'd read it twice, pointing out three grammatical
errors.

Everyone starts somewhere, her mind consoled her heart. Her
worth wasn't based on page-views, right? At least that's what she
told herself as tension tightened her gut. But if she got her house
clean—that was something tangible. She could see the shiny
floor. Breathe in the piney scent. It was a small sense of control in
her stay-at-home world. It was something she could point to and
give herself an imaginary gold star for. It proved she wasn't wast-
ing her life. That her noisy, overfilled, tiring days had meaning.

She didn't sit too long on that thought. It was time for action. Allyson closed the top of her laptop computer and rose. Within a few minutes a new sound had joined the crickets. The clacking of her sweeper on the floor. The scraping of toys as she swept them into a pile.

There, take that, she thought as her red curls tossed with her effort.

Out of the corner of her eye something caught her attention. The first pinkish light of dawn pushed through the kitchen window and beamed like a spotlight on one pink sock. The sock taunted her. "Do you see me? Are you going to leave me here? There's more mess from where I came from, you know."

She pushed the sweeper with fervor toward the sock. Her eyes widened as she noticed the block behind it. And the Matchbox car. *Swoop.* A dozen crayons, broken and scattered. She pushed them along too. It was as if Hansel and Gretel—or in her case Brandon, Bailey, and Beck had left a trail of bread crumbs, or rather toy box droppings, for her to find.

Happy Mother's Day.

A strand of red hair tumbled from her hasty up-do and curled on her cheek. She puffed her cheeks and blew it out of her face. Her hands tightened around the sweeper handle.

Children are a blessing, she told herself as she barreled forward. She moved to the den, organizing the toys in labeled bins. She moved to the sink next, scrubbed it with vigor. She opened the dishwasher. The lemony scent arose, like a balm to her soul. A clean, fresh scent.

Her hands moved with ninja speed as she tucked cups into the cabinet.

"KEEP CALM AND MOMMY ON," the mini-poster inside the cabinet door read, and Allyson set her chin in determination.

I want to believe Mommying is a blessing. I try. I really do. She wiped her eyes. But somehow I always end up feeling . . . like there should be something more to life than this. The room around her blurred just slightly.

What does it matter? She thought as she set the sweeper back into its spot in the laundry room. The house was cleaner now. Not perfect, but better.

Still the nagging wouldn't leave Allyson's gut. *Will I ever* feel *enough? Will it ever* be *enough?* And the question she'd written on her blog echoed through her soul.

Why do I feel this way?

CHAPTER TWO

Mom!" the voice stirred her awake. Allyson remembered the sweeping, wiping, mopping, cleaning, and the finally clean kitchen. Had she fallen back to sleep after that?

"Mom, Mommy!"

Her eyes fluttered closed again. Maybe she could doze off for one more minute. Just one more minute.

"MOM!!!" Her eyes popped open. She lifted her head and looked at the clock. *8:15.*

"Oh no."

She stumbled out of bed. Disoriented. Voices rose from downstairs, and she followed them. Dishes rattled. *Dishes!* The last time her three had tried to get themselves breakfast there was a half of a box of cereal spilled on the floor and then stomped on, crushed to a fine, fine powder.

She hoped it wasn't that bad. She rushed down the stairs, her heart pounding.

Allyson rounded the corner and then paused, peering into the kitchen. Her heart sunk. It was worse. FEMA worthy.

All three kids stood on chairs at the kitchen counter, with nearly every dish she owned spread before them. And in the middle, her giant punch bowl was filled with . . .

Oh no, oh no. Allyson's eyes narrowed. She rubbed them, refusing to believe what she saw.

"Surprise!" Brandon called at the top of his lungs. "We made you eggs!"

"With sugar!" Bailey chimed in, a silver tiara topping her head.

And with everything else in the kitchen, Allyson wanted to add, seeing the contents of her cupboards strewn all over the house. Her almost-perfectly clean house.

Three faces, three smiles, and Brandon stirring the raw eggs faster and faster, splattering as he did.

Allyson's lips pressed tight together as she took it all in. Hours. She'd given up hours of sleep . . . only to have her efforts destroyed.

"Mother's Happy Day!" Bailey called in a squeaky voice.

Allyson's mouth opened. She paused, trying not to have a panic attack. She knew it was a thoughtful, caring gesture. Instead, all she saw was salmonella.

Salmonella on the kitchen counter.

Salmonella on the handrail to the stairs.

Salmonella on the floor, the children. And for a salmonella phobia, it was her worst nightmare.

She thought back to last week. The same panicky fears had swept over her when Bailey had dropped her Barbie in a bowl of raw eggs. She'd burned it, not realizing it was Bailey's favorite doll, and she did feel bad about that, but that was then. This was now.

Allyson picked up the pump of hand sanitizer on the side table. "Okay, we—we're, we're going to play a little game. Everyone freeze!"

They did. Six hands jutted into the air. Raw egg dripped down their arms. The ketchup bottle Bailey had been holding plopped into the concoction. Giggles erupted.

Then Beck looked over at her with a twinkle in his eye. As if in slow motion, he dipped his finger into the raw egg mess and . . .

. . . and he lifted it toward his mouth.

"Beck, don't put that in . . . No!" Allyson's voice rose.

Oh no, no, no. He's going to eat it. He's going to put that in his mouth and be one of the four hundred estimated people that die of acute salmonella. She'd read it on a blog somewhere.

She rushed toward him, but too late. His finger went into his mouth and he grinned. Her stomach lurched. "Oh, here we go. Oh . . . salmonella!"

***

Allyson tugged hard, pulling the clothes off of Beck before realizing that all his diapers were upstairs. "Get dressed everybody. We're getting dressed!" She tucked her son under her arm and raced upstairs.

Allyson thought she heard the cell phone chiming in the living room. That and the sound of Bailey riding her trike . . . in the house.

15

Then she heard it. The crunch of the trike hitting the trash can. The sound of it spilling over. Its contents . . . the egg shells. Dozens of egg shells that she'd just picked up, splaying over the floor. Then came the quiet.

***

Sean rushed through the double doors of the airport with his carry-on bag in one hand and his document tube flung over his shoulder. His mind raced with excuses, but there were none. He told Allyson he'd try to catch an earlier flight. She'd wanted him to be home for Mother's Day. He hadn't promised her he could, but he still felt bad for not being there.

He'd tried to get his work done faster, but design issues had caused a delay. Then there were the canceled flights. At least he'd get home today. Maybe after dinner, and the kids were asleep, but that still counts as "today." Sean used his thumb to push Allyson's number on speed dial as he raced ahead, weaving through the people crowding the terminal.

He listened for Allyson to answer as he pushed forward. He pictured his family. His beautiful wife. What had he done to deserve her? And the kids. Maybe they were all snuggled up in bed. A happy little family on a beautiful Sunday morning. He rushed forward, telling himself that he couldn't miss this flight. A soft smile touched his lips.

I will get home today. Home to my wife. Home to my family.

Just when he prepared to leave a message on Allyson's voice-mail a small voice answered.

"Hello. How may I Field. Hello the Field. Hello Field residence please?"

Sean hurried up an escalator toward a packed line in security. His bag tugged on his arm. He wedged his phone between his ear and shoulder as he hurried faster. The sound of his daughter's voice. *His daughter's voice* brought a smile to his lips.

"How about you try this, 'This is the Field's residence. How may I help you?'"

"Daddy!" Bailey squealed.

"Hey, baby. Is Mommy there?"

"MOMMY!!!!! PHONE!!!!" Bailey's voice rung out, right in his ear, and he was certain then, that Bailey got her vocal chords from her mother. Sean cringed and pulled the phone away. *Loud. So loud.*

And as he heard her clomping up the stairs he couldn't help but smile, picturing his wife's angelic face. Picturing the home and kids she worked so hard to care for.

***

If there was only one reason to believe that evolution wasn't true, it was that moms only had two hands. Allyson definitely needed more than two hands to wrestle Beck into his church clothes.

She heard her small daughter's squeal and laughter downstairs.

"Daddy!" Bailey called into the phone. It was hard when Sean was away. Each day the excitement built for his return. Today was the day. She couldn't be more thrilled. Then again her husband had no idea what he was walking into. No parent ever did. From day one nothing had gone as she'd expected.

Beck wiggled faster, attempting to break loose. In all her years of daydreaming about a husband, a family, Allyson hadn't expected this. The tangle of mess, that family was.

"Bailey! I'm up here." She turned and called out over her shoulder. Turning back she scanned her bed—a mess of rumbled sheets. Beck was gone. How had he disappeared so fast? He'd fled, vanishing into thin air.

"Beck, Beck, where did you go?" She scanned her room, looking for him.

A soft giggle emerged from the other side of her bed, a small form darted past her—too fast for her to snag. She rushed toward Beck, and then paused as Bailey skipped in with the phone and handed it over. "Here's Daddy."

Beck or the phone?

She reached for the phone, desperate for Sean's voice. Even more desperate for his assurance that he'd soon be home.

"Sean?"

"Hello. Hey, Hon?"

"Sean? PLEASE tell me you're on a flight right now." She could hear that he wasn't. The sound of the airport din rose through the phone.

"It's Mother's Day. Happy Mother's Day. That's where we should have started."

"Yes, thank you, fine," Allyson interrupted. "I just, why . . . I need you on a flight."

"That's alright. That's alright. They canceled three flights on me, I changed airlines. I'm taking care of it. I got a direct flight."

Home. He'll be home soon. Allyson released a breath that she didn't realize she'd been holding.

Bailey reentered her room with arms outstretched with a drawn picture in her hands. She tugged on Allyson's arm with her free hand.

There was something in Bailey's bright eyes. Joy? Excitement? Mischief? Allyson couldn't tell, but she pulled the phone back slightly from her ear, giving Bailey her attention. "Yes, baby?"

Bailey's grin widened. "Hey, Mommy, I made you this."

Allyson took the picture from her daughter. Flowers and stick figures represented her family. For a four-year-old this was a Rembrandt.

"You made this for me?" Allyson leaned down, her face crinkling up into a smile. The eggs hadn't turned out well, but this . . . this was thoughtful. Her heart filled with joy as she scanned the figures again—her big stick figure body and three small images with circle heads and three fingers on each hand.

"Do you wanna know why I made you so big?" Bailey's voice was almost angelic. "Because you love us the most-est over everybody."

Still something didn't seem right. Allyson frowned, realizing what was missing—who was missing. "Where's Daddy?" she asked.

Bailey pointed to an orange shape with wings on the top left of the page. "Up on the plane in the sky, where he always is." Bailey's wide-eyed gaze looked serious.

"Ouch, that's not right," Sean's voice echoed from the phone, and Allyson's heart pinched.

Bailey reached down and picked up a marker she'd dropped before rushing off again. Allyson was about to call to her, telling her to put all her markers away, and reminding Bailey that she wasn't supposed to have them out without supervision, when Brandon's voice shot through the air.

"Mom! Beck's playing in the toilet again!"

"Oh, no, no. Not the potty. Not the potty!" Sean's voice called out over the phone. Loud, really loud, as if expecting Beck to hear him. Allyson smiled, imagining the curious looks on the faces of his fellow passengers at the airport.

"BECK!" Allyson raced toward him, and scooped him up. His hair was completely wet, dripping wet. He dripped on her. He dripped on the floor.

Pretend he was diving in the tub instead, yes, pretend that, she told herself. Allyson let her eyes fluttered closed for a brief instant, trying not to think about it.

And you call yourself a mother?

Allyson tucked Beck under one arm and then hurried downstairs determined to get those markers from Bailey before she made a bigger mess. She pressed the phone tighter to her ear as she took each step. Beck bounced on her hip.

"Sean, I don't know. I'm thinking, baby, that I don't want to celebrate Mother's Day ever again."

He gasped. "Why would you say that?"

She stepped down further and looked around again at the cyclone of her living room and kitchen. The very rooms she'd just cleaned a few hours ago. Obviously taming this home—these children—was beyond her control.

"You don't need to celebrate me, because I'm terrible at this. Really terrible." She paused at the bottom of the stairs, and Beck felt as if he weighed a hundred pounds on her hip. Or maybe it was her heart that weights her down. "In every single way. Do not celebrate me."

"What? Come on." Sean seemed impervious to her words. "You are an awesome mom, but kids get messy. Kids are messy."

From the corner of her eye Allyson spotted movement. Her daughter. The wall. Markers. Not the kid kind of markers.

Then as if realizing she'd been spotted, Bailey raised her hands like a bank robber who'd just been caught. Bailey's high-pitched voice rang out louder than Sean's voice on the phone. "I ran out of paper, so . . ."

Allyson's jaw dropped at yet another picture Bailey had drawn.

". . . so I did the rest on the wall," Bailey continued, her tiara cocked to the side.

"On the wall. On the wall?" Sean's voice rang out through the phone. "What kind of markers is she using? The come-off kind?" Then Allyson could hear him talking to someone in line next to him at the airport. "Do you have kids?" he asked. "Want mine?" But Sean's voice as coming through as if he was at the end of a long tunnel.

Allyson dropped her hand with her phone to her side. She dropped her chin to her chest, letting her hair fall over her face. Beck tugged on her ear and she let him.

Where can a mom go to wave a white flag? To surrender?

CHAPTER THREE

Allyson released a heavy breath as she parked her van into one of the last parking spaces at church. Clusters of families moved toward the front entrance. Girls in pretty dresses. Boys in coordinating outfits. The children nearly skipped with glee as they frolicked with happy smiles toward the church. And their mothers . . .

Allyson turned her attention to a group of women circled up, talking near the front steps. They were no doubt chatting about their wonderful Mother's Day breakfasts in bed, minus the egg shells and salmonella.

Sun backlit them, highlighting hair that perfectly framed their faces. Those moms looked rested, happy, and put together. Allyson doubted that any of them had wrangled with a toilet-diving toddler or interrupted a miniature Rembrandt-in-the-making who'd used permanent markers on the wall.

She focused on one woman with long blonde hair in perfect beach waves. The woman laughed as she tossed her hair over her shoulder. *Now that's a mom. Talk about perfect.*

I bet she has a nanny.

What's wrong with me? Why does everyone have their act together but me? She didn't even have her makeup on yet. At least she'd had enough foresight to toss it into her purse before she'd left.

Bailey climbed from her car seat and stood next to Allyson's seat.

Allyson pulled her mascara out of her purse. "Okay everybody, best behavior. It's Mother's Day!" She quickly dabbed her mascara onto her left eye, peering into the rearview mirror.

"Mommy, let me do it." Bailey said, leaning in close.

"No, baby, we're running really late today."

"Let meeeee!" Bailey's voice screamed out. "Let meeeeeeeeee!"

Allyson sighed. She was sure those other mothers could hear her daughter's screams.

"Shhh . . ." She handed Bailey the mascara wand. "Just one dab, okay?"

Maybe later she'd laugh about this morning. Maybe she'd be able to decompress with Sondra—Pastor Ray's wife. Sondra had been the first to welcome them into church six years ago. Allyson knew a good thing when she saw it, and she'd turned to Sondra time and time again. Sondra was her *Catcher in the Rye,* her crutch, Dr. Phil, Oprah, and Gandalf all rolled into one ball of goodness. Sondra's only perceived flaw was that the woman had no idea what autocorrect on her cell phone was.

Allyson held back a chuckle as she remembered the last text exchange Sondra's sixteen-year-old daughter Zoe had shared with her. At least it was something to brighten Allyson's spirits as Bailey dabbed the mascara on her lashes—well, mostly on her lashes:

Zoe / 7:31 AM
Mom, I feel sick.

Sondra / 7:31 AM
Just take some typhoid.

Zoe / 7:31 AM
WHAT?

Sondra / 7:32 AM
And a bowl of chicken noodle poop.

Zoe / 7:32 AM
Mom stop!

Ah, technology.

***

Sondra reached into the maintenance closet, without turning on the lights, and pulled the extra set of keys off the hook on the wall. With quickened steps she hurried down the church hallway. If she would have known Ray had bought her a red Mother's Day corsage she would have worn her red pumps. No matter, she walked with a quickened pace with her clipboard in hand. How a pastor's wife would survive without one she didn't know.

Her daughter Zoe, sixteen, bright, and way too adorable for her own good kept pace with her. Sondra had assumed that when Zoe came to be a teenager she'd stop trailing after her. Wrong. She'd walked these halls more times than not with Zoe chasing after her. Zoe used to chase after her and ask if they could eat out after church or maybe go to the park. The questions hadn't ceased, they'd just changed in nature. If Zoe was anything, she was persistent.

"Mom, slow down!"

"Walk with me, Zoe, just walk and talk."

Zoe huffed. "Mom, you're like the fastest person in the world."

Sondra unlocked the door and rushed into her husband's office. Piles of books and papers covered every surface. She didn't know how Ray kept track of anything. How he found anything. Actually, he didn't. That's what he needed her for.

She grabbed a solid blue tie from the back of his chair and zeroed in on his sermon notes on the corner of his desk, scooping them up.

"Mom, it's really, it's just a dance. And there's going to be some laser lights and some glow sticks and that's it."

Sondra shook her head, turning back to the doorway she'd just entered. "A rave is not a dance. Trust your mother."

Did Zoe think she was born yesterday? If her daughter only knew. Sondra pushed that thought from her mind. She didn't want to think of *that* . . . not now. Not here. Sondra tucked the back panel of her white blouse, deeper into her skirt with her free hand and continued on.

"But, Mom, a lot of the kids from church, they're even going . . ." Zoe looked to her with puppy-dog eyes. That worked when Zoe was five and she wanted a donut, but not now. Not for this.

She waved her hand her daughter's direction. "Uh-uh, no way."

Sondra rushed out of Ray's office and hurried down the hall, toward the back of the sanctuary. She smiled and waved as they passed the Johnson family in the hall—dear, faithful parishioners.

"Com'on, have a heart." The exasperation in Zoe's voice was clear, but that was her job, being the voice of reason when her daughter didn't have any.

She shook her head. "Zoe . . ."

"You always do this. You're going to murder my social life." Zoe's wide eyes and perky nose resembled the three-year-old she once was. Where had the time gone?

Sondra blew out a breath. She didn't have time for this—this conversation. Her internal clock sensed the minutes were ticking down until her husband was ready to take the pulpit. She quickened her pace. "Well, maybe your social life deserves to die. You know you're not allowed to date until you're seventeen. We have a winner."

Zoe paused beside her, lifting her hands in frustration. "And a loser." She motioned to her head. "I have 'preacher's kid' stamped on my forehead."

Sondra hurried into the atrium where Ray was being mic'd up by one of the technical guys. "Ah, there you are." He smiled. "Did you find my notes?"

"Right here." She handed Ray the notes. "Now, just one more thing . . ." She ripped off his checkered tie, replacing it with the solid blue.

"Where were they? I looked everywhere—" Then, as if realizing what she was doing, he glanced down at his tie. "And what's wrong with that tie?"

"The video guys say its strobing, so this is better." Sondra efficiently knotted it and then stepped back to eye her work. "Okay, looks good." She glanced up at him and smiled. "And the notes were on your desk. Corner pile."

"Oh." Ray returned the smile and winked. He was the most respected man in this church—a fine preacher—but he could still cause her heart to skip a beat with that playful look of his.

Unaware of her father's flirting, Zoe sauntered up to her daddy with her hands clasped behind her back. Sondra knew what she was up to, and she waited to see this unfold.

"Hey, Dad. You were awesome in the first service." Zoe batted her eyelashes. "And I was just wondering, uh . . ."

Ray slipped his arms into his suit jacket and shrugged his shoulders so that it slipped on with ease. "Sweetheart, I know what you are doing, but I've already talked to your mother and we agree." He pointed his finger at her and grinned. "Points for trying though."

"I didn't even get a fair shot." Zoe huffed and paced off.

He turned back to Sondra and a look of understanding passed between them. "Love you," he said.

"Love you," she whispered back. And she did love him, and loved this life as a pastor's wife . . . if she only had time to breathe. It was hard holding their little world together.

Sondra paused in the empty hallway, took a breath and composed herself. Putting on her best smile, she then waltzed into the packed lobby.

"Good morning." She shook Dave Piper's hand. Then she waltzed passed Bonnie Sue Johnson with a wave. "Somebody has a birthday, right? Nice to see you," she called to one of the choir members.

She motioned to Zoe to follow her. "Hey, did you get that recipe I sent?" she called to Tiffany, one of the young women in the college group. Tiffany nodded that she had.

"Nice to see you. Thank you for coming," Sondra called to a new couple that she'd seen for the first time last week. She moved their direction and then paused as another sight greeted her.

A frazzled and disheveled looking Allyson struggled through the door, holding Beck on her hip and dragging Bailey with one hand. Brandon trailed behind, but as soon as they got inside he darted away to play with friends.

Allyson wore shades, even inside. Large dark shades, and Sondra wondered if she'd gotten any sleep. By the way Allyson looked Sean had to be out of town. She'd seen that desperate, frantic Allyson before.

"Ally, hey, oh are you having a tough morning?" Sondra reached up and stroked Allyson's arms, and she brushed a few strands of red curls out of her friend's face.

"Sondra," Allyson's words released with a groan, "tell me it's going to be okay." The young mom was throwing out a lifeline. Sondra knew all Ally wanted was a glimmer of hope. But just like she had to disappoint Zoe earlier Sondra knew that she didn't have the answer that Allyson wanted to hear.

"It's all going to be okay. Just give it five years—seven or five," she muttered.

Allyson's shoulders slumped. "Years?"

"Do you want me to help you with the kids?"

"Brandon!" Allyson's voice split the air, and numerous heads turn their direction. Sondra followed Allyson's gaze to see the small boy racing around old Mr. McGregor who was trying to maneuver his walker. She bit her knuckle, and then breathed out a sigh of relief when Brandon darted away.

"Brandon, what are you doing?" Allyson called out, exasperated.

Beside Sondra, Zoe snickered, and Sondra wanted to ask her daughter, "Do you still want to date, sweetheart? Want to rush into marriage and motherhood and all that?"

Instead, Sondra took a step closer to Allyson. "Need some help?"

Sondra remembered what it was like trying to get to church with a happy Zoe, a dressed Zoe, a matching-shoes-on-two-feet Zoe . . . and she only had one child to wrangle.

Allyson squared her shoulders. "Help? No, I've come this far, Sondra. I'm going to finish this."

She motioned her little tribe of people forward, toward the children's wing. "Let's go, let's go. This way. Walk around everybody. Don't walk into them, walk around them!" Allyson sighed. Giggles erupted from the children and the small tribe moved forward, sort of, in a cluster of unproductive movement.

Before Sondra had a chance to offer her help for a second time Mattie Mae Lloyd approached, waltzing up as if she was coming to ask Sondra to dance. "Good morning, y'all. How is everyone?"

Sondra's lips lifted in a grin. "Great, Miss Mattie. Just wonderful today."

Mattie Mae's floral dress of pinks and greens was as bright as her garden. Pearls graced her neck, and her lipstick matched her pink sweater. Sondra also knew the large, yellow purse hanging from Mattie Mae's shoulder carried her large-print, burgundy, leather-covered Bible. Mattie never went anywhere without her Bible.

"Oh, Sondra, you are such an inspiration to me," Mattie Mae cooed.

Then she reached over and grasped Zoe's arm. "And sweetie, you are so bless-ed to have her as your mother."

Zoe nodded, as if agreeing and then Mattie Mae glided over to the nearest couple.

Zoe clasped her hands in front of her. "I'm just so *blessed*."

"Um-hum." Sondra offered yet another smile. Yet if the church ladies only knew . . . nah, she shook her head. They'd never find out.

***

Beck fussed as he clung to Allyson's side. She struggled down the hall, trying to keep up with Bailey and Brandon who raced ahead. The burdens weighing on her shoulders felt slightly lighter after seeing Sondra's smile. Everyone saw Pastor Ray's family as the perfect example, but Allyson had been around the mother and daughter enough to know no family was perfect, and knowing that gave her hope in the strangest way.

Now, she looked forward to seeing another glimmer of sunshine. Her best friend Izzy was graciously serving a one-year sentence, uh, a one-year *commitment* in the toddler nursery.

She and Izzy pretty much did everything together. In grade school Izzy was wild and popular, where Allyson was an introvert . . . with braces. Nothing much had changed, well, except for the braces part. As they neared the classroom, instead of going in, her two older kids returned to her, clinging to her.

"Let go. Let go. Let go," Allyson said to Brandon and Bailey who tugged on her arm. They released their grasp and then raced to the children's church room where Marco, Izzy's husband, stood waiting to sign them in. In his early thirties with dark hair, Marco was a lovable, huggable teddy bear of a guy, except for the huggable part.

Marco had a heart of gold, but he'd always had three irrational fears: luchadores, biker gangs, and small children. This made Marco especially vulnerable at Halloween.

"Izzy . . . They're talking to me again!" Marco hissed as Bailey and Brandon chattered away.

Izzy leaned out of the classroom door and peered down the hall. "You're doing fine, babe!"

Marco shook his arms as if trying to release tension. "I'm just supposed to check them in."

More eager than she probably should be, Allyson handed Beck over the Izzy. Then she adjusted her shades, making sure they were on straight.

Izzy, of course, was adorable, even with a half-dozen toddlers, including her twins, racing around her feet. How someone could look so good in a T-shirt, blue blazer, large-rimmed glasses, and a messy bun was beyond Allyson.

Allyson waved to leave.

"Hey!" Izzy called out, motioning for her to stop.

Allyson reluctantly did.

Izzy cocked an eyebrow and offered a serious expression. "Don't kill the messenger, but the Sunday School Coordinator said to remember your number this time."

"Yes, yes, okay, fine." She waved her hands in the air. "But please, please don't page me over something trivial."

Izzy's face scrunched up as if she'd just taken a bite of a lemon. "The fire department didn't think it was trivial!"

"Izzy," Allyson said flatly. "Look at me." She stepped forward and with one quick motion pulled her sunglasses off her face, revealing her right eye and the smudges of black mascara all around it. Bailey had gone wild with the wand, smearing it under Allyson's eye and on her eyelid before she could stop her.

Izzy winced and pulled back as if the spider-like swipes of mascara were really a spider. "Aaagh . . ."

"I just need an hour to myself. On Mother's Day. Please."

Izzy nodded. "Yeah, like me. With twenty toddlers."

Allyson turned, steepled her hands, and then gave her friend a quick curtsy. "Thank you. You're a servant." She pointed, and then hurried away before Izzy had any other messages for her.

"Sure! And fix the eye!" Izzy called after her. "It's weird . . . even for me!"

Allyson didn't have to be told twice. She hurried to the foyer bathroom and placed her large purse on the bathroom counter. She opened it, digging through the items—unpacking them on the counter. "Library book, diaper (thankfully clean), sippy cup, toy dog," she muttered under her breath as she tossed each item onto the countertop. She was looking for the baby wipes, but then remembered she'd used them all two days ago, cleaning the chocolate off Beck's face before his dentist appointment.

Well, plan B.

She turned to the get paper towels, deciding that rough, brown paper towels and tap water would have to do. She quickly swiped her hand over the automatic sensor, waiting to hear the rumble of the machine letting out one brown square. Nothing happened. She tried again, slower this time. Nothing. She tried waving her hand faster, and then she tilted her head to make sure there were paper towels up there. There were.

She swiped her hand again, nothing, and then she pushed her fingers up into the bottom rim, attempting to snag a piece big enough to yank out. It didn't work.

Tension tightened in Allyson's arms, and she closed her eyes slowly, telling herself to calm down. She took one slow breath, blowing it out. She'd heard that worked for some people, but obviously not for her.

Allyson eyed the paper towel dispenser again, wondering what it had against her. It was as if it knew that this was not her day and it taunted her by holding back. Frustration shot through her limbs.

"Work!" Allyson shouted at the machine. "Work!" She hit it once, twice, three times. "Why won't you work?!" her voice rose in volume, and she stamped her foot on the ground, just like she'd seen Bailey do a hundred times.

Just then, she heard the toilet flush, and heat rushed to her cheeks. Her heart rate quickened, and she quickly stepped back from the paper towel dispenser. With one smooth motion, Allyson swooped her hair down over her forehead so that the mascara eye wouldn't be so obvious.

Allyson held in her horror as Mattie Mae Lloyd exited the bathroom stall, slinking toward the sink with a swoosh of her floral skirt. Mattie Mae washed her hands, offering Allyson the smallest smile and a judgmental glance. Allyson fiddled with her hair, pretending like it had been someone else—not her—who'd just lost her cool. An invisible woman who'd just slipped out. *Yes, that was it.*

Mattie Mae flicked the water off her fingertips and then moved toward Allyson, stepping past her toward the paper towel dispenser. With one smooth motion, Mattie Mae swiped her hand in front of the sensor. With the hum of the machine, a paper towel slipped out.

She cast Allyson one more glance, dried her hands, and then strode out, her high heels clicking on the tile floor. The perfect church lady.

At that moment Allyson wished more than anything that the floor would open up and swallow up her, her junk purse, and her spider eye.

Compose yourself. The Lord worketh everything together for good, she told herself. Then she stepped forward and swiped her hand one more time, fully expecting a paper towel to emerge. Instead the machine didn't budge. Allyson half-laughed, half-moaned at the hilarity of it. Seriously?!

Finally, she found a handy-wipe in a side pocket of her purse and cleaned the mascara off her face. She hurried to the sanctuary, and let out the quietest moan when she realized it was full. Well, almost full, except for a spot half-way up next to a large man she didn't recognize.

With quickened steps she hurried up the aisle and reached the spot.

"Psalm 127 says that children are a gift from the Lord," Pastor Ray was saying from the pulpit.

Allyson squatted down next to the pudgy man with the receding hairline. She pointed to the empty spot next to him. "Excuse me, can I get in there?"

Instead of scooting over, or standing to let her in, he closed his Bible, turned slightly to the side, and pulled his knees against the pew, as if expecting her to get through a two-inch gap.

Why do people do that?

Pastor Ray's voice continued through the sound system. "That's why the position of mother is a high calling and one to be honored and protected."

Allyson attempted to slide in, but there just wasn't enough room. She then tried to step over the man's legs, but her pencil skirt only allowed her to stretch her legs so far. She did her best to wobble half around, half over him, and just as she thought she was clear, Allyson lost her balance and nearly fell into his lap.

"What are you doing? What are you doing?" the man frantically whispered under his breath, as if she meant to seduce him in church!

Scurrying, she quickly scooted herself over him, finally falling into the pew next to him. Her hair fell in front of her face as she landed with no grace. Then, attempting to compose herself the best she could, Allyson straightened her body and brushed the hair from her face, pretending as if nearly the whole church hadn't just seen her display.

And it was then she realized that all wasn't well that ended well.

Brushing her bare foot on the low pile carpet, Allyson winced and glanced over at his reddened face. "Uh, can I have my shoe?" she whispered. With the slightest shake of his head, the man scooted it over with his shiny black shoes.

Still staring straight ahead, trying to take in the pastor's words, Allyson slipped her foot back into her shoe. Heads were still turned her direction—those beside her, those in front of her—but she ignored the looks, pretending Pastor's Ray was speaking only to her.

"Let's be honest, I know what you're thinking," he said to the congregation. "Should I feel happy when my child sticks a Fruit Roll-Up in the DVD player? Or wakes up at 3:00 a.m. crying?" Pastor Ray motioned to his Bible as a ripple of soft chuckles erupts around the sanctuary.

"But I know for some of you, Mother's Day can be hard," he continued. "If you're like my wife, Mother's Day is when you examine all your efforts and wonder whether it's worth it when you have to sacrifice so much."

Pastor Ray looked to Sondra, his wife. "Or whether you're having an impact at all when that teen rebels." Allyson noticed Sondra and Zoe exchanging glances. Was the slightest motion of Sondra elbowing her daughter's ribs just her imagination?

"Or whether you're really a good mother by some measure that you've created in your mind. So as we get started today what I want to say to every mother here is that there is hope for you. I want all of you to focus in on what the Lord is saying to you—"

"Allyson!" It was Izzy's loud whisper that interrupted.

Allyson turned and noticed her friend standing at the end of the pew. Izzy crouched down in the aisle, uncomfortably close to the bald guy whose cheeks turned yet another shade of pink.

"Look, I know you didn't want to be paged," Izzy whispered, "but Beck has an *especially* large head and those are *especially* small pottys in the children's wing." Izzy winced. "But the good news is that we found the screwdriver and we got the seat off the toilet, but we don't know how to get it off Beck's head."

"What?!" Before she could stop herself Allyson's scream split the air. Somehow this made the salmonella incident seem like a cakewalk.

Pastor Ray turned her direction, and she could tell he was trying to keep his train of thought. "Our music minister, uh, he is going to come and, uh, lead us in song, and we are going to continue in worship . . ." Pastor Ray managed to say.

Allyson clenched her fists, and lifted her face to the ceiling—to God—breathing out a quick prayer for strength. Did He see her? Did God really see her efforts? Did it matter?

She released a shuddering breath and rose.

Happy Mother's Day.

CHAPTER FOUR

Sean held the bouquet of flowers in one hand, and carried his overnight bag in the other as he entered the house. The room was dim. The moonlight from the windows bathed the living room in a soft gray. For a moment he wondered if he had the right place. To say their home was a mess was an understatement. Every toy in the house was scattered over the living room, their extra blankets, and plastic cups, plates, bowls were too. Couch pillows made up a leaning fort that looked ready to tumble at any moment.

"Hey, Hon?" Sean called. "Ally?"

He noticed something else, on the floor a trail of chocolate wrapping papers led the way to their bedroom, and then into the closet. He peeked in. Ally was inside with her computer. There was a picture—a video maybe—of a bird on the screen. The door squeaked as he opened it farther.

He stepped into the closet. "Hey!"

Allyson was heaped on the floor. She cowered down as the light shined in, clutching a bag of dark chocolate.

She glanced up at him, and her lips curl up in a slight smile. "You're home, hi." Her voice was soft and raspy.

"What happened?"

Ally gave the slightest of shrugs. "Just taking a little break. Mommy time."

He slid down the wall and sat beside her. "Okay."

Allyson lifted the bag of chocolate up to him. "I ate the whole bag."

"That's okay." He tried to reassure her, and then breathed out. Sean cocked an eyebrow. "Seriously, the whole bag? Really?"

"Uh-hum," she muttered, appearing half-asleep. Or maybe in a chocolate coma. Yes, he thought it to be the later for sure.

"Actually, I'm hiding," she admitted. Her face looked beautiful in the glow of the computer screen, even with rumpled hair and a smudge of chocolate on her lips.

He reached up to brush a curl from her cheek. "From what?"

"The house. It's awful." She moaned.

"It's not awful."

Allyson tilted her chin down. "It's awful . . . it's so bad."

"Well, it's bad, but it's not awful . . ." He let his voice trail off.

She looked at him in disbelief, and he offered a slight smile. "Well, some of it is awful."

He noticed then what she was watching. It wasn't a video but rather a Ustream of an eagle's nest. "What do you have there?"

Allyson looked back to the screen. "Sondra posted it. I can't stop watching, and I—I don't know why."

He watched with her as a mother eagle tended to her babies in a nest. The image was gray and grainy. There was no sound. No action . . . it was the last thing he'd choose to watch.

"Weird," Sean muttered. He turned back toward the closet door and picked up the flowers he'd laid down, and then with sincerity he offered them to his wife. "Happy Mother's Day."

Allyson took the flowers and smelled them. Then . . . came the tears.

Her shoulders shuddered like a tree in a storm. "That's really sw-sweet." Her words came out as a sob.

Had he done something wrong? "Hon, what? They're just flowers."

"I'm gonna get up and clean. I'm gonna get up and clean." It looked as if she was forcing herself to hold back her tears. "I'm going to go right now. Here we go." Then she wiped away a tear and sat there, not moving an inch.

Sean waited, unsure what to do, what to say, how to help. He traveled for work often, and at first Allyson had seemed able to keep down the fort. But lately? As the kids had gotten older it seemed the three of them had teamed up on her. He'd been getting more and more desperate calls and frantic texts from his wife—and it wasn't like he could do much when he was away. And now that he was back—Sean still didn't know what he could do to help.

"I'm trying to make myself get up—to clean—but nothing's happening. I'm stress paralyzed," she finally said.

Sean scratched his cheek and eyed her. "I don't think that's a thing."

"It's not?" A mix between a sob and a roar emerged from Allyson's lips. That was new. After all the years they'd been married he hadn't seen anything like this before. He'd seen her "moments," but never a moment like this.

"Well, it *might* be a thing."

"I'm fine, I'm fine, I'm fine." She lifted her hands into the air, as if in surrender. "I ju-just need a second."

"I don't think you're fine." And he really didn't.

Her eyes focused on something near her feet. "I am, and ohhhh!" Her words were part excitement, and part despair.

Allyson reached down and picked up a pair of glittery strapped shoes, holding them in awe. It was as if she was a grizzled miner who'd just discovered a chunk of gold. Her mouth gaped open.

"I love these shoes. I haven't worn these in, like, in two years!"

"Uh." Sean cocked an eyebrow. "Well, they're uh, they're good shoes."

"They made my legs look so good!" Sobs emerged with her words and more tears. "I'm okay; I'm going to be fine."

"Honey, come on. It's okay. We'll make it okay. But . . ."

That's when she came to him, falling into his arms, relaxing into him as if she'd been waiting for this. Waiting for him to hold her up.

"I love you," she murmured. Two heartbeats later she was out. Asleep.

"I love you too." Sean's words were met with a soft snore.

He held her close, and then looked at the screen. "It's like an eagle, right?" he said, realizing Allyson was in la-la land and could no longer hear.

An eagle tending to her chicks . . . just like Allyson.

***

"Oh, not again with the bird!" Ray's voice blurted out as Sondra leaned over and looked at her computer. A soft smile curled on her lips, and a deep peace settled within. She didn't understand her obsession with this bird, and she didn't worry about understanding it.

Ray poured a cup of coffee and leaned close, peering over her shoulder. "You're watching a bird! It's a bird," he declared again.

She sighed and waved them away. "It's live! I might miss something."

Ray didn't seem to be listening, instead he shuffled around the kitchen, looking around the counter and opening drawers. "Hey. Have you seen my keys? I've looked everywhere for—"

Sondra held them up. Her eyes remained fixed on the computer, on the birds.

"I just don't ge—" His words paused as the mother eagle landed with a fish and let the little ones devour it. Ray leaned in, and Sondra smiled seeing him staring, frozen.

Yet her peace wasn't as prevalent two hours later as she sat with the other church ladies gathered in her den. Twenty women packed around like sardines. Twenty women she was supposed to be leading, guiding with spiritual truth. Did she dare tell them she hadn't even read the book they were supposed to be discussing? Thankfully Mattie Mae had.

"Mattie Mae, tell us what you got out of the book," Sondra had said. One question and she knew she could sit back for ten minutes and just let Mattie Mae go.

But it wasn't that easy to relax. Mostly because she could hear the kids in the other room. She'd begged Zoe to babysit, and her daughter had finally agreed . . . after the promise of a twenty-dollar bill and a trip to the mall.

A child's scream erupted and Sondra was sure it was Beck's. She looked back over her shoulder, looking at Allyson and noticed she hadn't even flinched at the sound. Instead Allyson stared straight ahead listening to Mattie Mae talk as if it was the most fascinating thing in the world. Sondra wondered if Allyson was sleeping with her eyes open. Or stress paralyzed. She'd heard that was a thing.

From the corner of her eye she saw Zoe waving her arms, trying to get her attention.

She glanced over. Zoe's long hair hung down and a small toddler was wrapped around her leg, tugging, pulling, trying to make her tumble. A half-dozen other kids played in the den, thankfully under some semblance of control . . . for the moment. A text message popped up on the cell phone in Sondra's hand, lighting the screen, and she glanced down.

Zoe / 10:51 AM
MOM, HOW MUCH LONGER!!??!!

Sondra typed out a response, hoping no one noticed. She offered Mattie Mae a smile and nodded.

Sondra / 10:51 AM
OYSTER BOON!

Then she glanced over at Zoe. Zoe looked at her phone. *What?* She mouthed.

Sondra pressed her lips together, pushed her finger into the typepad and typed out another quick message and pressed SEND.

Sondra / 10:51 AM

LKDBVAHIOUBNVWJOSD V

She glared at her daughter, hoping Zoe would pay attention to her text message and stay patient. Sondra glanced around the room. At least twenty women from church filled the space. Young, old, married, single. They were a faithful group. They sat on couches, her dining room chairs, and even extra chairs that Ray had brought over from the church. Reading together was a benefit, but gathering together—sharing each other's lives—was most important. Single lambs tended to stray. She knew that from experience.

The book club was one event that all the women of her church looked forward to, and she didn't want to disappoint them.

Couldn't disappoint them.

***

Allyson knew Mattie Mae Lloyd was talking, but the words only partly filtered in. For this one moment in the day she was sitting in a chair without kids climbing on her, tugging at her, or trying to brush her hair. She'd dressed and had put on makeup. The kids always knew they were going somewhere when she put on makeup. And for these thirty minutes she'd take what she could get. Peace. Sort-of quiet, if one could ignore Beck screaming in the other room. And hopefully a bit of wisdom too.

"Ya'll, it changed me," Mattie Mae was saying. "I mean, it is profound. I mean, I only read the introduction, but it is *revolutionary* in my life. Revolutionary."

Allyson smiled at Mattie Mae, and tried to think of the last time she'd actually read a book. Reading books was something she aspired to do, but she had three kids, so yeah she didn't read books. That was another benefit of being in a book club. It made her feel as if she did.

"I can feel it. Every time I go to the mall there is a parking space right out in the front," Mattie Mae drawled. "There's never a parking space right there in the front. But there is ya'll, every time. I'm not talking about the old one. I don't shop there any more . . . I'm talking about the new mall." The sun reflected off Mattie Mae's strawberry blonde hair, perfectly pinned up, and Allyson was certain she could smell Mattie Mae's White Shoulders cologne spray from where she sat.

Besides if Allyson wasn't at book club she'd be at home, still cleaning up the mess from yesterday. She felt bad waking up in the closet this morning. Well, she'd been fine, she'd slept in Sean's arms—her favorite place to be—but he'd been sore from trying to sleep half slumped over and half sitting up. And his eyes had widened even more when he'd seen the house in the light.

"Welcome home," she'd said with a kiss on his cheek as she handed him a bowl of cereal, since they were out of eggs. She made a mental note to pick up eggs after book club, and maybe hit the park with Izzy and her boys.

Allyson looked to Izzy who sat beside her. Izzy's gaze was narrowed, intent on Mattie Mae. Allyson knew she wasn't really listening. She was either rehearsing her grocery list in her mind, trying to decide if she wanted McDonald's or Chick-fil-A for lunch, or trying to think of anything else BUT the lyrics to "The Wheels on the Bus."

As subtly as she could, Allyson used her thumbs to tap a text in her cell phone.

> Allyson / 10:54 AM
> Sean says I'm stressed.

Izzy glanced at her smart phone.

> Izzy / 10:54 AM
> You are stressed. Very.

Allyson looked over at her friend and shook her head. "What?" Izzy mouthed, incredulous.

> Allyson / 10:54 AM
> Thx 4 that :-0
>
> Izzy / 10:55 AM
> You're stressed . . .
>
> Izzy / 10:55 AM
> I'm stressed
>
> Izzy / 10:55 AM
> Everybody's stressed.
>
> Izzy / 10:55 AM
> Look at Sondra . . .

Almost in unison, they leaned forward, gazing at her and slightly tilting their heads. Sondra looked normal/put together and completely focused on Mattie Mae's words, but her fixed smile and wrinkled brow gave her away. Even though she tried to give the impression that everything was okay—great even—Allyson could see behind the lines—the wrinkle lines on her forehead—that there was more on her mind than she wanted to admit.

Izzy / 10:56 AM
Sondra = MAJOR STRESS!

Allyson / 10:57 AM
So I got a Groupon,

Allyson / 10:57 AM
to Chez Magique

Allyson / 10:57 AM
5 STARS!

Allyson / 10:57 AM
Was thinking about a . . .

Allyson / 10:57 AM
NIGHT OUT?

Izzy raised her hand slightly, as if sending up a silent hallelujah and then typed in a text.

Izzy / 10:58 AM
YES! I need it! Wild!

Izzy / 10:58 AM
Gonna go buy a tube top.

Izzy / 10:58 AM
CRAZY!!!

Allyson attempted to hold back her chuckles. She glanced at Izzy through the corner of her eye and she pressed back a smile at the sight of Izzy sitting a little straighter, excited.

> Allyson / 10:59 AM
> You . . . Me . . . Sondra.

> Allyson / 10:58 AM
> THREE AMIGOS?

Allyson watched from the corner of her eye. Izzy pulled her lips in and her eyebrows shot up. She gave the softest nod as she considered the words she read.

> Izzy / 10:59 AM
> SONDRA? I like it!

Allyson smiled and then sent a text to Sondra next,

> Allyson / 11:00 AM
> NIGHT OUT. SAT. U IN?

"It's The Favor. I can feel it," Mattie Mae was gushing now. "I can feel it. It can make you a better cook. Take all your old recipes and rip them up. With The Favor you can zero in on what stores have the best bargains."

Mattie Mae turned to her friends, her face flushed with excitement.

Emma nodded her agreement.

Sondra was nodding along, too, as she listened to Mattie Mae. Then she looked down, reading the text.

"It's The Favor," Mattie Mae said.

"Yes, sister!" Sondra declared out loud. Then a shocked expression came over her face.

Mattie Mae beamed as pleased as punch that the pastor's wife was so excited about her comments, but Allyson knew the real reason for Sondra's excitement.

Sondra glanced over her shoulder at Allyson and Izzy and winked.

"Oh, Sondra, that's just the sweetest. Thank you."

Sondra turned back to her and nodded, forcing a smile. "That was, um-hum, yes . . ." Sondra tucked her dark brown hair behind her ear and then scanned the room. "Would anyone else like to share?"

"But we didn't even get to talk about when there is a discount involved . . ." Mattie Mae said, with eagerness in her voice.

The brightness in Sondra's face faded as Mattie Mae started in again. Yet Allyson didn't mind. When Mattie Mae started in it meant at least ten more minutes of no kids hanging on her. And as she partly listened to Mattie Mae, her mind had mostly moved to Saturday night. A night out with friends. That's what she needed. It would recharge her batteries. The angst had built up inside, and she knew the best way to release it was by eating good food that she didn't make herself, spilling her guts, and laughing with friends.

Saturday couldn't come soon enough.

CHAPTER FIVE

The kids were down for a nap, finally. And the house was back in order . . . mostly. Allyson sat down on the floor and pulled the lid off the small can of paint. When Sean had repainted the living room just last year, and had gone to buy new paint, the woman cashier at the hardware shop asked if he had kids.

"Yeah, I do," Sean had said. "Three of them."

The woman had handed Sean an extra pint of paint, in the same color. "I'm a mom of three myself. This is for your wife. She'll know what to do with it."

And she had. Allyson had used it to touch up scrapes on the wall from Matchbox cars and from crayon scribbles. And today she pulled it out again.

She dipped the brush into the paint and brushed it over the random scribbles along the wall. Bailey had indeed finished her picture on the wall when she ran out of paper. A cluster of stick figures was there. Five, not four, this time. Two big figures, three little ones. All of them together . . . as it should be. They were surrounded by red and blue flowers.

Allyson lifted her paint brush to paint over them, but then paused. Their little family. *Her* family . . . seen through her daughter's eyes.

A soft smile touched her lips, and she had an idea. She hurried to the hall closet where she had some old picture frames. She'd picked them up at the neighbor's yard sale last year and had plans for some type of Pinterest project, but she hadn't gotten around to it yet. She had the perfect idea for those frames.

Working quickly, she pulled them apart, and then hung the empty frames on the wall over Bailey's images. A large frame over the family picture, and two smaller ones over the flowers. A display of their lives from her daughter's eyes. She'd redeemed the offense, and it felt good. Not that she wanted Bailey to repeat it!

A lightness filled her chest as she looked at it. As crazy as this place got sometimes . . . this was *her* family.

Bailey woke up and wandered down the stairs. She was always the first one awake at nap time. It was as if the world had too much excitement happening for her to miss anything. Bailey paused at the bottom of the stairs and her eyes brightened as she saw her mother's handiwork.

She hurried closer, peering at the hammer in Allyson's hand. "Mommy, my pictures . . . why did you do that?"

"For Daddy." Allyson brushed her hand over her daughter's wrangle of curls. "So he can see our family together."

A grin filled Bailey's face from ear to ear.

She was still looking at the pictures, still smiling, five minutes later when Allyson heard Sean's car park. Allyson was folding laundry on the couch. One load down, five more that waited . . . but at least it was a start.

Bailey ran her hand down the length of her blonde, curly hair and continued to stare. "He's going to love this," she said. She tossed her hair around.

Sean walked through the door with quickened steps. She glanced up to him, and her throat thickened with emotion. He was home. Things always seemed right in the world when Sean was home.

"Hey, honey," she called to him.

"Hey." He walked over, a large smile filling his face. "Check this out." He had a hop in his step, and it was good to see. He handed her the document tube he'd been carrying, and then turned back to Bailey. As he leaned close Allyson got a whiff on his cologne, and her heart did a little leap. Yes, everything was so much righter when Sean was home.

Sean's eyes widened at the sight of the wall and the frames she'd added. "Whoa . . ."

Allyson waved her hand toward the wall. "Yeah, she said she wanted to be an artist when she grew up, so . . ." Her chest warmed with joy to see Bailey's pride. Bailey's cheeks plumped up as she smiled, and she swished from side to side basking in her father's approval.

"Whoa. That *is* awesome!" Sean hunkered down to get a closer look at Bailey's masterpieces. He kneeled before the pictures on one knee and then placed Bailey on the other knee, wrapping his arms around her.

"You know what?" Sean exclaimed. "You have a lot of talent. This wall may be worth something some day!"

"Okay, here you go." He turned around so she could climb on his back. "Alright." And then with a large smile on both of their faces he "flew" Bailey over to the couch, flopping her down.

Allyson took the lid off the document tube and pulled out the blueprint. She spread it on the ottoman before her, scanning the draft. It was a nice house, a large house that a real family would live in some day. Since they first started dating in college, *this* had been Sean's dream. Now he was living it. He made her proud, and it made it easier—okay, a little bit easier—to deal with his work trips when she knew Sean was doing something he loved.

"You know what I wanted to be when I was a little boy?" Sean asked. Bailey tipped her head in curiosity.

His expression grew serious. "A basketball player."

A giggle escaped Allyson's lips.

He feigned shock. "Don't laugh. There is a fine tradition of white, short basketball players." Allyson folded a small pair of jeans and set them to the side. Sean was the fun one, the silly one. He brought so much joy to their home, and she was blessed to be married to such a man . . . but in a way his joy made her feel deeper what she was missing inside.

Allyson laughed again, but deep down there was still that nagging feeling that something wasn't right. The house was cleaner today, yes, but nothing was fixed. It would just get dirty again *tomorrow*. The kids would get out of control again *tomorrow*. Life *tomorrow* would be the same as life today. More work. More noise. More stress. Is this what life had come to?

And Sean's talk of dreams hadn't helped much. No . . . not at all. An ache that had been just below the surface began to grow, and it refused to be pushed down. Even the smiles and laughter from a moment before couldn't keep it at bay.

Bailey turned her attention to Sean's architectural sketches spread before Allyson. She pointed. "What's this?"

Allyson leaned forward, peering down with her. "This is a house that daddy's making. Isn't it wonderful?"

Bailey pointed to a boxed-out space. "Is this a window?"

"Yeah, it is." Sean nodded, obviously pleased she'd been able to read the draft.

Bailey tilted her head and studied it. "If you move it over here then they can see the pool." She pointed to an opposite wall.

"Huh?" Sean scratched his head and then looked closer. Then his face brightened, and Allyson knew he liked that idea . . . and he most likely wondered why he hadn't thought of it.

"I have to go play, see ya." Then Bailey skipped off.

"Interesting," he said, and she could see he was making a mental note.

Allyson picked up one of Brandon's shirts that read, *Homework Kills Trees, So Stop the Madness*, and then turned to Sean, daring to open her heart. "You know what I wanted to be when I was a kid?"

He looked up from his plans. "What?"

"This." She gazed around the room wistfully.

Sean's eyes followed her.

"I wanted to be a mom. Marry a wonderful man, and I did. Have beautiful babies and raise them. And I did. I am." The words came out more as frustration than thankfulness, and Allyson pounded a soft fist on her leg.

"I don't get it, Sean." She blew out an exasperated breath, trying to hold back her tears. "*This* is my dream. I'm living it, and I'm not happy." She crossed her arms over her chest, pulling them in close. "How come I feel like this?"

Sean lowered his head, as if feeling defeat. "I don't know." She hugged herself hard. She didn't want him to feel this way. It's not like he had done anything wrong, and deep down she knew he couldn't fix it either.

Allyson returned to folding. "I'm a horrible person," she muttered. There. She finally said the words. She'd been feeling them. Almost from Day 1 of this parenting thing she had felt them, but they were words she couldn't voice. It was easier to put on a smile and continue on. Always continue on.

"No, you're not a horrible person."

Allyson peered up at Sean from under her lashes. She could tell he was trying to figure out what to say *to her*. What to do *with her*.

She swallowed hard. "I'm just tired. I'm sorry . . ."

He leaned closer to her, as if wanting her to pay attention to his words. "You don't have to be sorry, alright? You don't have to be sorry. You have to choose to do something for yourself. *Do something* for yourself. You have to do it. You're the only person who can do that—"

"Sean," she interrupted, but he continued on.

"It's the kind of thing . . . that, if you just . . ."

"Sean!" His name came out louder than she planned. She blew out a quick breath. "I—I don't need a lecture right now. It's not helpful in this particular moment."

"What?" He lifted his eyebrows. "I'm listening to you. I'm sitting here and listening to you. "

"I know, I know you're listening," she let her voice trail off.

"And I'm hearing you," he added.

She smirked. "You're doing *both* of those things? Listening and hearing?" Her eyes widened and she pressed her lips together.

He chuckled. "I am, I'm very talented." He pointed a finger into the air. "And I'm showing marked improvement. You have to give me that. I want credit."

The doorbell interrupted their banter.

Allyson looked to the door. Her mind raced, trying to remember if someone was going to stop by. No, she didn't think so. She looked to Sean, and her heart sank when she saw the guilty look on his face.

"Who is that?" she asked.

Sean released a heavy sigh. "That would be Bridget."

"What?"

"Yeah, I called Bridget and I invited her to dinner . . . and I forgot."

"Dinner?" Allyson's mouth gaped open. She hadn't even thought of dinner, and that was a problem. No, actually the problem was that her family expected to eat . . . every single night.

"Open up, you community of losers, let me in. I'm hungry," Bridget's voice filtered in from outside.

He cast her a look that said, *Forgive me?*

"It's fine. We'll just whip something up." Sean circled his hands in the air, and then he rose and moved toward the front door.

"Oh, we'll just whip something up? Because that's how that happens." She tossed the towel she'd been folding onto the couch. "We'll do it together. Looking forward to whipping something up . . . together."

∗∗∗

Allyson opened the door to see Bridget standing there. Petite, blonde, beautiful, Bridget had been such a darling girl when Allyson and Sean were dating. Allyson had met Sean's half-sister at her seventh birthday party. She'd worn a pink Cinderella dress and had long blonde ringlets. She'd embraced Allyson's neck and planted a wet kiss on her cheek when presented with "glass slippers" that were made of a really hard, uncomfortable looking plastic. Yet the years hadn't been easy on Sean's sister.

"Hey, what took you so long?" Bridget asked as she strode in with baby Phoenix on her hip. She wore tight jeans, mid-Goth makeup, and Allyson noticed new hot pinks streaks in Bridget's blonde hair with some purple ones added in for fun. Nice.

Thankfully Sean felt super guilty for inviting Bridget over without warning, so he entertained the kids while she cooked. Spaghetti with sauce from a jar. Frozen dinner rolls and salad . . . the easiest meal on earth.

But then came the dinner conversation. Allyson tried not to wince as Bridget spilled all the details of her life and even showed off her new nose ring. Bridget always said awkward things. Bridget had no filter. At least dinner tonight wasn't as awkward as last week when Bridget wanted to show off her stretch marks.

Allyson breathed a sigh of relief when dinner ended and no new words were said that her kids would pick up and have to be grounded for tomorrow.

Sean—still feeling guilty—dismissed the kids from the table and set to work clearing it. Allyson stayed seated wondering just how far his guilt would take him. All the way to filling the dishwasher? This would be fun to see.

Sean cleaned off her plate, and then moved to get Bridget's.

Bridget swatted at Sean's hand. "Hey, I'm not done with that. Give it back." Then her scowl disappeared and a smile quickly replaced it.

"So, great news. I got an extra job. We needed something more so I picked up a night shift at a bowling alley." She stabbed her salad with a fork.

Allyson spooned another spoonful of carrots into baby Phoenix's mouth, and she felt her eyes widen. A lump formed in her throat as if she'd just swallowed a whole carrot. Allyson had no doubt that Bridget did need extra money. Her Prince Charming had turned into a frog and had leapt away as soon as he could, running from all responsibility. The problem wasn't Bridget's need. It was her ability. How could the single mom add in one more thing to her already part-time job and school? Allyson knew exactly how . . . and sweat beaded on her brow.

"That is unbelievably cool," Sean exclaimed, obviously not putting two and two together.

Allyson looked to baby Phoenix. Ten months old and the sweetest thing. She supposed if Bridget needed help—

No. Stop that!

Allyson's mouth gaped open, and she bit her knuckle. *Oh no, here it comes. She knows I compulsively take care of people.*

In the pyramid of codependence, Allyson was the peak, and all the dependent people filtered down from there. Sometimes they were shuffled slightly, depending on need, but always . . . always their needs were met by her.

My kids, her kids, other kids, kids at the park I don't know, stray animals. I can't say no.

She gritted her teeth and focused on Bridget. Her eyebrows lifted as she waited for the words to come. *10 . . . 9 . . . 8 . . .*

Bridget turned to her. "I start on Saturday night, and I was hoping you could watch Phoenix while I work."

And then a realization popped in her head. And Allyson glanced over to the calendar on her fridge and the big red circle that she'd drawn around Saturday.

"Saturday night?" she hurriedly said. "Oh, um, normally yes. I'm glad you brought that up." Allyson winced and turned to Sean. "Because I planned a Moms' night thing . . . for Saturday." She gritted her teeth.

"What?" Sean turned, a look of disbelief on his face. "You planned a moms' night?"

Allyson scratched behind her ear. "Yeah, I planned one."

Bridget's mouth gaped open. "What? You always watch Phoenix on the weekends. I was sort of counting on you when I got the job." She pointed at Phoenix with her fork.

"Yeah, um." Allyson fought against the urge to tell her it would be fine—that she could do it. She pressed her lips tight and looked to Sean.

Instead of anger at her making plans without asking him, his face brightened. "You know how a flight attendant goes through the safety thing?" He talked with his hands, emphasizing his words, walking back toward them. "You know when you have to put on your oxygen first before assisting others?"

Allyson's brow furrowed, and she wondered where he was going with this. "Are we flying somewhere? Is this what we're doing?" She cocked her head to the side.

"You need your oxygen mask, Allyson. You need *your* mask on, before assisting others." He pointed his fingers to Allyson, then to Bridget and then back to her. "Right? Before you can help others."

Bridget sat up straighter, obviously not happy with where this conversation was going. "Wow, Sean, we get it." She bobbed her head from side-to-side. "It's a metaphor. I think we both . . . we got it."

Sean pointed at his sister, like a school teacher pointing out a top pupil. "It's a very good metaphor, thank you for pointing it out."

He looked to Allyson. "You will go Saturday night. Saturday night," he repeated as if making a mental note of the day. He pounded the table with his finger, emphasizing his words.

"Saturday night," she echoed softly, partly in disbelief that this was going so well.

"You will go Saturday night?" This time his words were more like a question than a statement. "Really?" Disappointment flashed on his face.

"Oh no!" Bridget whined, catching on to the change in her brother's countenance. "Sean's not going to be able to play video games on Saturday night with his loser friends!"

"First of all, that's low." Sean pointed at her, the big brother coming out. "You don't even know Kevin."

"I know Kevin."

Allyson knew Kevin, too, and for once she found herself on Bridget's side. Obviously they had the same opinion this time.

Kevin was Sean's best friend. They met when they were in the fifth grade. They started playing video games as juveniles. And they were still playing video games like juveniles.

The worst part was, Kevin WAS a kid. And Sean always justified this relationship, even though it revolved around childish things.

So usually on Saturday nights as she was trying to put the kids to bed Allyson heard something like this . . . loud, way too loud coming from the den.

Don't stand right behind me, move over, move over.

No, no, back up, back up. I just died.

I didn't shoot you. The guy behind you shot you.

And no matter what anyone said, Sean not only justified his relationship with Kevin, but his habit too.

"I use video games to transition from work stress," he said defensively. "That's my oxygen. I put mine on."

He moved his fingers as if he was playing a Gameboy. "Video games equal oxygen . . ." Then he pointed to Allyson. "So I can help you put yours on, and you can help the rest of the world."

Allyson scooped up another spoonful of baby food and tried to hide her smile. It was just something about her husband she had to accept . . . as hard as it was at times. "Thank you." She swooped the spoon into the baby's mouth.

Bridget didn't seem quite as amused, especially as Sean launched into fix-it mode. "Who's going to watch the baby? What about Joey?" he asked.

Bridget smirked. "Uh, no."

Joey was Bridget's ex, and the father of baby Phoenix. He was a fun guy, in a noncommittal, allergic-to-all-responsibility kind of way.

"No, I tried that." There was a sense of sadness, more than anger as Bridget said those words, and it about broke Allyson's heart.

"Here's the thing." Sean puffed out his chest. "You're going out, and I'm going to watch Phoenix."

"You're going to watch Phoenix?" Allyson asked.

A smile touched his lips. "I will watch Phoenix, big brother to the rescue once again, and everyone's happy."

Bridget straightened in her seat and then tossed back her hair. She could ask for help—and she often did—but Bridget's defenses rose up and red flaming arrows shot from her eyes every time someone accused her of being a charity case.

"I don't need your charity, and I certainly don't need your metaphors." She pounded the table, open palms. Then she rose and lifted Phoenix out of the high chair with a swoop. "So I'm going to go and get you to bed. Because that's the responsible thing to do, because I'm so responsible. Later."

"See you later," Allyson said, unsure if she was thankful or guilty over how this went down. Probably both.

"Look for your oxygen!" Sean called after Bridget. "You'll find it."

Sean let out a large, heavy sigh. "I thought that went well." His words disagreed with the look on his face, but Allyson remembered something else. Something very important she forgot to mention.

The words spilled out before she could hold them back. "And also, Marco is bringing the twins over because he's afraid to watch them alone." She offered a weak smile. "Surprise!" She added in a sing-song voice, and then winced. "Sorry."

"That's a lot of kids." Sean put on a brave face, and Allyson remembered why she loved him. She promised herself then that she'd get her oxygen, and make his sacrifice worth it.

Five more days. Just five more days.

CHAPTER SIX

Allyson crossed out the last day on the calendar page. FREEDOM she'd written in big letters on Saturday, and now today was the day.

The house was quiet, too quiet, as she got dressed. But she didn't want to think about that—worry about that. Sean was here, and he was taking care of the kids. Tonight was her night. This was her oxygen.

She went to her closet and pulled out her rhinestone, studded stilettos. The shoes that she had just cried into a few days before. She smoothed her dress, slipped on her heels, and then put on the rhinestone bracelet and matching earrings she'd gotten two anniversaries ago but had never worn. Then Allyson took tentative steps to the bathroom to finish her makeup. Her ankles wobbled a little as she walked, and she realized it had been a long time—too long—since she'd worn heels like this.

Standing in front of the mirror Allyson was pleased with what she saw. It was better than the jeans and soft tees that she usually wore.

With soft swipes she put on her lipstick. Her hair was pinned up in a Betty Grable sort of way and it looked . . . nice.

She stepped back from the mirror, and for the first time in a long time she was happy by how she looked, pleased even. She picked up a small bottle of perfume and sprayed her wrists. The scent of orange blossoms drifted up. Perfect. Then with tentative steps she walked down the stairs, pausing by the door to glance at their kids. They were glued in front of the television watching an old *Tom and Jerry* cartoon, Sean's favorite, but he was nowhere to be seen. She glanced at the time on her cell phone and hurried outside. She had just enough time to pick up Izzy and Sondra and make it to Chez Magique in time for their reservation.

She hurriedly exited the house, snapping her clutch closed as she walked, and spotted Sean wrangling Beck's car seat out of her minivan.

Sean froze when he saw her. His jaw dropped. He eyed her from head to foot and back up again. "Wow."

She tugged on the bottom hem of her dress, hoping it wasn't too short, and offered a tentative smile.

"Wow, honey, you look amazing."

"Are you sure tonight's okay? Because I'm starting to feel guilty again."

"It's fine. Com'on, yes. You're gonna have fun. I've got this. I'm not going to call you unless it's a natural disaster. And then I might not even call you. The house may be flying . . ." He waved his hands from side to side for emphasis. "And I'm not even calling you at that point."

She chuckled, relief flooding her. He cared for her . . . he really did, and he wanted this for her.

"Promise me that you'll do one thing," Sean continued, his voice softening to almost a whisper. "Promise me that you'll do whatever it takes to unplug and just breathe."

Allyson closed her eyes. She blew out a heavy breath. Peace filled her just thinking about that. Her husband was so sweet. She didn't deserve him. She didn't deserve this . . . but he was right. She needed it.

She let her eyes flutter open. "I promise."

Then, with the sweetest smile, Sean handed her the keys for her van.

Peace filled her, but it was short lived. The roar of a car's engine interrupted the quiet moment. She recognized that sound. Her head flipped around, and a red Chevy Nova parked in the street.

"Uncle Kevin!" Brandon called out as he raced out of the house.

Man-boy Kevin wore torn jeans, a ratty T-shirt, and a green sweatshirt that had seen better days. Brandon leapt into Kevin's arms with abandon.

Kevin nodded to her as he strode past. "Allyson." He hoisted Brandon up on his arm like a trophy.

"Kevin?" She lifted one eyebrow and turned back to Sean.

"Yeah, Kevin's coming," he muttered, scratching his cheek. "He's gonna help with the kids." He swallowed hard. "He *might* help with the kids."

She lifted the other eyebrow.

"He's here to help. He had a free night," Sean hurriedly added.

"Kevin is babysitting?" she hurriedly asked.

"No, I'm babysitting." Sean pointed to himself. "Kevin's just here."

"Get in here, Stout Flipper, let's do this," Kevin called to him.

Allyson turned back to him. "What?"

"It's gamer time." Kevin growled.

She turned back to Sean who wore a pained expression.

"Please tell me you're not going to play those violent video games—"

"Double kill!" Brandon called out.

She gasped. "—with our son." She shook her head in disbelief.

"Triple kill!" he shouted louder.

"You know, you're going to have to define violence." Sean guided her to the van. "Because do you know that Lego game you bought? Those characters shatter like into a million pieces."

Her mouth circled into an O. Was he really saying this . . . as if she'd change her mind and agree with him? "What? What?!"

"That—that Lego game is sick. Right?"

Allyson gasped, unsure with how to respond. Was he joking? "I—I . . ." No words came.

Sean motioned take large breaths. "Just breathe, breathe."

He took a deep breath, and then blew it out, as if expecting her to mimic him. Anger buzzed in her temples and quickened her heartbeat. But she had a choice. Was this a battle she wanted to fight? Not tonight it wasn't.

She tilted back her head and sucked in a long deep breath, stroked the back of her neck with her free hand, trying to will away the tension, and then released it.

Sean's hands pressed together, as if in prayer, and she knew he was holding back the urge to usher her into the van. She told herself to leave. To walk away. This wasn't a battle she needed to fight at this moment.

"I don't want to know." She opened the van door, blinking rapidly. "Not tonight, because I love everybody," she said, forcing a smile.

"Destroy them all!" Brandon bellowed. His words broke her feigned calm.

Allyson spun around and rushed toward Kevin. She took two steps, and Sean caught her arm.

Allyson waved her small purse toward Kevin as if it was a weapon. "Okay, do you know what childhood friends do eventually?"

Kevin smirked. "Oh, just say it."

She bobbed her head like Queen Latifah. "They grow up!"

"There it is!" Kevin called out.

"One night, dude!" Sean scolded him.

Sean ushered her into the van, and quickly closed the door behind her. Her hands trembled as she grabbed the steering wheel, but she decided again not to let this bother her.

Let it go. Let it good.

Seeing that she was staying put, Sean relaxed his shoulders and took a step toward the house. "Okay, good. *I* have to breathe," she heard Sean mutter from the other side of the glass.

Allyson put her key into the ignition, and told herself that Sean was right. It was only one night. One night for her—for her friends—and as she pulled out she pushed all thoughts of Triple Kill out of her mind.

Well, mostly.

∗∗∗

Izzy stared at the white pregnancy test in her hands. Her breaths came fast, quick. "Izzy. Breathe, breathe."

She held it up, noticing two pink lines. Just like the three previous tests she'd taken. She had dressed up in a new coral-colored skirt that fit strangely tight around the waist. Her intense hunger prodded her to take the test. Not the small "Oh-I-wish-I-had-something-to-eat" hunger, but the "food-must-enter-my-body-now" hunger that she only experienced when she was pregnant with the twins.

A knock sounded at the door. Unless it was the pizza man, she wasn't interested.

"Hold on!" she shouted.

She placed a hand on her hip, and studied yet another test. "This is beautiful!" She tried to convince herself. But she wasn't very convincing.

She put the lid down on the toilet, sat, and then stared at the test. "Oh crap!"

Marco needed full, detailed daily instructions for the two kids they had now. What was she going to do when another one . . . or two . . . joined them?

She rose and hurried out the bathroom door. Marco was standing there with his list in hand. It was one night. ONE. Did he seriously have to freak out like that?

She rushed past him to the kitchen to get her phone, hoping there was a text from Allyson telling her she was almost there.

"I know you'll do great!" she called to her husband.

Steak? Chicken? Both? Would she look like a freak if she got two appetizers too?

Izzy moved around the kitchen with frantic movements. She lifted potato chip bags and blankies. She moved boxes of cereal and toys looking for her keys and purse.

"Okay, I mean I have the wipies," Marco said as he followed her. "And I have the diapers. I have no red dye because I know it drives them crazy, right. But you said there were three emergency numbers." He scanned the list she'd left him again, waving it as if it was defective. "But I only have two, Izzy. Your mother's and—"

Izzy lifted a hand, halting his words. "Stop second-guessing yourself." She paused and glanced into his eyes—his glazed over and terrified eyes.

"You know I'm actually not." He swallowed hard and leaned against the counter, repeating the words she'd seen him rehearsing in the mirror just an hour earlier. "I have full confidence in myself and my abilities as a father."

She offered him what she hoped was a reassuring grin. "It's one night. I believe in you."

Marco gritted his teeth. "And you should . . . n't."

Izzy lifted her eyebrows. "I mean, what's the worst that can happen?"

"Serious injury, death." Marco's voice quivered. "They can get maimed. I can lose both children!!" Marco fanned himself with his hands. "We have to turn the air on. Oh, it's getting hot in here. I feel hot!"

She nodded and then turned toward the door. "So, good luck!" she called back as she hurried out.

Twenty steps and she found herself at Allyson's van and swung open the door.

"Ah, you look gorgeous!" Allyson squealed.

Izzy climbed into the car with a determined set to her chin. "Okay, I want to have crazy fun. Get me out of here. Now!"

"You got it!" Allyson pursed her lips. "Yes, ma'am." She started the car with flair, and they were off to pick up the third Musketeer.

Allyson turned on the radio. A crazy cool rock song played, and they danced in the front seat like they were eighteen again and they had their daddy's car for the night. Izzy lifted her arms and rocked out to the beat. Allyson gripped the steering wheel and rocked her shoulders as she drove, digging the song.

For one night they weren't going to have to pause their dinner for a potty break. Didn't have to cut someone else's hot dog into tiny little pieces or refill a sippy cup. They could talk at a normal tone and speak of other things other than poo poo and farts. Just the idea of it was a magical thing.

And Izzy forced herself to push those pregnancy tests out of her mind. Tomorrow . . . tomorrow she'll think about how this was going to add a tilt to her already unbalanced life.

***

Ten minutes later they were at Sondra's house. She wasn't answering her texts so they went to the door. Allyson could hear voices inside. Loud voices!

"Whose credit card is that going on? Oh, no, no. You're never wearing those," Sondra exclaimed. "Over my dead body, and my credit cards won't work if I'm dead."

Allyson bit her lower lip, wondering if Sondra knew they were there. Sondra always was so . . . well . . . under control. Surely this was a fluke. Or . . . could it be her friend wasn't as put together as everyone always thought?

"Everybody's wearing them!" Even through the door Zoe's teenage voice was LOUD.

Izzy went to knock, and then paused. Izzy was usually the brave one, but she seemed unsure about interrupting this awkward moment. Allyson winced as she reached up. She knocked just loud enough to let Sondra know they were there.

The voices paused for a moment, and Allyson released a breath. Then, unexpectedly, they started up again.

"I'm not wearing them, and your father's not wearing them, thank God!" Sondra exclaimed. The door opened, and she poked her head outside. Her dark, short hair was perfectly in place and she wore her perfectly-practiced pastor's wife smile. "I'll just be a second."

The door had opened just wide enough for Allyson to notice the jean short shorts in Sondra's hand . . . obviously the item of dispute.

As quick as it opened, the door closed again. "Oh, wow, Ally's not wearing them!"

Not two heartbeats passed when the door opened again, and Sondra's serene smile was convincing, surprisingly convincing. The store hanger and short shorts remained in her hand. "So, whose car are we taking?" Sondra asked sweetly.

Allyson clapped her hands together and did a little hop. "Can we take Ray's?" She motioned to the vintage Mustang parked behind the house. It was so much nicer than her minivan and didn't smell like stale French fries.

Sondra wasn't moved. "I can't be seen riding around in Ray's mid-life crisis, and anyway it's a cop magnet."

Behind her, standing on the landing of the second story steps, Zoe held a cluster of shopping bags in her hands. A single braid hung over her left shoulder, and stray curls framed her face. She was adorable, which was probably the reason Sondra was so protective.

"I am so sorry that I want to go out with a guy that I met from church!" Zoe lifted her hands for emphasis and the bags rustled together. "How wild of me. Wow, I'm so crazy."

Sondra offered another half-smile. "Hold on."

"Okay." They stepped back. The door closed again, but Sondra's voice was clear through the door.

"You're not going anywhere until your father gets home. And he's going to agree with me when he gets home . . . so good luck with that!"

Then she swooped out of the house as if an entourage awaited, which it sort-of did. "Here I come," Sondra said in a sing-song voice.

"Yeah!" Allyson let out a little cheer, and Izzy shook her hips with excitement.

In the van, Sondra insisted on taking the back seat, mostly because Izzy wanted to control the music. Izzy waited with anticipation, with her fists balled and ready to pump the sky, as Allyson started the van again. Only this time there was only silence as they pulled out and drove out of the middle-class suburb and onto the highway.

Allyson pushed out her bottom lip. "The radio was working a minute ago."

Izzy fiddled with the knobs. "Why does it keep going out?"

"Because my daughter spilt apple juice on it." Ally hit the dashboard. Hard. Doing that had worked before.

The large hit worked, and the music blared once again. Allyson resumed her head bob and Izzy shook her balled fisted in the air to the beat. They were young. They were together. Tonight was going to be a great night!

Amidst drum beat and blaring lyrics, a squeak of a voice came from the backseat. "Kind of loud," Sondra said.

Allyson pushed out her lipsticked lips and glanced in the rearview mirror, noticing Sondra wearing a skeptical church lady face.

"Sorry!" Allyson called back to her. "The volume doesn't work either." She glanced to Izzy and they continued their seat dances.

"Whip out a CD," Sondra offered. "Oh, do you have any Amy Grant?"

Izzy paused her bouncing, and she leaned closer to the stereo. "Um, let me check." She reached her fingers toward the buttons.

"Oh no, don't touch that!" Allyson blurted, but her words came late. Too late.

"A B C D E F G!" Elmo's voice blared through the radio. The screeching puppet voice startled her. "Ah!" She swerved slightly into the other lane. Headlights moved quickly her direction, and she jerked back into her lane again.

Izzy tried to press the "stop" button, but it didn't stop. She pushed more buttons, but the "volume" or "off" button weren't working either.

Allyson wrinkled her nose. *Dang apple juice.*

"It happened once before. It's fine!" Allyson called out. She pounded the dashboard over and over again, but it didn't help. It didn't stop. Allyson felt invaded . . . by Elmo. Could she ever leave her role as mommy behind, for even one night?

Finally, they arrived at the restaurant. Even the parking lot looked upscale as she pulled into a space right under the streetlight. It was a little farther from the door than other spaces, but totally worth the protection the light offered.

"H I J K!" Elmo continued to sing, and with one swift movement Allyson turned off the van and pulled out the key.

Sondra let out a weak sigh as she unbuckled her seat belt. "Well, now I know my ABCs." Leave it to Sondra to always try to find the bright spot in things.

"You always park this far away?" Izzy asked, glancing back at the restaurant.

"Good news is that I got a good parking spot. Right under the light. Safest spot," Allyson chirped.

"Oh yeah, I read that blog," Izzy said offhandedly.

Allyson pulled out her cell phone from her purse and noticed there was a text message . . . from Sean. Her heart sunk a little, and she wondered if things had already gone awry. Then she paused and smiled as she read his words.

> Sean / 7:33 PM
> Unplug. We got this.

She stared at the word "Unplug," then looked over to Izzy and Sondra. There was a sense of rightness to the three of them being together. Just them.

"You know what, ladies?" Allyson tilted up her chin and moved her gaze from one face to the other. "Tonight is our night . . ."

They both looked up to meet her gaze, and she continued. ". . . And we look good!"

"Um-hum," the both said in unison.

"Let's do it," Izzy said.

Allyson stepped out from the van and closed the door. Stars twinkled in a clear evening sky. The weather was warm. Not too hot. Not too cool. The streetlight cast a warm glow over her washed and waxed van, and together they moved toward the restaurant.

Allyson hadn't been on this street in over a year, and the property owners had given it a face-lift. Large flowerpots filled with flowers lined the brick-faced building

Stepping under the portico outside of the restaurant was like stepping into another world. Small, white twinkling lights had been wrapped around white pillars. It was as if someone had pulled the stars in the sky and had created a tunnel for them to walk under.

Allyson walked in the middle with Izzy on one side and Sondra on the other. She didn't know if it was on purpose, but their strides matched hers. A light wind came up, stirring her hair and lifting it off her shoulders. They looked good. They looked like Charlie's Angels, she was sure. A few people looked up from their outside tables and watched them pass. Did anyone guess they were three stressed moms? Not tonight. Allyson could almost hear the theme music to go along with their stride.

Then, unexpectedly, Allyson's ankle turned. She shifted slightly, and thought she would tumble to the ground, but then caught herself.

Just one moment . . . can't I have just one moment of grace? She righted herself and continued on, hardly missing a step. If Izzy and Sondra noticed her fumble they didn't say a word, and she liked that. They were good friends indeed.

CHAPTER SEVEN

They entered the small restaurant and the aroma of garlic, fresh bread, and expensive perfume greeted them. Allyson paused for a moment, realizing this was so different from the restaurants that she usually ate at with Sean and the kids. Instead of loud, kid music, a soft harp played. Instead of the dings and buzzes of video games and the loud clunks of skeeball, low conversation and murmurs filled the room. She glanced around. Every table seemed to be full, well, except for the one that waited for them. She'd been diligent in making a reservation. Izzy and Sondra stood by the large plant in the foyer near the door as Allyson stepped forward.

A hostess wore a slinky red dress and a large silver statement necklace. She had perfectly arched eyebrows, flawless skin. Her black hair was pulled into a high, tight bun, and she smiled as she greeted them.

"Welcome to Chez Magique. Your journey awaits." Her voice oozed out like frosting from a squeeze tube.

Allyson nearly squealed as she approached. Giddiness bounced in her belly and threatened to escape. "Ohhh." She cooed and briefly glanced back to her friends, then back to the hostess. "Field. Party of three."

"And what is your name?"

Allyson's smile fell. She cleared her throat. Her eyelashes fluttered, sure she'd pronounced her name clearly. "Fie-ld," she repeated.

The hostess pursed her pouty lips as she used the computer mouse to move over her computer screen. "I cannot seem to find your reservation on my scroll." She punctuated every word and pushed her lips down into a slight frown. "Uh, sorry."

Allyson's mouth gaped open. "But, I. I—"

The woman leaned forward slightly and stretched her hand to Allyson, as if trying to ease her concern. "It's only a two-and-a-half-hour wait, totally worth it," she said in a valley girl drawl. "And during that time you're more than welcome to observe the art in the gallery." The hostess motioned to the wall behind Allyson, and then she smiled and nodded as if pleased with herself that she'd come up with the perfect solution.

Allyson's eyebrows scrunched down. "I—I don't want to observe the art."

The woman reflected her scowl. "I know it's really exhausting, right?"

Desperation clawed at Allyson's throat, and she willed her pounding heart to still. It didn't.

"I—I scouted, I planned. I got the Groupon. I made a reservation. I did everything that was required of me, so there must be some mistake." The words spilled out, untamed.

The woman offered a sympathetic smile. She waved her hands and flashed her painted nails as she spoke. "How about this, why don't I go back and talk to my visionary for you?"

Allyson wrinkled up her nose. "Your what?"

The woman's sweet plastic smile dropped, and she took on the look of an impatient cab driver. "The manager," she growled.

Allyson's eyes darted from side-to-side, and she hoped Izzy and Sondra couldn't hear. This was their night. She was their event planner, and once again she was a big, huge failure. "Oh, yeah," she whispered.

"Uh, wait here." The hostess strode off toward the kitchen, taking little steps in her too-high heels.

Allyson sighed. Frustration coursed through her, and she leaned on the counter for support. Her feet hurt, and she remembered why she hadn't worn these type of shoes in two years. A nice dinner out would be worth the pain . . . but as of this moment she questioned if that would happen. She turned back toward her friends.

Sondra strode up and placed a hand on Allyson's arm. "Everything okay?" She clutched her small purse to her chest.

Allyson released a heavy breath and stopped her stilettoed foot. "No. They lost our reservation. The wait is two and a half hours. This is going to totally ruin our night."

From the corner of her eye she noticed Izzy grabbing a plate of half-eaten appetizers that had been abandoned at the bar. Izzy moved to the waiting bench by the front door and sat, shoveling the fancy nachos into her mouth as if she hadn't eaten all day.

Allyson puffed out another breath. Is this what their night had come to? Her best friend sneaking leftovers since Allyson hadn't been able to fulfill what she'd promised?

Sondra smoothed down her dark hair. Every strand was perfectly in place. "You know what? Everything's going to be okay." Sondra's voice was calm, too calm for the situation.

Allyson spread out her arms, in defeat. "There is a man-child playing death video games at home with my son," her voice rose with every word.

Sondra's voice was calm. "Ally, Ally, relax. I'm sure that Sean has everything in control. Everything's going to be alright. Relax."

Sondra, always the levelheaded one. But even the mellow words of her pastor's wife could not diminish the angst she felt inside. She'd left her husband and kids at home, but she hadn't left her frustration with man-child Kevin there. She hadn't left her annoyance with Sean back in the driveway, no matter how she pretended she had. Instead, she played it all out in her mind again.

I bet Sean's playing some game with the kids, something like cops and robbers and it's gotten totally out of control.

She could see it—see it so clearly in her mind's eye. Kevin and Sean tied up in chairs, backs to each other, wrapped up in packing tape, their arms pinned down so they couldn't move.

Her eyes fluttered closed, and she could picture the toddlers running wild. Screams echoed off the walls and cabinets. Packing tape strung from every chair, table, and wall to the center of the den. Allyson resisted the urge to bolt from the restaurant— resisted the urge to jump in the minivan and race to their rescue.

She swallowed hard, trying to keep her heart from pounding and opened her eyes.

The house was most likely a plane wreck, and in total chaos. The kids most likely were running—with scissors—as unwholesome music blared from the computer games. Bailey probably jumped up and down, dancing wildly to the music.

Then there was the worst part . . . Brandon playing death video games, and Kevin going into meltdown mode since he admittedly didn't like kids.

"I didn't sign up for this. I didn't sign up for this!" She could hear Kevin screeching in her mind.

Allyson also bet that Marco was all freaked out, crouched in the kitchen, and overwhelmed. Sean would try to control things as he always did, and he'd swagger over to Marco, with Kevin still attached to his back, and offer the *Braveheart* speech. "This is your moment! Fatherhood . . . man it up!"

And one of the twins would be in a video game coma, which was going to make him have nightmares and which would make Izzy mad at her on Monday. Yes, she played it all out in her mind.

She didn't have time to ponder it any further, because someone walking by caught Allyson's attention. She recognized the dark hair and the swagger. "Joey?" He was dressed nicer than usual.

She'd at first been impressed with Bridget's ex-boyfriend when she'd brought him to meet them. Joey was handsome and engaging. He always dressed nice, and he seemed to have his act together. But it was just for show. He didn't have a job. He didn't go to school. He floated through life using that charm of his to get people to like him, to help him out . . . but charm could only get one so far.

Joey paused before her. Surprise flashed on his face, and then something else. "Hey. Hi Allyson." Joey's surprised looked turned into a worried one as he adjusted his tie. He looked handsomely sharp. A fedora was pulled low on his brow, and he looked as if he'd just stepped off the set of *High School Musical,* or maybe *Glee.* "I, uh, didn't recognize you without your kids."

"What are you doing here?" she asked. She fingered her thin gold necklace.

He fiddled with his fedora. "I'm just meeting somebody."

Allyson swayed slightly. How was he able to waltz in so easily and she got stopped at the front door?

She awkwardly pointed to her friends. "We're just having dinner, a little moms' night out." *Or at least that was the plan.* This wasn't turning out anything like she thought. She still waited to hear about the table. Izzy was eating someone's leftover food. *Gross.* And Sondra was now on the phone . . . so much for unplugging.

Joey offered a half-smile. "Yeah, Bridget told me."

Sondra's voice rose as she spoke into the phone. "No, Zoe, I told you that you cannot take your father's car. And if you know where you're going, just tell me where it is. It is so simple." Sondra motioned with her free hand as she spoke as if Zoe were standing right in front of her. She looked so prim and proper in her cream-colored skirt, white blouse, and tan jacket, but frustration flashed in her eyes.

Some ladies' night this was.

Joey stood their awkwardly for a moment as if trying to decide what to say, and then his eyes widened and he darted stage right like the Roadrunner. "Have a nice night."

"Okay," she spoke between clenched teeth.

Joey didn't get too far, though. He returned, looking like a repentant puppy who was trying to get on his master's good side. He walked close and leaned in, trying to play it cool. "Hey, if you talk to Bridget, don't tell her you ran into me. Okay?" His eyebrows flickered up and he made a quick exit once again.

"What? Why?" she called after him, but Joey didn't pause this time, didn't turn, and didn't acknowledge that she was talking to him. "Joe—"

Allyson's words were cut short by the hostess returning. She took small steps, and her arms swung from side-to-side, as she gingerly approached the hostess desk. Behind her was the man who Allyson assumed was the manager . . . or visionary as the woman called him. He was dressed in all black with a burgundy scarf on his neck. He stood behind the hostess with a hand on his hip, as if he owned the place. Maybe he did.

The manager was bald on top, which didn't bother her, but he wore a scowl—which did. At the distasteful look in his eye Allyson had a bad feeling she wasn't going to like what the hostess had to say.

"Okay, so after a consultation with my superior, there is a very special table that awaits you . . ." The hostess's smile was bright. Too bright. ". . . that awaits you next Saturday, because *that's when you made your reservation.*"

Allyson's own smile fell. "No, no, I didn't. I called on Monday . . ."

She pasted on a grin. "You did. You called and you spoke with Brie." The hostess peered over her shoulder to a young blonde woman sitting at a table alone. The young woman offered a slight wave, obviously knowing they were talking about her.

"Yes, yes." Allyson remembered that was the woman's name now.

The hostess nodded. "Brie's really pretty." Then she returned to the conversation at hand. "And you said, 'Next Saturday.'" The woman lifted her eyebrows waiting for a reply.

"Yes, next Saturday, as in the next available Saturday, the next one that exists. The next one to be." Allyson forced a chuckle.

"No, next Saturday would be the Saturday immediately following the current week you are in." The hostess pointed her fingers downward.

"No, it's the one immediately following whatever day it is." Allyson wrinkled her nose. "That's what *next* means."

"Uh-um, no," the hostess said with a wry little smirk. "That would be *this* Saturday. As in like this pen." She lifted a pen and clicked the end of it, and then placed it back on her stand. "As in this little mousey thing." She lifted it up and showed her, then returned it to her mouse pad.

The hostess lifted the restaurant's phone next. "As in this phone. 'Oh, hello.'" The hostess raised her voice an octave, as if pretending to hold a conversation between two people. *"I'd like to make a reservation for this Saturday."*

Then she lowered her voice. "'Oh you mean today? Yes, you may.' See like that. But you didn't say *this*, you said *next*." She placed the phone back in its cradle.

Allyson closed her eyes and squished up her face. Pain throbbed at her temple and her mouth felt dry. She opened her eyes and glared at the hostess. "I don't care what I said."

Allyson held back the urge to scream. She gritted her teeth. Heat rose to her cheeks and neck. She forced herself to remain calm . . . but she wasn't doing a very good job. "Just get me a table," she gasped.

Sondra rushed up to her side. "Okay, Ally. I think she gets the idea." Sondra closed her eyes and offered her pastor's wife smile as if that would make everything right.

"Yeah, you're getting a little angry," the hostess's valley girl voice drawled. "And it's, like, doing something ugly to your face." She motioned to her own face and winced.

Allyson's eyes grew wide. She fixed her gaze on the hostess, unsure she'd just heard correctly. She had a dozen ways she wanted to respond. A few choice zingers came to her, but they wouldn't help. Allyson swallowed her pride, pressed her lips to hold back a short comeback, and then relinquished herself to a moment of desperation. "I'm sorry. I just . . . Can you help a girl out?" She flaunted her doe-like eyes and leaned in, melting into the podium.

"This is my first time out, like, in forever," Allyson hurriedly explained.

"Ahh—" Sondra cooed, as if comforting a child. She wrapped one arm around her and squeezed.

"I'm wearing heels, and I'm carrying a small purse." Allyson lifted it and shook it for the woman to see. "I just want to sit with my friends and enjoy a meal without three little people clawing all over me." Her hands stretched out and clawed the air for emphasis.

The hostess wore a pasted-on smile and nodded slightly.

Sondra leaned in. "So let us know when a table's available?" She nodded and offered her prim, pastor's wife smile.

The hostess smiled wider and nodded, yet from the look in her eye she was certain Allyson had lost her mind. "Okay, I'll do that."

Sondra wrapped an arm around Allyson's shoulders and led her to where Izzy sat. Ally took two steps but the emotion overwhelmed her. She could not wait. She could not sit on the bench by the front door. She could not let this night be ruined. Instead of walking toward Izzy, she circled around Sondra and headed back to the hostess.

"I just—I need a break because my job never ends." Her voice carried strains of desperation. Allyson leaned over and ran her hand up and down in front of the woman's computer monitor. "Can you please just check your scroll?" Her voice squeaked with every word, and she could feel the muscles in her neck growing taunt. "And change your scroll, please!"

The manager took a step forward. Ally expected him to say something. Maybe he'd offer a bit of grace and find them one teeny, tiny little table, in a small little nook, in a far of corner.

He leaned forward as if he was going to say something and the hostess turned and their eyes locked. Commiseration passed between their gazes. The manager lifted his eyebrows, and then the hostess turned back to them.

"Visionary has decided that you've disturbed the aura and you have to leave." The hostess's voice was firm.

"What?" The word shot from Allyson's mouth. "What! This is a restaurant. This used to be Mike's Barbecue!"

The visionary—the manager—growled. He pointed a finger. "How dare you!"

Sondra's hands were on her arms again. She turned Allyson away from the people eating in the restaurant, away from the hostess, away from the visionary, away from all Allyson's hoped for—longed for—plans. Sondra led her with small quick steps.

"There's no aura." Allyson scoffed to Sondra, looking back over her shoulder. "Really, aura?"

The manager covered his mouth, and from the look in his eyes he wanted to explode.

Allyson also noted something else in her retreat. His eyes weren't the only ones on her. Many diners had paused eating to watch. *Lucky people,* she wanted to call to them.

Yes, all those lucky people who used *this* instead of *that* when they called to make a reservation. She envied their use of the English language. She also envied the butternut squash raviolis and seared tuna sitting before them.

Izzy jumped up from where she'd been sitting. Her mouth look full, and she chewed, trying to swallow down the rest of the appetizer. Instead of following Allyson and Sondra out, Izzy rushed up to the hostess. She placed the empty plate before her. "So good," she gasped.

At least her friend got something to eat. Allyson's own stomach ached, partly from anger and partly from hunger. She'd purposefully had a light lunch that day so she could enjoy the evening meal.

"Goodbye," she heard the manager mumble.

And as she walked out the door she wished she had a closet to retreat to, and a bag of chocolate to retreat with . . . as if that would make things better.

CHAPTER EIGHT

The air was cool, crisp as they walked outside, back into the night. Allyson didn't know whether to laugh or cry. Was that a moment? Did she just have a "moment" in front of everyone in the restaurant? She'd come to fix that problem. To fix herself, and what had happened? Instead, she'd just made a big mess. Now there would be no dinner. Now there would be no conversation. Now there would be no unplugging. Allyson's breaths came short, fast.

And this . . . this was worse than mascara on her eye. It was worse than her meltdown in front of the newlyweds. She'd lost control in front of her friends. She was getting worse, not better. How could she return home worse than she started? Sean would be so disappointed, and then who knew what tomorrow would bring? Yet another failure to heap upon all the other ones.

"That's okay. It's okay. I didn't want to eat there anyway," Izzy said as she followed Allyson and Sondra out. "Just need to eat somewhere," she said in a weird, deep voice. "Soon!"

Allyson looked from Izzy to Sondra. Sondra's face held a look of compassion. "No big deal Ally. We can do this another night—" Her words were interrupted by the buzzing of her phone. She reached into her purse for it.

Allyson threw up her hands in frustration. "No! We are not doing this another night. Tonight is our night. Tonight is NOT a failure!"

Instead of responding to her, Sondra pulled her phone from her purse. She answered it.

Allyson gasped, and then looked up to see Izzy texting. Texting!

"Marco is so clueless sometimes," Izzy mumbled.

"Just one second." Sondra lifted a finger. Then she leaned over to talk into the phone.

"Zoe, I told you not to go ANYWHERE till Dad got—"

"So we're gonna just . . ." Allyson didn't finish her sentence, but it wasn't like anyone noticed. They were pulled away, into their devices. They were like bugs drawn to a light, and it was futile to fight.

Allyson stood in disbelief, and for the first time she saw it . . . really saw it. These women were so intent on keeping the plates spinning where they *had been*—maybe where they felt they still should be—that they were missing the "now." Is this what Sean meant when he said he wanted her to unplug? Did that mean more than just getting away for a bit? Did it mean unhooking yourself from the worries and cares that never seemed to go away? Was that even possible for a mom?

Even as she'd been here at the restaurant she'd thought about what was happening at home. She'd made up horrible scenarios in her mind. She'd carried anger about death video games . . .

and she'd even been so focused on creating a special moment that she didn't realize she was *in* a madness moment. And from the intensity of her friends' faces, as they talked and texted, they didn't realize that either.

Sondra pointed a finger into the air. "Ah! Zoe! Zoe, listen to me, don't go anywhere."

Izzy gasped. "Uhh . . . Marco forgot the wipes, I mean seriously." Izzy continued to stare down at her phone. How common of a look that was. Izzy was always texting on her phone. Always walking without looking. Even now she walked along the sidewalk like a zombie, glued to her phone.

Allyson looked from one woman to another, and she wondered if things had been simpler in the past before women had the ability to connect with everybody at once. Did people enjoy being together more in the past? Because from the way things were now, there really wasn't such a thing as "together." Not when everyone else "out there" had the access to butt in at any moment. Not only the access but the accessibility—the welcome.

Izzy stepped from the sidewalk into the street like a phone zombie. She didn't see the car coming. Allyson rushed out into the street and she wrapped her arms around her friend. Izzy paused and struggled slightly. She lifted her head and had the same startled, displaced look that Brandon always got when he was woken up for school.

"What?!"

A car zoomed by, missing them my inches. The air pushed against them, and Allyson looked to the spot where Izzy would have been if Allyson hadn't stopped her. *Smashed.* She pulled Izzy back to a safe place and then grabbed the phone from her hand.

"I'm saving your life!"

Izzy looked at her in disbelief. "What?"

Then Allyson hurried over to Sondra.

"I'm sorry. I'm going to have to go," Sondra apologized to them, holding up her phone.

Allyson could see the worry in Sondra's eyes. Sondra wanted to be there for Zoe, but Allyson knew Zoe well enough to know she could handle things—everything—herself. How was Zoe ever going to grow up if Sondra ran to her every time she had a small little issue?

"No, you're not going to do that!" Allyson grabbed the phone from Sondra's hand too. And then she started running with both phones. Running as fast as her stilettoed feet would carry her.

They could be turned away from the restaurant, but she would not allow her friends to be turned into phone zombies. She would not let Sondra go "save" Zoe, when she really didn't need any saving. If they couldn't have a nice dinner, at least they could have each other. Friendship was food for the souls. That was written somewhere, Allyson was sure. Or at least if it wasn't it should be.

She was saving their lives. She was saving them in ways they didn't realize. They had to unplug so they could remember what the real world was all about. So they could be a part of it again.

Her heels clicked against the asphalt as she ran. She didn't have to look behind her to know that the other two women followed. Their shouts and their own heels clicking on the pavement gave them away. She hurried faster so they wouldn't catch her. Hurried faster so she could get to her van before they caught up.

They ran, but as if in slow motion. Allyson tucked her small purse up under her armpit and pulled up Izzy's phone, reading the text and returning an answer, typing with her thumb.

"I'm sure Marco can find the rash cream on his own!" she called. "I have full confidence."

Izzy stopped and stood there in disbelief. "Except he can't."

"He can't," Sondra echoed, taking Izzy's side.

"Sean told me to unplug. He said unplug and this is me UNPLUGGING." Allyson's voice was near frantic now. Her heart pounded, and her hands tingled with nervous energy. She looked to the older woman. "Okay. I'm listening to my husband, Sondra, it's biblical, right?"

That was the first time Allyson ever used that excuse, but it seemed to work. Izzy's mouth was open, and she looked to Sondra.

Sondra opened her mouth as if to say something, but then paused and scratched behind her ear. Sondra didn't have a defense for that because it was biblical indeed.

Allyson opened the minivan door, and then she shoved Izzy and Sondra's phones into her center console, between the front seats, closing the lid on it with a loud click. She pulled her own cell phone from her purse and tossed it in. An energy surged through her as she did that. A freedom that she hadn't expected. She was unleashed. She was in control. And her friends would appreciate it; too, she was sure, once that got those frantic looks off their faces.

Allyson stepped back and eyed them. "No phones!" Allyson waved her arms like a baseball umpire calling out that someone was safe. "No phones. So this is what we're going to do." The words spilled out, and then she realized that she didn't have a plan. What were they going to do?

"And we're gonna . . . We're gonna . . ." She looked around as if the answer was hanging in the air around her, and that's when she saw it. The new bowling alley, *Down Ten Alley*, that had just opened up. She'd heard that it was the happening place. It wasn't a fancy dinner, not by a long shot, but they could have fun. She pointed that direction. The blinking lights on the bowling alley building beaconed her, beaconed them.

"We're going bowling! Yes! Bowling."

Izzy and Sondra looked at each other in disbelief. She read their looks. They believed that she had lost her mind . . . and maybe she had. Allyson smoothed her hand down her black dress. Who said that one couldn't get dressed up for bowling? Maybe she'd start something.

She pumped her fists in the air like she did in junior high when she'd pretended she was a cheerleader. "Who wants to go bowling? I know I do." Allyson's smile widened. "Sondra?"

Sondra's eyebrows lifted, and her face froze into an awkward smile, like Bozo the clown. She looked to Ally from the corner of her eyes. "Fine, absolutely."

That was all Ally needed to run with this. She didn't ask Izzy. Allyson knew that Izzy would come along. She didn't have a choice. Her cell phone was locked up in Allyson's van, and Ally had the keys. She had no way to call Marco. Besides there was food at the bowling alley. It was the closest food. Yes, Izzy would come.

Allyson hurried ahead, across the parking lot to the bowling alley. The wind picked up slightly and blew on her neck, and she knew what she had to do. As she strode ahead she reached up and pulled the pins from her hair. It tumbled down, falling down her back and over her shoulders. Allyson tossed her curls from side to side. If she was going to be free tonight, they were going to be free.

She glanced over her shoulder to the two women who followed her. "I'm letting my hair down, ladies!" She let out a whoop.

Izzy and Sondra looked at each other, still in shock, but they continued moving forward. That had to be a good sign.

Allyson did a little jig. "Bowling! Yes!"

"Fine. Absolutely," Sondra said going along with it with as much enthusiasm as a church lady could muster.

"I'm not wearing vending machine socks." Izzy's voice carried through the night air.

And as they neared the front door, the scent of sweat, socks, and French fries greeted them. It was something at least. It was something.

CHAPTER NINE

If Sean had learned one thing as a father it was that the best way to handle a houseful of kids was to get them out of the house. Staying in the house meant a messy house. Getting out of the house, his kids could mess up some other place and he could walk way. Someone else would pick up the pizza crusts off the floor. Someone else would wipe up spilled milk. Someone else would have to Windex fingerprints off of every glass surface, even those ones that you were certain the kids couldn't reach. As long as he kept Beck out of the bathroom, and made sure he didn't go toilet diving, he'd be good. He'd also win points from Allyson for NOT allowing Brandon to play violent video games. It was a win, win, win.

He stood beside Kevin's car with the kids buckled up inside of it. That's another thing he'd learned—not to unbuckle kids until the very last moment. Car seats saved lives. Car seats saved a dad's sanity. He was sure that the person who'd invented them liked the idea of *restraint* just as much as safety.

He and Kevin moved to the back of his car, leaning against it.

Sean looked up to see Marco's car driving toward them. It jerked and swerved as he pulled up into a parking space.

"Whoa." Sean and Kevin jerk their heads back, in unison.

Marco swatted at something inside. Then he wrestled himself out of the car, stumbling. As soon as he was out he quickly slammed the front door as if something was trying to get out—something was chasing him. It took a moment for Marco to catch his breath. Catch his balance. Sean could see the twins quietly strapped in the backseat. *Dude, what's your problem,* he wanted to ask.

"You alright?" Sean called to Marco.

Marco lifted his hands into the air, as if trying to wave off their worries. "Yeah, I'm fine, under control. Can you help me get my kids out?"

Sean moved closer to the car. He looked inside and noticed white spots on the seats—like bloops of spit-up. Yet Marco's toddler boys were too old for that. Then something small and fluttery darted at the window, hitting it, trying to get to him.

Sean flinched and jumped back. "Whoa, what was that?" His arms and hands flew over his head, and he ducked down certain that whatever that thing was it was going to go through the window and get him.

Marco cast his gaze down to the ground. "A bird."

Sean's eyes grew wide. "A bird?"

"Yes, it's a bird, okay? My kids, they wanted to bring the pet bird."

Sean's jaw dropped open. "And you let them?"

"I didn't know it was going to be flying all over the place!"

The bird continued to dart around inside the car, and the twin boys in the backseat watched nervously.

Sean glanced at Marco again. *Rookie.*

From his stance, and the look on his face, Marco appeared as if he was going to dart. Of course, Marco always had that look after Izzy had the twins. Sean had always found humor in that. Marco had seemed so freaked out about having one child that God gave them two, right from the start.

Kevin glanced into the car in disbelief. Sean was sure this wasn't the evening his childhood friend had been planning. Not at all. He pointed to the cage on the floorboard of the passenger's seat. "Why don't you put it in the cage?"

Marco bounced with frustration. His fists swatted the air as if pummeling down Kevin's question. His large body bounced a bit too. "Don't you think I thought of that? Look, it was in a cage!" He threw his hands up. "The locking mechanism is not intuitive."

The bird flew around and then landed on the head rest. Moving with slow movements, Marco opened the door. "Stay Mama!"

Kevin offered a wide-eyed look as if Marco had lost his mind. "Its name is Mama??" Marco's hair was tossed and wild, as if he hadn't brushed it in days. Now his eyes were wild too.

Marco puffed out his chest. "Izzy was the one who let the twins name her."

Kevin scoffed and then swatted his arms around in the air, mimicking the flying bird. "You've got a bird flying around, Marco."

Marco slowed opened the door and leaned in. "I don't think he's scared of it. I think he doesn't want to hurt it," commented Sean.

Finally, they got the kids out. It took ten minutes to unbuckle them, tame them, and hold them. Sean put Beck into the stroller. And he held Bailey on the crook of his right arm. Marco walked with one twin in each arm. Brandon walked by Kevin. Kevin was Brandon's favorite person. Allyson believed it was because they were at the same mental age, but Sean knew it was because Kevin didn't treat Brandon like a little kid. Brandon felt appreciated, grown up when he was with Kevin. They didn't always play death video games, but when they played Kevin always invited Brandon to join in. Sean just wished Allyson understood that.

They stood before the family play center. Treetop Family Adventures. Sean knew that once they got inside it would be loud. It would be crazy, and the kids would love it.

"Okay, so here's the plan." Kevin's tone was serious, and he glared at the front door with intensity. His mission tonight wasn't getting to a new level, so he'd make this place, their fun, his mission. "We take them inside, stamp their hands, and they can't get out. Like *Shawshank Redemption*."

"Love it," Marco replied.

They all continue to stare, and Sean tightened his fingers around the stroller's handle. *Let's do this thing.*

***

The clang and clatter of bowling pins being knocked over, and of balls clunking down the long wooden lane filled the air.

Sondra offered to go first, and Allyson almost felt bad for swiping her phone away. She could tell that Sondra was trying to get into it. Trying to make the most of Allyson's flub.

Sondra picked out a ball, careful not to chip her fingernail polish, and she put her fingers inside the holes. She approached the lane with determination, and then a woman's voice filled the air.

"Oh, hey!" Mattie Mae Lloyd called out. A huge laugh erupted from her lips. Everything was bold and loud about Mattie Mae. Today she wore a bright pink sweater, green skirt, and green headband. She waved to Sondra and looked pleased to see their pastor's wife having fun, letting loose. Mattie Mae wore a black bowling glove on one hand—the sign of a true bowler. Allyson wouldn't be surprised if she was on a league.

Sondra appeared shocked by Mattie Mae's eager wave. "Oh, hey," Sondra said meekly. "Hey." Her words were lost in the sound of pins tumbling on other lanes.

And instead of leaning over, exposing her legs any more under her skirt, Sondra sat the purple ball at the end of the lane and gingerly kicked it with her foot. The ball rolled slowly halfway down the lane and then dropped into the gutter. She strode nonchalantly back to where Izzy and Allyson sat with a little hop to her step. Sondra didn't even look back. Obviously the people around her were more important than if she'd knocked down any pins.

What a balancing beam Sondra was on, Allyson realized. Sondra wanted to have fun for Ally's sake but not too much fun to make the church women a few lanes over believe that she'd "gone wild" at the bowling alley.

Sondra approached were Izzy was sitting. "Why don't you go ahead?" She pointed to the lane. Izzy rose and moved to take a turn, her full skirt swishing as she walked.

Sondra eased herself into the hard plastic chair across from Allyson. "That threw me a little bit."

But then the worried look on Sondra's face changed to one of feigned excitement as she leaned forward and fixed her eyes on Ally. "Well, this was a good idea, Ally. Fun night after all!"

Allyson was thankful for how easily Sondra let things roll off her back. She wished she was more like that. If Sondra was on a canoe on a raging river, she'd be the one sitting there calmly, letting the motion of the current carry her, and swaying along in peace whether it be bouncy or calm. Allyson on the other hand would be trying to row against the current. She'd move from bank to bank, and try to make her own way, and in her struggle she'd get waterlogged, and flip, and find herself soaking wet and on the opposite bank from where she wanted to be.

Why can't I be more like Sondra?

Allyson pushed that question from her mind. Maybe that had been the whole point of this night, to learn to be more flexible. To learn to find peace no matter where she was. To let things go. To go along for the ride, and so far she had failed completely. She took a deep breath and focused on Sondra's gaze.

"I am really sorry about the horrifying display out there." She drug out the words and her eyes darted to the side. "I actually think I'm going a little crazy."

Sondra's brow furrowed as she listened, and then she shook her head, dismissing Allyson's apology. She offered a compassionate gaze. "You were just having a moment." She reached over and patted Ally's hand.

She leaned forward, offering a confession. "Yeah, well it was like my fifth one this week."

Sondra didn't seem surprised, or even horrified. "It happens to everyone."

A half-laugh emerged from Allyson's lips. For some reason she didn't believe Sondra. She laughed again under her breath. "Really? Somehow I can't picture you having *a moment.*" Sure, she'd seen Sondra blow up at Zoe a little, but that was different from Allyson's display in front of total strangers.

Sondra smiled a knowing smile, and Allyson waited for what she had to say. But then, Sondra's look changed and she put on the peppy, happy face again.

"So how's the blog going?" Sondra asked instead. She played with the straw in her drink cup; as if that was the most important thing she had to think about. She took a sip from her drink and then wiped the corner of her mouth with a finger. Sondra had no reason to worry. Her hair was perfect. Her makeup was perfect, and there wasn't even the smallest smudge on her lipstick.

"Oh, the blog." Allyson bounced a little in her chair, and tilted her head to the side, trying to find the right words. "It's—it's not coming, really at all." Allyson lifted up her straw and swirled it around in her cup. "I can't—I can't really find anything worth saying." She rested her elbow on the table and then rested her cheek on her hand.

"And almost every time I sit down to try . . ." Allyson stretched out her hand for emphasis. ". . . I just end up watching that eagle's nest. You've completely ruined me."

A smile lit Sondra's eyes, and she leaned close. "And Ray thinks it's crazy."

Allyson laughed. "And you know, seriously. I can't stop watching. It's like crazy." She placed an open hand on the table, feeling the cool Formica under her fingers. Allyson closed her eyes and let her words tumble out. "I don't know . . . she's so . . . there. You know?"

Allyson pounded soft fists on the table. "Like, she's peaceful. Happy." She glanced up and realized that tears rimmed her eyes. "Are you . . ." Allyson swallowed, laying her heart on the table between them. "Are you . . . happy?"

The burden came again. Heavy. Big. And it settled on her chest. It was always there, even though she tried to ignore it. And sometimes—like now—it seemed heavier than others.

"Look, Ally. Life is not about a . . . parking space." Sondra briefly glanced over Ally's shoulder to where Mattie Mae was still bowling. "It's not about God taking away all our problems and making everything perfect." She clasped her hands together. "It's about finding . . . meaning and joy and purpose in . . ." She motioned to the space around her. "This. In the crazy. In the chaos. It's about knowing God is with you in the good days and the bad days." Sondra reached over and took Allyson's hand again.

"Yeah." Allyson lowered her head and looked to Sondra's hand on hers. Then she looked up at her, peering up under her lashes.

"And does my faith give me that?" Sondra continued. "Yeah. It does. Am I always 'happy' No. That's a fantasy." It made Ally feel better. She wasn't the only one with these struggles and issues. And she knew that God was there—with her—no matter what. But still . . . well, she just wished it was easier to change.

Allyson released a sigh. Some of her pent-up tension released with it. "I think I'm up." Ally stood to bowl. She moved to get her ball.

"Hey Ally," Sondra called after her. Her voice was low. Allyson turned back.

There was a softness to Sondra's face that Allyson hadn't seen too often. A tenderness and maybe even vulnerability. Allyson leaned over, placing her hands on her knees, to hear what Sondra had to say.

"Thanks for inviting me tonight." Sondra offered a shy smile. "You know, it's the first time anyone from the church has invited me to something like this." She shrugged. "First time in five years." She forced a soft laugh, as if it hadn't bothered her . . . but Allyson could see that it had.

Allyson stood straighter. "Of course."

Sondra looked back to the table. Her lips were pressed into a thin line as if she was trying to hold her emotion in. And if Allyson wasn't mistaken, there was the hint of tears in Sondra's eyes as she looked back to her drink. Sondra lifted it up and took a sip.

Allyson turned back around slowly. For so long she had thought Sondra had everything together, but maybe that was just a show. Was it better to explode or better to hold everything in and keep everyone else at arm's length? For the first time Allyson wondered if one was just as bad as the other.

Izzy hurried around Allyson. She placed a hand on Allyson's arms and pointed to the balls. "Hey, go."

"I'm going. I'm going." Allyson stepped closer. Izzy walked around her and then sat in the chair that Allyson had just left. She settled in and then leaned forward.

"Hey, can I ask you something? A little free advice?" Izzy asked, leaning close to Sondra.

And then, as if someone had just pulled down the shades on a sunny day, the look on Sondra's face transformed. The vulnerability was gone. She took off her Sondra hat and put on her pastor's wife hat again.

Allyson released the breath she'd been holding, and in that moment Sondra looked differently in her eyes. Sondra wanted to help everyone, but how often did people want to help her? She tried to be everyone's friend, but who reached out to befriend her? Allyson had been so worried about her mommy meltdowns that she hadn't even taken time to really listen to Sondra's concerns.

As she picked up the bowling ball and hurried to the lane, Allyson wondered if it was suffocating being the one who everyone confided in. Especially when hearing everyone else's confessions, worries, and fears did nothing to help your own.

CHAPTER TEN

Marco / 8:00 PM
Called 10 times, where R U?

Marco / 8:00 PM
IZZY . . . HELP!!!

Sean / 8:00 PM
Ally, don't freak out.

Marco / 8:00 PM
I'm freaking out-of-control

Sean / 8:00 PM
Got everything under control

Marco / 8:00 PM
Totally out of control!!

Sean / 8:00 PM
Just need to chat.

Sean tried to ignore the sounds of video games behind him as he spoke into his cell phone. He'd tried to text Allyson, but she hadn't returned the text messages. He knew Marco had tried to reach Izzy too.

Sean had seen the frantic look in Marco's eyes as he'd tried to get a hold of Izzy. "This is bad. This is bad," Marco had repeated over and over.

Finally Sean gave in and called Allyson. He knew she'd be upset—really upset—if he didn't try to reach her. There was no answer to her cell phone, so he decided to leave a message. It made him happy that Allyson had taken his advice to unplug. She'd also obviously encouraged her friends to do the same since no one was responding.

Sean pictured the women in his mind's eye, sitting around a small café table. Talking, laughing, and tasting everything that everyone else had. When he usually went out to dinner he never wanted anyone to touch the food on his plate, but girls were different. They not only enjoyed their food, they wanted others to taste it too, and enjoy the moment with them. It's as if the food tasted better if someone else oohed and aahed over their selection.

After four rings, Ally's voicemail came on, telling him to leave a message. After the beep he started in.

"Hey Ally, it's me, just wanted to let you know that everything's going great here. Uh, we're all good. We're going to take a little trip to the hospital." He tried to keep his voice calm, his tone light. And he thought he was doing a good job, but over his shoulder Sean could hear Kevin's voice, and Kevin was anything but calm. After using up their tokens, and finishing up their games, Kevin and the kids had ventured over to the prize counter to redeem their prizes.

"Are you kidding me?" Kevin's voice rose above the noise of the arcade room. "You want 50 tickets for this plastic spider?" The dinging of a pinball machine filled the air, but Kevin's voice was louder. "That's extortion!"

Sean continued leaving the message, keeping his voice even-keeled. "Beck got stuck in the Rocket to Mars game," Sean said as unemotionally as if telling her they'd had chicken strips for dinner. "They didn't have to use the Jaws of Life this time, thank goodness."

Sean looked over to Beck who was sitting next to him, chowing down on a piece of candy and holding an unwrapped sucker in his hand. Allyson never let Beck have a big sucker like that—choking hazard.

Beck looked around, watching the colorful, flashing lights around him, taking in all the noise, and he didn't seem to have a care in the world.

"He's free now," Sean continued on the message, "but the fireman said he had to be checked out. A matter of policy. So I'm gonna take him. Which is convenient because I kinda dislocated my shoulder trying to get him out of there. Funny thing." Sean smiled, knowing full well that Allyson wouldn't think it was funny.

The fireman approached as Sean talked, angling the stretcher so that it was more like a chair, and urging Sean to lean back into it. Sean turned around and lifted his leg over Beck, so that his legs straddled the young boy. Then, as gingerly as he could, Sean leaned into the stretcher. His youngest son allowed the EMT to move him, so that he sat between Sean's legs. Beck's small tennis shoes stuck up next to Sean's larger ones on the stretcher. It would make a cute picture for him to post on Facebook . . . well sort of. Allyson wouldn't be amused.

Sean tried to adjust against the back rest, but pain shot through his shoulder. As long as it was immobilized in the sling it didn't hurt too bad, but even the smallest movement caused searing pain to course through him. His heartbeat quickened, and his stomach lurched. For some reason the pizza he'd just gobbled down wasn't sitting too well.

As Sean allowed the EMTs to situate him on the stretcher, he could see Kevin still at the prize counter. Kevin leaned forward, eyeing the teen boy on the other side as if on a face-off.

"We spent $50 in tokens and got 200 tickets. I want something of equal or greater value," Kevin declared. "Like a—"

"A puppy!" Bailey cut in, her blonde hair bouncing on her shoulders as she bobbed with excitement. Brandon stood next to her, nodding in agreement.

Kevin pointed to Bailey excited. "Yes, like a live animal. I want something like a live animal. Like a turtle or a pet pig. I want a pet pig."

An EMT leaned close, looking into Beck's eyes in a pin light, checking for a concussion and breaking off Sean's view of Kevin and his other two kids.

"Me and the Beckster are kind of cruising on our own," Sean continued on his message to Allyson, "but they need the minivan to move the kids around. We know where you are. So we're just going to slip into the parking lot, and we're going to switch the cars around and take the minivan." He took a breath. "Marco texted Izzy that, so she knows that—"

A beep sounded, letting him know that he'd run out of time for his message, and then the call dropped. Sean looked down at his phone, and he was jolted a little as the EMTs rolled him and Beck past the video games and toward the front doors.

"I'm pretty sure she got most of that," Sean mumbled to himself. Just as long as Allyson got the part that he was taking the van and leaving Marco's car. That was the most important part of the message. Sean could hear Marco's voice trying to help the ticket counter guy and Kevin come to some type of compromise.

"What about the bouncy balls? Kids like bouncy balls!" Marco said.

"Marco, that's a choking hazard." Kevin's voice was far from patient. "Why am I the only one who knows this stuff?"

***

The music at the bowling alley blared! Blared! Sondra resisted the urge to cover her ears. They'd been "so lucky" to be there when the bowling alley switched over from regular to cosmic bowling. This meant that they turned off the lights, turned up the music, and turned on the black lights. From Sondra's experience, more noise and less light never led to anything good.

Sondra watched as Izzy bobbed and carried a plate of nachos from the snack counter. That had to be Izzy's third trip up there. She'd spent more time eating than bowling, not that Sondra minded. She liked being with her friends, but bowling wasn't her favorite. She wasn't coordinated, and she was too self-conscious to let herself go and have wild fun.

She envied Allyson in that way. Allyson didn't hold anything in. Instead, she let it all out—all her frustration, all her worries, all her annoyance. Sometimes she let it out in inappropriate places, at inappropriate times, but surely that had to be better than holding all of it bottled up inside, right?

That was the hardest thing about being a pastor's wife, Sondra supposed. She knew everything, but couldn't speak a word about anyone, lest she be considered a gossip. There were times she wanted to cry, but didn't want to alarm anyone. There were times she was furious with Ray, but didn't want anyone to look negatively upon their spiritual leader.

There were even times she wished she could ask advice about how to deal with Zoe, but how could she when she was the one who was supposed to have all the answers? Her greatest fear was that she'd say the wrong thing or do the wrong thing and Zoe would walk a dark path, just as she had. But who could she even relate that fear to? No one.

"It's time for the Dance Cam," the DJ called over the sound system. People around them cheered. Izzy continued toward them with a little hop to her step and a sway to her hips. And even though Sondra didn't think it was possible, the music grew even louder.

Sondra pushed all the thoughts and worry from her mind, and she covered one of her ears with her hand. "That is loud. Very loud." She winced, wondering if her ear drums were going to burst and realizing how very old she'd gotten.

"Okay, who wants to be on the Dance Cam!" the DJ (who was responsible for this loud ruckus) called out. He wore shades and an oversized jean jacket, retro 80s style. He had a Fu Manchu mustache and sat at a high podium with a microphone in one hand and a small video camera in the other. His body bobbed along to the beat, letting everything loose and encouraging all of them to do the same.

Sondra watched on the small overhead monitors (which normally screamed out how low her score was) as the Dance Cam fixed on a beautiful African-American woman who was standing near the lanes. The spotlight moved to her, and the woman beamed. She lifted her arms and shook her hips in an adorable way. Oh, what would it be like to feel so unencumbered, so free, without worrying all the time what others thought?

"Get on the Dance Cam and get some free bowling, just like Ashlee," the DJ called to the crowd. The crowd cheered again. "Look at the lady out there, busting a move."

Ashlee threw back her head and laughed. And even though Sondra couldn't hear the laughter over the sound of the music, the transformation on her face was clear.

"Everyone give it up for Ashlee!" the DJ said as the spotlight dimmed.

Izzy finished her sashay across the bowling alley, and sat down across from Sondra with a huge plate of nachos covering with everything they had in their kitchen . . . including pickles.

Sondra eyed Izzy's plate of nachos. "Okay, so how far along are you?" She'd been around enough women to know how a pregnant woman acted. Izzy had thought no one had seen her sneak that appetizer earlier, but Sondra had. And now this. That was the role of a pastor's wife. To notice everything and to, most of the time, look the other direction. But it was hard to deny Izzy's pregnancy when she was sitting here scarfing bowling alley nachos as if she was a beggar who'd just sat down to a banquet table.

Izzy paused and glanced up at Sondra, as if pretending she hadn't heard correctly. "What?"

There was worry in Izzy's gaze, and Sondra guessed that she'd just found out. This pregnancy was most likely a surprise, but Izzy would come around. Marco would freak, but Izzy would come around eventually.

"Well, you're—" Sondra pointed to the nachos. The normal overhead lights went out and black lights flashed off and then back on. A cheer rose up from the people surrounding them.

"Pregnant? What, no." Izzy shook her head. "Because if I was I would be freaking out that my husband would be whimpering in the fetal position like he did last time."

Izzy's mouth kept moving, she kept talking, but Sondra couldn't make out her words.

Sondra leaned forward. "I have to be honest with you. I didn't get any of that!"

The music increased in volume, and she wondered how this had happened. She'd prepared herself for a nice, quiet dinner . . . and now this. She covered her ears again.

Of course she couldn't let Allyson know how disappointed she was. Poor dear. Allyson had tried her hardest. That was another role of a pastor's wife. To applaud everyone's honest efforts, despite the results. And to hide her own disappointment. Always hide her disappointment. Always hide.

***

Allyson strode up to Sondra and Izzy with a little dance and a hop to her step. They were sitting across from each other at the small table. The two women leaned in close, trying to carry on a conversation. Seeing that, warmed Allyson's heart—or maybe it was the heat from all the sweaty bowling people. Either way, she was warm . . . and she liked seeing her friends together.

So this wasn't the night she had planned. It wasn't quiet. They didn't have a plate of fine food in front of them, but they were together. Tomorrow they'd most likely be laughing about how things turned out. They'd make fun of each other: "Do we want to go to the park *next* Saturday or *this* Saturday?" And they'd brag about their bowling scores, no matter who won.

Allyson laughed as she swayed her hips and kicked one of her bowling shoes up in the air behind her. "Six pins down, ladies. Beat that, Sondra!"

Allyson danced to Izzy's side with a bounce in her step, her shoulders pumping up and down to the music.

Sondra rose and paced for the lane with a determined look on her face. She was going to have fun if it killed her.

Allyson moved to sit and she noticed something—someone serving a table six lanes down. *Bridget!* Bridget had gotten a job here—at this bowling alley. Of all the luck!

She whipped around, wondering if she should say something to Bridget. She still felt guilty for not being able to watch Phoenix. She was supposed to be someplace with her friends, getting her oxygen, and here she was, living it up, breathing hot air, and sort of flaunting her fun and friends in Bridget's face.

The music continued its loud beat and the quickening of Allyson's heart followed.

Izzy must have noticed Allyson's panic. Izzy looked up at her. "What?"

Allyson pressed her lips together in a tight, thin line. The muscles in her neck cinched down, and she slightly shook her head. "Moral dilemma."

Allyson couldn't hear Bridget's footsteps behind her, but she sensed her nearing presence. Her shoulders tightened up.

"Ally!" Bridget called to her.

Allyson turned, her black skirt swished around her legs as she did. She ran her fingers through her mess of ringlets, trying to act natural.

Bridget approached with a tray of empty beer bottles and cans and placed them on their small table. "Hey, what are you guys doing here?"

Allyson forced a smile. "Hey, Bridg." She shrugged her shoulders. "You know, glow-in-the-dark bowling?" She sweeps her arms wide, exaggerating her words for Izzy's sake. "Which is just SO fun!!" Allyson rolled her eyes up and grinned.

Bridget didn't look that impressed. "It's actually not that fun." There was a weariness about Bridget. Even though she was young it seemed she always had dark circles under her eyes, most likely from balancing all she did with work, school, and baby.

Guilt pounded a stake back into Allyson's heart. She bet Bridget would love to be out with friends, even if it was bowling, and even if it wasn't fun. When was the last time she'd done something like that?

***

Sondra sauntered up from bowling. She hadn't wanted to be here, but she had to admit she was starting to have fun. This time she'd stuck her fingers into the bowling ball, and she swung it like she'd seen the others doing. When her hand fully extended, the ball had dropped off her fingers and it rolled straight down the lane and hit six pins. She did a small hop and looked back, but Izzy and Allyson weren't watching. Instead, Allyson was taking to a young woman. Sondra thought she recognized her. Yes, she believed that was Sean's half-sister, Bridget. Sondra had seen the young woman only a few times over the years, but she had said many prayers for her. Ally had been heartbroken so many times when Bridget had made one bad choice after another. They couldn't fix the messes that Bridget found herself in, but they could pray, and they had done that often.

Sondra's ball popped back up, and she hurried back to tell the others to watch. "Did you see that?" she called to the others. Then she saw it. Bridget had placed one of the trays she'd been using to clean the tables on THEIR table, and that tray was filled with beer bottles and cans. Sondra didn't take the time to look over her shoulder to see if Mattie Mae Lloyd had already spotted the bottles. Instead she rushed forward.

"Oh, no, no, no . . ." Sondra grabbed four beer bottles with one hand and two beer cans with the other. They clinked together, and she walked toward the trash can, as if using her body to shield what was in her hands. "Oh, we can't have this. Oh, this doesn't look good . . ."

"Okay, anyone else who wants to be on the dance floor?!" The DJ shouted over the microphone. Loud, too loud.

"Oppa Gangnam Style!" the music blared. She hurried, looking for the trash can, and then . . . like a light beaming down from heaven, the spotlight landed on her.

Sondra spun around. She clutched the bottles and the cans to the front of her, and she shifted from side to side trying to figure out which way to go to escape the lights.

A cheer rose from the crowd and then she looked up. There she was . . . on all the monitors . . . with beer bottles in her hands!

"Dance! Dance! Dance!" The people call out.

Dancing was the last thing on her mind. She froze. Her knees grew weak. Her head grew light and she told herself to breathe. Waves of panic grew higher and closer within, and no matter how much she told herself to move—to escape the light—nothing happened.

"Dance!" the DJ called.

"THESE ARE NOT MINE!" she called out. No one heard. Between the loud noise of the music, and the DJ over the microphone telling her to dance, her explanation was lost—even to her own ears.

"Wiggle, do anything," the DJ called.

She turned to the side, paused, and wondered how to escape this. Not only escape the light but escape the moment, the sight of her with beer bottles in her hands. Surely this had to be a bad dream—no make that a horrible nightmare.

Swallowing hard, she looked across to where Mattie Mae Lloyd sat. There was enough light to see Mattie Mae, her bright sweater, her hair perfectly in place, and her condemnation.

"These aren't mine. I don't drink. Oh, no. Oh, no, no . . ."

Mattie Mae stood, her mouth circled in an O, and then she turned and ran the other way. She seemed too excited as she rushed off. She couldn't wait to find someone she knew and tell them what she'd seen—what Sondra had been doing at the bowling alley. Sondra had no doubt that, by the end of the night, phones would be ringing off the hook as dedicated ladies called each other on the church prayer chain, and urged each other to offer prayers for their backslidden pastor's wife.

The light stayed, but the only jiggling happening was the erratic heartbeat within. "Okay, I'm just going to throw these away—"

Then, as quickly as it shone on her, the light flashed off.

"Boo!" the crowds around her called out. She scanned their faces and saw their disappointment.

She lifted up the bottles again. "These are not mine." Her voice was no more than a whisper.

Did anyone care?

A loud buzzer sounded. DANCE FAIL popped up on the monitors. She focused on the second word, and the word pounded in her head to the beat of her heart: fail, fail, fail.

"Now that was embarrassing," the DJ called over the sound system.

Embarrassing . . . is an understatement. Sondra hurried away, into the glowing darkness, seeking out the trash.

***

Wiggle, shake. Do something! The words replayed in Ally's mind and she had to admit that she'd called out too, telling Sondra to do *something.* They were here, so they might as well make the most of it. She'd seen the panic and the fear on Sondra's face, but Allyson didn't understand why she worried. Everyone could see she was just cleaning up the table. Anyone who knew Sondra knew that not one drop of alcohol would ever touch her lips. More than anyone Allyson had ever met, Sondra stuck as close to the straight and narrow as she could. If the straight and narrow was a shoulder-wide path, Sondra treated it as a 3.9 inch-wide balance beam.

Sondra, her face pale in the black light, hurried off toward the nearest trash can.

Bridget pointed to the place where Sondra had stood. "Uh, that's a dance fail."

Allyson looked back over her shoulder to the monitor. Her lips lowered into a frown. She wrinkled up her nose and scratched the back of her head. "But she tried. She tried though. She tried hard."

Allyson watched as Sondra slinked by with the bottles and cans in her hand.

"Fail," Bridget whispered, pointing up to the monitor.

"But she tried. But she tried. But she tried," Allyson said one more time as Sondra slinked away toward the trash can.

Bridget nodded, hurried to her tray, picked it up, and then hurried away. Seeing her go, Allyson rushed after her. "Hey . . . um, actually, I was just wondering . . ."

Bridget paused and turned, waiting with tray in hand.

"So who did you wind up getting to babysit Phoenix tonight?"

Bridget stroked her neck. "Oh. I just asked Joey to do it." She smirked. "You were right. He owed Phoenix some daddy time." She lifted her eyebrows and her eyes widened.

Panic struck Allyson's heart. "Joey, Joey, as in your ex-boyfriend? That Joey?" Her hands flailed around as the panic tried to escape. She'd just seen him. On a date . . . and without his son.

"Yes, yes, that Joey. Why?"

Ally looked from Bridget to the other women, and back to Bridget. "No, um." A sinking feeling hit her gut and she wanted to tell Bridget anything but the truth, yet she had to know. She had to know that Joey didn't have the baby. And . . . where was he? That's what worried Allyson the most.

"Why?" Bridget asked again.

Allyson froze. Her mouth opened, and she felt like the most horrible person. First, for not watching Phoenix, and then for having to tell Bridget the truth.

"What's going on?" Bridget's face took on a panicked look.

Allyson swallowed hard. "There's something I need to tell you, Bridg."

CHAPTER ELEVEN

Bridget stormed into the fancy restaurant, looking all around for Joey. She'd never been in a place like this. Joey had never taken her out, hardly ever, and now he was here . . . with another woman. And he didn't have their son?

She stalked up to the hostess, looking past her. "Hey," Bridget managed to mumble. Fear grabbed hold of her gut and wouldn't let go.

"Welcome to Chez Magique." The hostess waved her arm, welcoming her in. "Your journey awaits you—" The woman was smiling. Pretty. Annoying. In her way.

"Great. Okay, thanks." Bridget hurried toward the dining room.

The hostess rushed up to stop her, her high heels clicking on the tile floor. She stood before Bridget, stopping her. "Oh, wait!"

Bridget considered pushing her, getting her out of her way.

Phoenix. Where is Phoenix? It's all she could think about.

"You need to wait here," the hostess said with an arch of her brow.

Bridget squared back her shoulders. "Are you kidding me? Move!" One punch . . . that's all it would take to have this woman sprawling.

"Oh, I will not move." The hostess smirked and looked down her nose at Bridget as if she was some pest who needed to be squashed out. She laughed under her breath, as if Bridget just made the most ridiculous demand she'd ever heard.

Bridget's fists balled up, but a voice broke through.

"Uh, yes you will." It was Allyson. Bridget looked over her shoulder to her, not realizing she had followed. "Or so help me . . ." Allyson cocked out her hip . . . "I'm going to take this aura in here" . . . she circled her finger, as if encompassing the room. "And murder it." She pointed to the ground with emphasis, as a warning.

Bridget's jaw drop. She'd expected Ally to tell her to have good sense—to calm down—but not this.

Behind Allyson, Izzy and Sondra rushed in, like Clint Eastwood rushing into a bar fight. The shocked looks on their faces as they heard Allyson's words were priceless. They scurried back toward the bench by the front door, trying to hide themselves from the fists that were about to fly.

The hostess gasped. She pushed out her lips and glanced from Bridget to Ally. "You're kidding me."

"No." Ally's stance—her words—were unmoving.

Bridget didn't expect the hostess to back down, but she did.

"Whatever." The hostess threw up her hands and walked back to her computer. "My mistake."

Gasps arose from behind them, and Sondra and Izzy sat by the front door.

That was all the permission that Bridget needed. She stormed into the room filled with fancy tables, yummy smells, and startled diners . . . with Allyson right behind her.

***

Sean took his keys from his pocket and opened the door of the minivan. Even though he'd cleaned it out earlier it still smelled like French fries and chocolate milk. He'd told Allyson more than once that they should stop letting their kids eat in the car, but she said it wasn't practical. Between story time at the library, soccer practice for Brandon, and Awana nights at church, there were just some meals that needed to be eaten as they went.

He slipped the keys back into his pocket and was glad again that she'd get this break. Allyson just worked too hard and never got a break. He looked over at the restaurant and smiled, thankful she was able to relax for once.

Marco approached hurriedly and handed Sean the birdcage. "Here's the bird."

Sean adjusted his arm in the sling. "The bird?" He blinked slowly not believing this.

"You gotta take the bird." Marco thrust the cage to him. "There's no way the boys are going to get into the car without the bird." He tilted his head to the side, in a plea. "Just take the bird."

Reluctantly, Sean took the cage from Marco. It swayed in his hand.

Kevin stomped over. He held Bailey under his arms and carried her out in front of him as if he carried a sack of potatoes. She hung there and swayed, as if she was a rag doll. At least she didn't make a peep. Maybe she knew that with Kevin it didn't make a difference.

"Where's the car seat?" Sean asked.

"What?" Kevin looked at him with uncertainty.

"Everybody knows you need a car seat," Marco piped in.

Kevin didn't say a word, but he winced.

Sean pointed back to Kevin's car. "You've got to get the car seat, that's the whole point."

Kevin winced and then turned and walked away, still holding Bailey out in front of him.

"What am I going to do with a bird?" Sean lifted up the cage and peered at the small parakeet inside. He/she looked innocent enough.

Sean put the birdcage in the passenger's seat. The night wasn't turning out like he planned, but he still had everything under control. They still were getting things taken care of. He had a new plan. Sean always liked to have a plan.

They'd pull out the van, and they'd park Marco's car in the same spot. Marco assured him that Izzy had the keys. Then, he'd head to the hospital in Kevin's car, and Marco and Kevin would take the van and watch the kids at Sean's house. Sean shut the driver's side door. His hands gripped the steering wheel, trying to hold back his fears.

He was sure—pretty sure—that his friends could handle the kids. The women wouldn't take that much longer for dinner, would they?

Sean started the van and put it in reverse. He started backing out slowly, but then the radio blared Elmo's voice: A B C D E F G! Sean jumped and his foot hit the gas, toppling the birdcage to the floorboard. Slamming on the brakes, the van stopped right in the middle of the road. The slightest fluttering and sound of birds' wings brushed past him. He turned off the van to stop the music, and Mama landed on the top edge of the opened window. Then, before he could react, the bird lighted and flew out of the window.

"No!" Sean gasped, reaching his hand after it, but it was too late. He opened the door and jumped from the car.

Marco's voice cried out, and the tall, big-boned man jumped from the car and ran to Sean's side. "Sean, tell me that was not my bird! Tell me that was not my bird that just flew out of the window."

Sean tried to explain, but just as he opened his mouth another car—a small black sports car—zipped into the empty space where the van once sat. Sean stood there with his mouth open. He'd just pulled out. It was clear they were going to use that spot.

A man in a black suit and white shirt climbed out of the car. He looked like one of the male models on the magazines at the checkout stand, and he strode with the swagger of James Bond.

"Hey! Hey!" Sean called out to him.

The man didn't flinch. He didn't break his stride. He just continued forward, looking ahead to the restaurant. Finally, he glanced over to them, and gave them a passing glance as if they were trees rooted there in the middle of the road, not people. He reached his hand back and clicked the lock on the key fob in his hand. The lights flashed on the sports car and it made a beeping sound, letting him know it was locked up.

Watching him, Sean suddenly felt defeated. He'd lost his parking spot, yes but he'd lost much more . . . his pride. The man just disrespected them, and he hadn't stepped forward to do a thing about it.

Kevin rushed forward with Bailey on one arm and the car seat in the other hand.

"Hey, that's our parking spot!" Bailey shouted.

"It's all under control." Sean held up his hands, not wanting to get into it now. The last thing he needed was to follow that man into the restaurant and disturb Allyson's night. "We'll just park down the road. I'll leave another message so they know where it is."

"Leave a message? Leave a message?" Kevin's voice rose with emotion. The vein in his right temple bulged to the beat of his heart. Boom. Boom. Boom. It had always done that when Kevin was angry, upset, or otherwise intense, like when he came in contact with a surprise zombie horde in his game.

Desperation was clearly on Kevin's face. He didn't understand why everyone had to get so worked up . . . about everything. When one was a dad, he had to learn to go with the flow. Things weren't usually as big of crisis as one tried to make them up to be. Kids were resilient. Drama happened on a daily basis. You could either deal with it, or crumble under the weight of responsibility.

"Just go in and talk to them," Kevin spouted.

Sean leaned forward and pointed to the restaurant. He shook his head. "No! I'm not going in there."

"You've got to go in there." Kevin clung to Bailey as if she was a teddy bear, saving him from this nightmare he was in. "This night will never end . . ." His words gushed out. "That's why you've got to go in there."

Sean waved his hand to the restaurant. "I said. I promised. I vowed." He emphasized each word with a jab of his hands. "And then . . . then I'm just going to walk in?"

Kevin's eyes widened, and his eyebrows nearly touched his hairline.

Sean waved a hand to the restaurant and lowered his voice. "I'm not going in there. It's a matter of principle. Okay?"

Marco gasped. He looked to the sky and blinked slowly twice, as if he too was in the middle of a bad dream and he didn't know how to wake up.

Sean pressed his fingertips to his forehead, trying to formulate the plan. "Okay, we'll leave Marco's car down there for the girls, you guys take the van and kids to my house and . . . Gosh, this is confusing. Marco, park your car in that open spot. The girls will find it. Kevin, give me your keys."

Marco looked as if he was going to cry. The craziness disappeared from Kevin's face and he shrugged. That's one reason why they'd remained friends so long Sean guessed. Kevin escalated quickly, but he calmed easily. Sean knew that Kevin would go along with him . . . and Marco would go too, mostly because being left alone with his kids was as frightening to him as facing a group of angry luchadores or a biker gang.

"I have to get back to the hospital and check on Beck," Sean said slowing, trying not to overwhelm them.

"Beck's fine." Marco and Kevin said in unison.

"Did you hear the fire guy?" Sean's voice rose an octave. "It's policy." He circled his hand in the air. "Now make the transition."

Marco's face scrunched up again, reminding Sean of the face that Beck made when he was hiding, trying to fill his diaper. "But what about my bird?"

"I have an idea." Kevin pointed to Marco. "I saw this on *Animal Planet* once." He held his arm out even with his shoulder, like all those guys did on the bird training shows. His fist was balled up. "They come back," Kevin said.

Sean smirked, and then he realized Kevin was serious.

Marco eyed Kevin, and then did the same. "This?" He held out his arm, fist balled up.

Kevin hurried the direction they'd seen his bird fly. "Mama!"

Sean's lip curled up. He looked to Kevin in disbelief. "It's not a falcon."

***

Sondra sat by the front door of Chez Magique wondering how this had happened. For the five years since they'd started pastoring this church, she'd done so well at running things. On keeping things in order. On maintaining control. On presenting a good image, but now it was all crumbling.

She couldn't get Mattie Mae Lloyd's startled expression off her mind when she'd seen her holding those beer bottles. How could that have happened? Out of all the moments for the Dance Cam to sweep down. Was someone out to get her or something? And now this . . .

She looked to where Ally and Bridget . . . yes . . . that was her name . . . hurried to confront the nice-looking young man in the center of the restaurant. Ally in her black skirt and heels. Bridget in her tight jeans and bowling shirt, streaks of pink streaming through her long, blonde hair.

Ally had shared prayer requests for Bridget many times during the years that they've become friends. Bridget had struggled since she'd become a teen, had made bad choices, and then found herself pregnant. Even though Sondra had compassion for the young woman, it had made her even more determined to make sure Zoe didn't make the same choices. It was so easy to get off track.

One little compromise easily led to another, until you no longer recognized the person looking at yourself in the mirror. Sondra remembered what that was like. She'd been that young woman. She didn't want Zoe to have to deal with the same pain. Same shame. The same permanent markings.

Sondra could hear their voices raising, even with her face hiding behind her purse.

Outside the doors she could hear shouting in the street too. "Mama, mama!" a man called with a frantic voice. She didn't dare look, lest anyone think she was involved with them too. The hostess had already been giving her the stink eye since they'd returned.

"I am not overreacting!" Bridget yelled from across the restaurant. Sondra looked into the dining area, and she was almost certain that she saw the small crystals on the chandeliers quiver as Bridget's words bounced off of them.

"Now!" Bridget's voice escalated even more, and the hostess picked up the phone.

Sondra wrapped her arms around her tan leather clutch and pulled it tighter to her chest, anticipating the hostess's words to come. Sondra scooted closer to where Izzy sat, and she again lifted up her clutch to hide her face. She hoped the hostess didn't remember that Ally was with her, and by transitive property Bridget was too. The last thing she needed was for anyone to think she was part of this.

Ever since she'd married church-boy Ray, she'd done her best to live on the straight and narrow path. And when he graduated from seminary and then became pastor, staying above board was even more important. To have anyone question her reputation was to mar his . . . and she couldn't do that to her husband. He was too good of a man for that.

From the widening of the hostess's eyes it was clear the dispatcher had agreed to send a squad car.

"Chez Magique." The hostess' voice still sounded smooth, controlled as she spoke into the phone. "The reason? There is a crazy lady in our restaurant, and she just brought her crazy baby sister."

Sondra dug around in her purse, pretending she was looking for something. It didn't matter what she was looking for, just as long as her face wasn't seen.

"A crazy baby sister, or a mini her," the hostess continued. "There are two crazy ladies now. One crazy lady, now two crazy ladies. Chez Magique," she repeated.

Sondra looked to Izzy, and Izzy stared her down. Izzy lifted her eyebrows as if expecting Sondra to have an answer, a plan.

Why did everyone always come to her? Look to her? Sondra shrunk down farther into the cushioned seat. She didn't know how to get out of this. Ally had the keys to the van. And her cell phone was in the van too. She needed to fix that. She needed to text Ray and let him know what was happening. He needed to know in case word got back to him about what his wife had been up too . . . and maybe he'd have advice.

Izzy continued to stare, and Sondra shrugged. She had nothing. No answer. No solution. No way to get help, and it was the feeling she hated most. After all, others counted on her to do the right thing—to be the good example.

***

Marco ran with his arm extended down the street in front of the restaurant. "Mama, Mama!" He called to the bird, but he saw nothing. He heard nothing. The night was quiet. There wasn't even one chirp. He didn't know what he expected. Was Kevin right? Had he indeed seen this on *Animal Planet*? Would Mama come down and sit on his arm if he called?

Marco tried to think back. They'd lost the bird a few times in the house. The bird wasn't like a dog. It didn't come to them when it was called. Instead, when Mama got free, it liked to sit in the big house plant that Izzy had in the foyer by the front door. It would sit there, perched, as quiet as a mouse while the kids—and sometimes Izzy—ran wild trying to find it.

That gave Marco an idea. He rushed over to the bushes just outside the front doors of Chez Magique. He looked around, starting at the bottom, but he didn't see anything. Kevin rushed ahead, looking into another tree. Kevin paused, and his eyes grew wide. He looked to Marco, pointed to the tree, and then he flapped his arms.

Marco rushed forward. "Do you see her? Do you see my bird?"

"Shhh . . ." Kevin frowned, and then he went through his hand motions again. He flapped his wings—uh arms—and then pointed to the tree.

Marco looked up just in time to see the bird lift from the tree limb and head their direction. He jutted out his arm, balling his fist, preparing a place for it to land. Instead, the bird dive-bombed Kevin.

The bird looked like something from a horror movie, swooping down, poking Kevin's head and then flying up again.

Kevin jumped and screamed like a girl. He flapped his arms and swatted his head and then turned in a circle. He squealed and jumped up and then down, as if a flock attacked him—not just one parakeet.

Marco took a step back, trying to see where it went. His heart pounded. If he didn't get that bird he'd never hear the end of it. He could picture it now. The boys up all night crying and sobbing and asking for Mama. Izzy would be crying too. She always did when she didn't get enough sleep, which had been often lately. He didn't know if he could take that—handle that.

The bird dive-bombed again.

Kevin swatted at it again, spinning in circles. "Marco, Marco!"

Marco grabbed the front of Kevin's shirt, "Where's my bird? Where's my bird?"

Kevin stopped his motion. His hair was flopped all over his head. He was staring down at Marco's feet, panting heavily.

"Where's my bird?" Marco asked again. Then Marco followed Kevin's gaze down to the ground.

"You stepped on it." Kevin's voice was a monotone.

Marco wanted to drop to his knees in horror and disbelief, but he didn't want to get bird parts on his pants.

"I'm dead."

CHAPTER TWELVE

Hot, seething anger pumped through Bridget's veins. She should have expected this. Should have known this would happen. She'd put her trust in Joey too many times, only to have him completely fail her. She'd trusted that he'd love her when he said he did. She trusted that he'd be by her side when she decided to have the baby. He told her he'd get a job and then find an apartment for them. That they'd be a happy family. None of it had happened. None of it.

Instead, he'd shacked up for a while with someone else—Caprice. Thankfully, that had been short-lived. But he still continued to make excuses why he hadn't come around after Phoenix's birth. That's why she'd been so surprised when she'd called and he'd agreed to help her. She'd thought he'd changed . . . obviously not!

Bridget trampled into the restaurant area, weaving around small tables, and looking for Joey. She finally found him at a table near the back. He was dressed in a shirt and tie. Of all things! And with him was a blonde. Beautiful wasn't a good enough description. She was gorgeous, well-dressed, and put together. Both jealousy and fury fought for a rightful place within Bridget.

Unable to tame her emotions, Bridget stormed up to the table. The click of heels on the tile floor told her that Ally was right behind her. She knew the other women wouldn't follow. They didn't know her. They didn't care.

She reached the table and paused, jutting out her chin. "JOEY!" Bridget stretched forward, leaning on the chair for emphasis.

Joey jumped to his feet, startled, as if he'd just seen a ghost. "Bridget?!?"

Then he looked past her to Ally, who'd sidled up beside her. "Seriously?" he asked Allyson.

Bridget fumed even more. As if he had any right to accuse her sister-in-law.

"Where's Phoenix?" her voice bellowed, and her heartbeat pounded in her temples. It took all her restraint not to pound him. "I leave Phoenix with you for one night and—" She gripped the back of chair tighter.

Joey tried to appear calm. "He's . . . fine. Someone is watching him."

She hated when Joey did that. The sky would be falling, and Joey always tried to play it cool. Bridget glanced down at the table and noticed they weren't eating dinner, but dessert. Joey had often taken her out for dessert. She at first thought it was romantic until she realized he was just being cheap and didn't want to pay for a whole meal.

"So you can take some tramp for chocolate cake?" Bridget's voice rose. "Oh that's great." She reached over and shook the woman's hand. The woman's skin was perfect. Her nails were manicured. The woman cast Bridget a sympathetic look, which just made her madder. "Hi, I'm Bridget."

Bridget turned back to Joey. "So, where is he?"

"This is not what it looks like," Joey told the blonde.

"So who has him?" Bridget urged, louder.

Joey pursed his lips together. He looked down at the table. Worry filled his face. His chin slightly trembled, and he refused to answer.

Finally a word escaped his lips. "Bones." He winced and looked up at her.

She didn't know what to do. What to say. He was joking.

She laughed and smiled. She waited for Joey to crack a smile too. Surely this had to be a joke.

But Joey didn't smile. He didn't change his worried expression. Horror splashed over her as if someone had just poured a glass of ice water over her head.

"Bones?" she gasped. "Bones from the tattoo parlor, Bones?"

Joey shrugged as if his explanation made complete sense. "Yeah, yeah. He said he could hang there until I can pick him up."

Bridget's face scrunched up. She tilted her head, sure she misunderstood. She frowned at him. "He's *at* the tattoo parlor?"

Joey shook his head as if she was the one who'd lost her mind. "He's not getting a tattoo!"

Joey looked again to his date. His look was worried, as if he was concerned about what she thought. Bridget fumed. He cared more about impressing the date than about their son— their SON.

She stomped her foot and lifted her face to the ceiling. "You've got to be out of your ever-living mind!" The words burst from her lips.

Joey reached out, and his hand barely touched her arm. "Bridg, you have to stop overreacting."

She gasped, pulled her arm away, and looked back at him. "I am not overreacting!"

Bridget lunged for Joey. She pushed her pointed finger into his chest. "I'm gonna kill you, kill you!" Bridget didn't care about the other diners. She didn't care if Joey was embarrassed. All she cared about was Phoenix. Was he worried, alone, scared without her? The anger pulsing within was hot and thick, but worry ached deep down in her gut.

Allyson's hand wrapped around her wrist, pulling, tugging, trying to pull her back. Bridget knew she could stay there and continued to unleash her fury. She could give him a few more choice words. She could pummel him with her fists, but what good would it do? Joey would always be worthless Joey. The most important thing for her to do was to find Phoenix.

Bridget submitted to Allyson's tugging.

Allyson guided her along through the tables and the diners. Everyone in the restaurant was silent. Every eye was on her. Some diners had paused with their forks halfway to their lips, but all she could think about was Phoenix. Her baby.

"Yup, yup. Okay," Allyson mumbled under her breath as she pulled Bridget along.

Bridget spun around one more time to face him.

Joey's eyes were wide, and she pointed at him, hating him for what he did . . . and what he'd made her become—this crazy woman. She hated him for leaving Phoenix like that. "I'm going to kill you . . . in your sleep!"

"Okay, let's go." Allyson's voice was way too soft, way too calm. Of course it wasn't Ally's baby who was missing. No one loved her son as she did. No one.

She turned back around and moved to the front door of the restaurant.

And then, to make things even worse, she heard Joey behind her, trying to shrug off his actions. "It's—it's just nothing," he said to his date.

Steam blew out of her ears.

Yeah, to him it may be nothing. But to Bridget, Phoenix—her son—was everything.

Everything.

Bridget burst out the front door, fighting hot tears. Fresh, cool air hit her face.

Allyson and the others followed her out. She paused on the sidewalk right outside of the restaurant. There was a gathering of people waiting for tables, but otherwise the night air was quiet. The road was empty. The sky was large, and suddenly she felt so out of place . . . and so small. So helpless.

Bridget paused her steps. The other women looked at each other, trying to figure out what to say. Not knowing what to do.

She didn't know what to do either, well, not exactly. She knew she had to get her baby. A tattoo parlor? Really?! But how could she get there? It was all the way across town.

Her thoughts jumbled all together. Had Phoenix eaten? Was he crying? She was sure Bones meant well, but when is the last time he'd cared for a baby?

"How am I supposed to get him?" She threw up her hands and then dropped them. Allyson stopped right in front of her.

Inside her stomach quivered as if it was made of Jell-O. "I took the bus to get here. If I leave work I'll be fired. On my first night. On my first night. I need this job, Ally!" Bridget wiped her tears. She had rent to pay and she was late on her phone bill. She needed a new phone too. The crappy one she had kept cutting out and dropping calls. Then there were diapers—so expensive.

Bridget looked to Ally, and all she got was a blank stare. She needed help, but what had Sean said, that Allyson needed her oxygen? Suddenly Bridget felt so very alone in this with no place to turn.

What am I going to do now?

***

Allyson's heart pounded even after they'd left the restaurant. Bridget's voice had echoed all over the room, and every table had gone silent as they quieted to hear her words. Bridget had been angry. Fuming. Joey deserved it though. Allyson had to admit she'd do the same if she'd been in Bridget's place.

She couldn't imagine her kids being treated in such a way . . . by their father. Yes, Sean made unwise decisions at times—or at least decisions that she thought were unwise (i.e., violent video games), but he'd never pawn them off onto someone who wasn't responsible. He'd never taken them to a tattoo parlor . . . left them there.

Allyson stood in front of the swanky restaurant and knew what she had to do. "I have the van." She spread arms wide, feeling like superwoman. They were here for a reason. It was meant for her to see Joey for a reason. They'd run into Bridget . . . for a reason.

She clapped her hands together. "We'll run. We'll pick him up. We can fix this and get back on schedule." She tried to make her tone light. She looked to Izzy and Sondra. "Best night ever will only be on pause for thirty minutes."

Izzy's eyes grew wide behind her glasses. "And then do what with a baby?"

"I haven't gotten that far yet!" She moved toward the parking spot with quicken steps. "Let's get the van!"

Allyson looked under the streetlight, and she stopped dead in her steps. Her—her van was gone. A small, black sports car was parked right where she'd left her van. *It was gone!*

"Where's the van? I parked it right there." She turned back to her friends. "Remember, I told you that it was right under the street lamp?" She pointed. Her jaw dropped and goose bumps rose on her arm. Goose bumps of fear.

"It only takes a couple of seconds to steal a car." Izzy's eyes looked even larger behind her glasses. "Always lock everything up. That's what Marco says."

Bridget covered her face with her hands, and Allyson knew she wasn't worried about the car. She was worried about Phoenix and how to get to him.

Allyson looked up and down the aisle of parked cars. There wasn't a minivan for as far as she could see. "I did. Am I crazy?" Ally grabbed her hair. She could not believe this was happening. How much could happen in one night? How much?

There were a group of people standing around the entrance to the restaurant, most likely waiting for a precious table. The thief had some nerve to steal a van under a streetlight, right in the full view of others. Who would do that?

"So what do I do? Do I report it to the police?" Allyson looked to Sondra, seeking an answer.

Sondra covered her mouth with her hand, as if in shock. She looked into her purse and then back up to Ally again. "With what phones?"

Allyson closed her eyes remembering. The phones, they'd put them all in the console. Whoever had stolen the van had their phones too!

She bent over, hands on knees. "Oh, no. No, no, no, no, no . . ."

Bridget stared at them in disbelief. "You don't have phones?"

Izzy clenched her teeth and looked around. "Okay, I'm freaking out now."

Bridget waved her hand toward the bowling alley. "My phone's back at work. We can just use mine."

"Okay!" Allyson took two steps in the direction of the bowling alley, and then she paused. She spun around, motioning to Sondra and Izzy. Then she pointed to the people standing by the Chez Magique entrance. "Can you ask them and see if they saw anything?"

They turned and hurried back to the front of the restaurant.

Bridget ran back to get her things, Allyson asked if she could use the phone behind the counter. Next to her, the kitchen smelled of French fries, hamburgers, and artificial cheese. Allyson's stomach growled and she told herself that after they got Phoenix that she'd get something to eat. Something not made by a sixteen-year-old whose only culinary skills included putting a basket into a deep fryer.

She picked up the phone and dialed. Her small purse was tucked under one arm, and her hand rested on the back of her neck. Her neck was sore, from tension for sure. How could this . . . this happen? After everything!

A dispatcher answered, and she explained about her stolen van and the location she'd last seen it.

"Describe it?" Allyson wrinkled up her nose. "There were a bunch of bumper stickers on the back . . ."

The DJ still danced, the music still blared, the bowling balls still crashed, and the pins still tumbled. Allyson pressed the corded phone receiver into her ear as she tried to describe her van to the operator on the other end of the line.

"There's a fish bumper sticker, but it's pretty faded." She winced slightly and let her eyes flutter closed. "Eat organic."

Then, remembering the other stickers, she lowered her voice and turned her head away, making sure none of the other customers could hear. Heat rose to her cheeks. "My homeschooler is smarter than your honor student."

She shook her head and waved her hand. "And a bunch of others that I don't really want to talk about, but you get the idea!"

Allyson listened as the dispatcher told her they were going to ask their officers to keep an eye out for her van.

From behind her she could hear Bridget's voice. "It's an emergency! It's personal!" Bridget said to the guy working in the kitchen. Bridget approached and pulled on a flannel shirt over her bowling shirt. She paused before Allyson with intensity in her gaze. "I called a cab."

"Okay, okay." Allyson hung up the phone. A cab it was. She wondered what Sondra and Izzy would think of that. Another twist in their already U-turned night.

CHAPTER THIRTEEN

Bridget climbed into the front seat of the cab. She'd never ridden in one before, and she didn't have money to pay for it. She assumed that since Allyson agreed to it that she'd cover the bill. Surely it wouldn't be too much, right, just to go across town to get Phoenix.

The three women were sitting in the back. Bridget was sort of surprised that they all came along. They seemed worried about Phoenix, which made her feel good. At least they cared a little bit. She was sure they were horrified—like she was—by the thought of Phoenix being in a tattoo parlor. She'd doubted they'd go in.

The security, or privacy, or whatever window between the front and back seat was open. Bridget glanced over her shoulder and saw that they were clustered around it.

The driver seemed to be driving too slow. If she were driving, if she had her own car—which was something else she needed money for—she'd have her foot pressed to the floorboard. She'd be going as fast as she could, and if a cop tried to pull her over she'd explain about Phoenix, where he was, and how she needed to get to him.

She looked around at the streets they drove past—and the buildings—and they didn't seem familiar. "Are you sure this is the fastest way to Davis Street?"

The driver had an English accent. He seemed proper. He'd made sure they'd buckled up. He wore a fedora, and looked like someone who should be at home penning spy novels, not driving a cab.

"Absolutely the fastest way," he spoke with a crisp British accent that sounded so real it had to be fake.

Bridget had been to Bone's tattoo shop many times, and he seemed to be going there in a roundabout way. Maybe he was doing it for a bigger bill, but if that was the case she did not have time for this.

"Shouldn't you cut over on 8th?" Bridget asked.

"He should take the expressway." The pastor's wife said from the back, leaning through the window, breathing down their backs.

"Are you from England?" It was Allyson's friend Izzy talking. Izzy was cool in a spacey sort of way. She'd been nice enough to Bridget. She'd even given Bridget some of her sons' baby clothes when Bridget had Phoenix. It was a nice gesture, but the ducky and monkey decorated clothes really were not Bridget's style.

"Me, from England?" The cabbie answered. "No, I just watched a bit of the BBC and picked up the accent."

Bridget looked over at him and rolled her eyes.

"I'm a cabbie, love. It's my occupation."

"Why do people from other countries always sound smarter?" Izzy said in that wispy voice of hers.

Bridget pressed a fist to her forehead, turned her head toward the window and closed her eyes. Seriously, they were going to talk about stupid stuff like this?

"Because we are smarter, which is why this is the fastest way," Cabbie answered.

Didn't they know that it was only going to distract the cabbie and get him headed the wrong direction? He wasn't even from his country. Who knew how long he'd been there. Maybe he really was heading the wrong direction.

Bridget wanted to tell them all to be quiet. To tell them just to chill, but they were all she had—this crazy bunch of women, and she needed them. At least at this moment she did. She clenched her fist and held back her words, her frustration.

"Then can you just . . . speed up?" It was Allyson's voice. The one she knew well.

Thank you, yes, just please freakin' speed up . . . she wanted to add.

"You're all very lovely." The words rolled off the cabbie's tongue. "But I'm not getting a ticket for you four."

Bridget tapped her cell phone against her head, wanting to explode. Wanting to go ninja on them all. She was using more self-control than she had in months, and she told herself that they'd be there soon.

Allyson gasped in the backseat, obviously feeling the same frustration. "Look, we're trying to find her baby who happens to be stuck at a tattoo parlor." Her voice rose with emotion.

"Yeah, well, that's none of my business—" His voice trailed off and then he paused, as if Allyson's words were finally sinking in.

His head jerked around, and he looked at her. "Wait, are you having a laugh?" Shock registered on his face. Horror. His eyes widened, and he looked back to the faces cramming the window, as if trying to see if they were serious.

As he did the cab started speeding up, yet he was looking backward at the ladies instead of the road. Their taxi was quickly approaching the back of another car.

Bridget sucked in a breath. She grabbed his arm, trying to get his attention. "Road, road, road!" He turned back around, and his eyes widened. He yanked the steering wheel and jerked the car into the fast lane, barely missing the back of the other car.

Bridget breathed a sigh of relief, but her heart still pounded. And it would pound until she had Phoenix in her arms again.

"Right, right," the cabbie said, trying to downplay their near miss. "Onwards!"

He situated himself, and then looked straight ahead. He sat quiet for a moment, completely focused, and seemed to speed up a little. Then he turned to her, "I'm sorry, where are we going again?"

Seriously?! Bridget held back the string of words she really wanted to say and then gave him the address again.

***

Allyson released a breath as they exited the freeway. She knew now that they were close. Even though the drive probably only took fifteen minutes, it seemed to take forever. She'd watched

Bridget in the front seat, and her heart ached. At every flippant comment, Bridget seemed to jump out of her skin.

Allyson had spent a lot of time with Bridget, and she was usually bothered by how much of a teenager she still was—so focused on her looks, on guys, on television, and on her phone. Not to mention the inability to tame her tongue. But being with her now helped Allyson to see a new side of her. Allyson was even impressed by how much she *didn't* say on this drive . . . maybe having a pastor's wife in the car had something to do with that.

As they drove, Allyson felt a connection with Bridget that she hadn't felt before. Bridget was a mom who really loved her kid. Yeah, she needed Allyson to watch Phoenix often, but unlike Allyson she didn't have a Sean. She didn't even have a good relationship with her parents. She counted on Allyson not because she was just trying to shrug off her responsibility—okay, maybe sometimes she was. But mostly she probably really needed help. Tonight made it so clear why that help was necessary. There was no one else to turn to—no one who could be trusted anyway.

They pulled up to a street lined with old brick buildings on the wrong side of town. A neon sign lit up the window. A cluster of motorcycles were parked outside, and Allyson wondered what type of guy this Bones fellow was. If his name was any indication, he didn't sound pretty.

Bridget jumped from the front seat of the cab and darted into the tattoo parlor first. Sondra and Izzy followed, and Allyson climbed from the car and then paused. Cabbie had opened the driver's side door and was standing. He'd crossed his arms and was resting them on the top of his cab, watching them.

She lifted her hand and splayed her fingers, waving to him. "Can you wait just five minutes?"

"Is that an actual five minutes, or 'a ladies night' five minutes?"

Allyson shrugged. "How long can it take to get a baby?"

Allyson entered and the first thing that struck her was the scent of hospital soap, ink, incense, and something that smelled like damp woods. She paused just slightly as she walked in, and looked around. The walls were lined with posters of skulls, snakes, and cartoon ladies.

The room was dim, as dim as the bowling alley had been, without the black lights. A front counter sat in the middle of the room and behind it sat an African-American guy with a massive Afro and a day-old beard and mustache that was nothing more than a shadow on his face. He wore a sleeveless hoodie, a jean vest with studded front pockets, and an intricately designed black tattoo on his arm.

He was handsome. Well, Allyson just assumed he was handsome. His eyes were covered by large, reflective aviator glasses, reminiscent of Tom Cruise in *Top Gun*.

Sitting to the side were a line of bikers that looked like the guys from *Duck Dynasty*. They flipped through biker and automobile magazines as they waited for their turn under the needle.

The desk guy was flipping through a magazine too, as they entered, and he barely glanced up as they paused before him. The buzz of a tattoo needle could be heard from across the room.

Bridget leaned on the tall counter. "Bones here?"

The desk guy glanced up briefly. "He's working."

"Can you go get him?"

"Yeah, because he apparently has a baby in the back," said Izzy.

"I need to talk to him right now."

"We really need your help."

All four women were talking at once, and four fingers wagged as they leaned over the counter.

Allyson's voice rose above the others. "Her boyfriend Joey was supposed to be watching him . . ."

"I need to talk to Bones right now!" Bridget bounced as she spoke.

"Whoa, whoa, whoa, simmer down, ya'll." The front counter guy rose and spread out his hands, trying to calm them. "I can't even understand what you're saying right now, like." His voice was soft, as if he was only half-awake. "Chill for real." He shook his head and his Afro tossed from side to side.

"We're here to get Phoenix!" Bridget smacked her lips and motioned with her hands.

"That's what I'm talking about." He reached out a fist to fist-bump her. "Phoenix rising out of the ashes." His fist bump turned into open-splayed fingers that wiggled as they rose, as if rising from smoke. "Number 97 over there, but I suggest you do it on your back." He nodded to the wall of designs and spread his hands. "Because it'll be really pretty like." He flapped his hands, as if mimicking a bird's wings flapping.

"No, no, no." Allyson's voice joined in with the others as they tried to explain that he'd misunderstood."

"Shhhh . . ." Bridget interrupted their protests, and then fixed her gaze on the desk guy. "No, Phoenix is my baby!"

"You got a picture? Because Bones needs a picture." He mimicked drawing with his hands. "To get the tattoo perfect because those little guys are hard to draw."

Bridget flipped her head around to look to Ally. "Am I speaking English?" Then a strand of her hair hit Allyson's face as she flipped back around to look at the man's face again. "No, no boss. None of us wants a tattoo!

"I don't want a tattoo," Izzy muttered to herself, as if confirming Bridget's words.

The guy pointed and then made a clicking sound, "Yeah, you do," he said not believing her.

Ally looked to Sondra, and the pastor's wife awkwardly shifted from side-to-side and said nothing. She didn't try to interject, didn't try to jump in the middle of this. Allyson knew why. This was out of her comfort zone, like a moon walk to Mars type of out-of-the-comfort-zone. Sondra looked at the ground and said nothing.

"Phoenix is my baby." Bridget pointed to herself, speaking in a slow, clear voice, trying again. "And he's in the back." She pointed to the back and then to the others. "And we're here to pick him up."

Allyson nodded along as Bridget talked, as if doing so would help him understand better.

"Why would someone bring a baby to a tattoo parlor?" The desk guy smirked. "That's dumb." He offered a soft chuckle. "I mean that's really dumb."

"I know. It's totally dumb," the women agreed, everyone talking at once again. "I mean that's really dumb."

He removed his aviator glasses, pleased with their response, and then it was Sondra's voice that rose above the others. One clear word rang out. "Illegal."

Without hesitation the desk guy rose, slipped his glasses back on his face, and hurried to the back. Wow, Sondra knew what it took to get him moving. No one else moved. The long bearded guys still waited. Someone else continued to give a man a tattoo, the *buzz, buzz, buzz* causing Allyson's skin to crawl.

Allyson glanced over at Sondra, wondering what she thought about being in a place like this. Sondra stood with her arms crossed over her chest, pressing her tan clutch to her. She moved stiffly and looked around at the lava lamp and the art on the wall. She seemed uncomfortable and Allyson guessed that Sondra had never been in a place like this before. Why would she.

Then Allyson noticed that one of the bearded guys was giving Sondra the eye. He wore a black leather vest with a lot of patches. Tattoos covered his arms that she supposed had one time been muscular but weren't any more.

Sondra glanced over at him and a smile rose above his long white beard, and he winked. Allyson gasped. The man was hitting on her. She wondered what Pastor Ray would say about that!

Sondra nodded to him in return and gave him a sweet church lady smile. "Hello," she said as simply as greeting a new person who walked into church.

Bridget didn't act so calm. She lifted her face to the ceiling, as if there was an answer there. Allyson could see her hands trembling, and her face had lost a lot of color. She stood in one place, but shifted from side-to-side as if not knowing what to do. As if worry crawled like a million ants over her skin.

"Okay, I am officially freaking out!" Bridget seemed to choke the words out.

Allyson reached out her hand and tried to calm her, but she felt the same tension tightening her own gut. "Bridget, it's going to be okay." She hoped her words sounded convincing. She prayed that things would get wrapped up soon and everything indeed would be okay soon.

The desk guy moved through a curtain that separated the front area from the back. His huge Afro was backlit from the light in the back room. He shook his head as he walked to them, which wasn't a great sign. They all moved toward the counter. Bridget gripped Allyson's arm, as if leaning on her for support.

"Okay, there is no baby back there." He pointed his thumb behind him, toward the back. "Which is awesome. You guys had me." He shook his head and then slowly settled back into the chair. "I thought you were from the health department or some-thing . . ."

Bridget threw down her arms and started breathing hard. Allyson turned to her and motioned for her to breathe, to breathe.

"I thought you were going to arrest me . . ." the front desk guy was saying. "Or maybe worse, cut off my hair. Like what . . . what would happen if you cut off my hair?" He pressed his hand against the front of his hair.

Bridget turned back to the desk, placed her hands on it, and leaned forward, trying to get his attention.

"It's okay though," the desk guy droned on. "Bones is going to help you when he's done. Everything's okay." He gave them the okay motion with his hand. "Like, we're good."

Allyson felt her mouth falling open. Surely he had to be joking. Hadn't he heard what they'd said? Allyson looked to Bridget. Her face was white. It looked like she was going to faint, and Allyson wondered if she should make Bridget sit down.

Instead, Bridget straightened up and pointed a finger. "What?! I need to talk to Bones, like, right now."

The desk guy cocked an eyebrow and then looked to her in disbelief. "You don't rush art," he said softly. Simply. His forehead folded in disbelief at her request.

"What is wrong with you?" the words erupted from Bridget's mouth.

"Are you kidding me? Are you kidding me?" Allyson found herself saying. Then everyone started talking at once, and she couldn't hear herself over the noise.

"We need to get the baby!" Allyson said, but her words were drowned out.

Bridget stood on her tiptoes, making sure her voice was heard over all the rest. "Are you hearing what everyone's saying?" She called out and then hit her open-palmed hand on the countertop. "I'm going to call the police!" She shrugged.

The man rose to his feet again. One of the bearded guys in the waiting area also stood, and then hurried to the back. It was like a floodgate, and seeing him a whole bunch more hurried out.

"Whoa, whoa, whoa, like calm down." The desk guy motioned to all the hardened bikers who were rushing out of the front area and moving past the curtain into the back. "Look, you're scaring everyone." He waved his hands, clearly upset. The serene, passive look from his face had hardened into a frustrated one. "Seriously, I'm going to have to ask you to leave and take your little 'Housewives of Ohio' with you."

He waved them away. "Seriously." Then his face grew calmer again, and he pointed to Izzy. "Especially this one, she's been eying me all night."

Izzy's mouth dropped open and she gasped, and then her brow furrowed.

The women stepped back from the counter. Allyson placed a hand on Bridget's shoulder, hoping to reassure her. They weren't going to get anywhere here—not with this guy.

"Follow me," Sondra said, motioning to them. She waved them forward.

He pointed to Sondra and shooed them out. "Follow Mama Bear. That's right."

They moved to the door, and then the desk guy pointed to Izzy. "I'm just kidding . . . you're cute."

She snarled her nose. "I'm married!"

"I love you . . ." he mouthed, and Allyson didn't know whether to laugh or run up and punch him in the nose. Obviously he was not "all there" . . . which was one reason why a person didn't leave a baby at a tattoo parlor!

They walked outside, and it was colder now. The wind had picked up, and her hair fluttered around Allyson's face. It was getting later. The night was getting darker.

They paused outside of the door, and Allyson found herself looking to Sondra. Surely Sondra would have the answer. Surely Sondra would be able to figure something out.

Sondra released a slow heavy breath. She turned around, and eyed the street as if the answer would come hiking toward them.

"So what should we do?" Bridget's voice sounded desperate. "Should I call the police?" She lifted her hand in desperation.

And instead of turning to Sondra for advice, Bridget turned to her.

"Ally?" Her voice was no more than a squeak. A mix of sadness, worry, and confusion filled her face.

Me . . . she wants advice from me?

Allyson looked around. She lifted her small purse and waved it. She'd been carrying it around all night. It was as if she was on a runaway train—one she didn't know why she'd gotten on in the first place. But she had no ideas. No answers. "I—I don't . . ."

Not waiting for her answer, Sondra moved and paced for the alley.

She carried her purse like a clipboard, and her straight-back stance was the same one Allyson had seen her take as she strode into meetings for the Women's Missionary Union.

"Okay, ladies, follow me," Sondra called out. "Back door."

Relief flooded Allyson. Someone with an answer. She didn't know if it was the right answer, but at least they were moving again.

CHAPTER FOURTEEN

Sondra breathed out slowly feeling a little light in the head. Walking into the tattoo parlor with the lava lamps, the abstract art, the incense smell, and the psychedelic music that was like a low hum in the background took her back to her teen years. Just standing in there she felt young again. Stupid. She remembered how she'd worked so hard to fit in. And where had it got her? In a lot of trouble. Well, not a lot according to the authorities or anything, but she had made choices by following the crowd that she knew better.

Sondra walked with determined steps toward the alley. Being in the tattoo parlor had made her feel eighteen again, which was probably close to Bridget's age. What would she have done if she'd had a baby then? She shook her head slightly not wanting to picture it. Considering that, she knew Bridget was trying. She knew she cared for her son . . . and the baby was in trouble. That was a mission worth walking down a dark alley for. She just prayed that nothing would jump out at them . . . or rather, no one.

Dear Lord . . . here we go . . . she prayed silently.

She rounded the corner and noticed how disgusting it really was. It was as if the people in these buildings had been dumping their junk there for years. There was old tires, shopping carts filled with who-knows-what, piles of soiled bedding, and garbage bags that had been torn open and scattered—by creatures that she didn't want to think about.

Graffiti covered the wall, which meant that human creatures had been down that way too. Hopefully they weren't there now. And . . . she hoped they wouldn't show up.

Sondra lifted her head slightly as she continued on. The other women followed her tentatively. Even Bridget held back a little, as if wondering if this was the best idea.

Sondra did her best to navigate around trash cans, cardboard boxes . . . foreign, sticky substances . . . She didn't want to know what that was.

The women were quiet, watchful, as they walked.

A horrible stench rose up the farther they walked. Sondra resisted the urge to cover her nose and mouth. From somewhere in the distance a fireman's siren blared. Sondra breathed in and out in measured breaths, the same way that she'd learned to do in Lamaze when Zoe was born.

She stepped over a puddle of something-that-wasn't-rainwater and almost laughed to herself thinking what Mattie Mae Lloyd would think to see her here now. Something else to add to that list for the prayer chain.

Sondra brushed her hair out of her face. She accidentally kicked a small, metal trash can and it made a loud bang, causing her to jump. "Oh!"

She pointed to a pile of trash. "Careful there."

"Eewww . . ." Allyson said.

She scooted by a shopping cart and tried not to gag. "Don't touch that." Sondra pointed out. "It has hair in it."

A small squeak sounded behind her, and she was sure it came from Allyson. "Oh, wow. Oh, germs. Germs everywhere!" Allyson said in alarm.

Sondra led them along, and finally stopped beside a peeling wooden door with a rusty handle. From the position of the door in relation to the building she guessed that this was the one from the tattoo parlor.

Sondra reached for it and pulled. It moved just an inch or two and stopped. Locked. She wiggled it harder, but nothing worked. It didn't budge.

Suddenly she wondered what she was doing. She didn't know anything about this Bones guy. She didn't know how he'd respond to someone in the alley. She didn't know what he was hiding behind that curtain. Whatever it was it most likely wasn't good.

Sondra turned. "This is a bad idea."

She moved toward the street, and she didn't have to tell Allyson that they needed to get out of there. Ally darted toward the street, as if wanting to get there first.

But it was Bridget, the youngest, the one with the most in the game who rushed forward back toward the door.

"Oh, no, no, no. We need to get to the bottom of this. I have to find my son!" She rushed forward, pounding on the door with her open palm—hard, fast. It was clear she believed that the answer to finding her little boy was on the other side of that door.

"Open this door! Open it—"

There was a loud squeak and the door jerked open. Bridget jumped back, hands in the air. She cried out in fear and Sondra found herself crying out too. All of them did.

A large form filled the doorway. A dark shadow. A man jumped out, carrying a double barrel shot gun. He wore a black leather vest with patches, a black bandana on his head. He was beefy and every inch that wasn't covered with ink was covered with hair. He bellowed.

"I ain't got money back here so turn yourselves around—" he bellowed. Then, seeing the women standing there, his look of dominance and terror turned to one of curiosity.

Instead of shrinking back, Bridget smiled and stretched out her arms. "Bones! It's me, Bridget."

Before her eyes the Big Bad Wolf turned to Santa Claus. He reached for her, and Bridget threw herself into his arms.

It took all of Bridget's reach to wrap around his waist. Bones pulled her in tight, and Sondra's eyes rimmed with tears. *This is better than a Hallmark commercial.*

Pressed into his leather vest, Bridget's smile was squished lopsided.

"Bridget? Hey, Baby Girl!" Bone's voice takes on a fatherly tone.

Bridget's hand splayed open on his chest and for the first time Sondra noticed that Bridget's fingernails were painted different colors. Pink, green, black . . . they were all different colors. A lump grew in Sondra's throat. She was so young, so . . . needy. From the way she allowed herself to fall into Bone's hug, it was clear that Bridget was just looking for someone to care for her. And in her longing she found herself to be a mom. A mom who didn't know where her son was.

"What are you doing back here?" Bones asked.

"I'm just here to get Phoenix." She patted Bone's chest and then pulled herself back and looked up at him. Taking another step back, Bridget looked around his large frame, as if trying to peek in the door behind him.

"Where is he? Joey said he dropped him off with you . . ."

Sondra peeked in. The walls were painted green and pictures of tattoos were pinned onto the wall. There was a lounging chair and other things set up for tattooing. She guessed it was the penthouse of the tattoo shop.

Bones nodded. "Yeah, yeah, he did."

Bridget glanced back at the women, and Sondra could see a look of hope in the young mom's gaze.

"Man, I love that kid," Bones continued. "Do you ever notice how he snorts when he starts to laugh? He's adorable, he really is."

Then, as quickly as he started talk about Phoenix he switched his attention and turned to Sondra. He leaned forward and pointed.

"Have I seen you before?" he snapped.

Sondra's blood turned to ice water in her veins. She'd been around many guys like him before. She'd allowed herself to go into places where characters like this hung out. She had stories. A library of stories held within. Locked up with a lock and key stronger than the lock that had kept Bone's back door shut.

Of course she couldn't admit it. She couldn't tell these ladies that. She couldn't give it away.

Sondra's jaw dropped, and she narrowed her gaze. "My husband's the pastor of First Baptist." She tried to keep her voice as even as possible. She lowered her head and looked up at him from under her lashes.

"Nah, that's not it." He shook his head and then turned back to Bridget as if he'd kept one train of thought the whole time.

Regret filled his face. "I can't go more than an hour without a smoke. Awful habit. I also know you should not do that around a baby," he said, trying to explain.

Then, in the next breath, he looked back to Sondra again.

"Bonnaroo?" Bones asked.

Sondra knew of that place. It was a music festival in Tennessee, not too far away. She'd heard stories of the music, the drinking, and the out-of-control fans. She'd never been there and it was a place she definitely didn't want Zoe to go to.

The other women chuckled under their breath, obviously trying to picture that.

"No." She shook her head again slowly and tried to give him a warning look. He *really* didn't need to keep prodding.

"Hmm . . . Could'a sworn—" He bit his fist.

He paused to think for a minute.

Bridget waved her hands in front of his face, trying to snap him out of it.

"Bones! My Baby!?!"

"Anyways," he continued. "I called Caprice to take him until Joey gets back."

Bridget stared up at him, disbelieving. She ran her fingers through her hair. There was anger reflected on her face. Anger that was different—even from the anger that she had toward Joey. If steam could come out of Bridget's ears, Sondra bet it would.

"Caprice Stephens?" Bridget spit out the name. Then she forced a smile and softly pounded Bone's chests with two fists. "Joey's ex." A hard chuckle escaped her lips.

"It's okay. She don't smoke." Bones said, as if his explanation made complete logic. "She's a nonsmoker."

Bridget turned and headed down the alley even before Bone's finished. She walked with quick steps, angry steps. She didn't even care where she was going and kicked a pile of trash to the side.

"Do you need her address?" Bones called after her.

Bridget paused, and swung around with ferocity. Her hair flipped over her shoulder, and her face was scrunched up with anger. "No, I know where she lives!"

Allyson rushed after Bridget, and then Sondra followed with Izzy by her side.

Sondra turned to look back over her shoulder. "Thank you."

She stepped carefully as she moved through the mess, and she could feel Bone's eyes on them as he watched them go.

"You ladies should stay out of alleys, now. There are some unsavory types of fellers who hang out back here," he called out with concern.

After all these years Sondra had never thought she'd find herself back in a place like this. It was a night of surprises and rediscovery, to be certain. She just hoped that next stop was to discover Phoenix . . . and now that they knew who had him they should have no problem finding the young boy. Right?

CHAPTER FIFTEEN

Bridget stormed up the steps of the ramshackle house and pounded on the door. "Open this door, now!" The wood of the door was unyielding, and she pounded harder.

Pain shot through her knuckles. Pain pierced her heart. If anything happened to Phoenix, she didn't know what she'd do—how she'd ever forgive herself. She shouldn't have trusted Joey. This wasn't the first time he'd disappointed her. He'd been so handsome and so charming when they'd first met. He'd listened as she'd told him about the trouble with her parents. How she never felt she'd ever live up to their standards. He told her he understood. He told her he loved her. And as soon as she found out she was pregnant he was gone—out of the picture.

He'd come back, of course, just long enough to get her hopes up. All she wanted was a happy family like Sean and Ally had. She didn't want Phoenix to have to grow up without a mom and dad in the home, but now Joey had done this . . . had passed off his responsibility to someone else. And then Bones had passed off sweet Phoenix to Caprice—the person who Joey had started dating after her.

"Open up! Let me in!" Bridget shouted. Ally joined her, help-ing in the pounding. Sondra and Izzy stood a few steps behind them, providing backup she supposed.

Behind her the cabbie called out. "Hey!"

Bridget turned to see what he wanted.

"Hey, what's going on, love?" The cabbie walked up to the end of the sidewalk. He stretched out his arms toward them. Behind him the taxi was still running. The light bar on the top of the taxi glowed—one of the few lights on the darkened street. The meter was still running too. "Would someone please . . . communicate with me?" He approached the steps of the house.

All four women stood with Bridget on the porch. Bridget was about to call back to him that they were just going to pick up Phoenix, and then they'd be out of there, but she heard the sound of footsteps and then the door squeaking open. She turned back around.

A disheveled-looking guy dressed in a black undershirt, wear-ing a worn ball cap opened the door. His eyes were blurry, look-ing like he had just woke up from a nap. Bridget recognized him immediately. It was Caprice's new man, Hank.

He leaned against the doorjamb with one hand. "Hey, what's your problem?"

Bridget crossed her arms over her chest. "Where's Caprice?"

"She went out, man." He shook his head.

Bridget bit her lower lip. The tension building within her had eased as they'd pulled up. Phoenix had seemed within arm's reach, but now the agony came back in a wave.

"Went out where?" Her throat felt tight and she pushed the words out.

His eyes were only half-open. "She didn't say. Who are you?"

Ally leaned forward. "We are here to pick up baby Phoenix, my nephew."

"My son!" Bridget's knees grew soft.

Hank wiped his nose and just stared at them, acting as if they were images on a television show he was watching. Bridget balled up her fists, about to come unglued.

"Ah, right, right, right. Your baby has been screaming his lungs out. Yeah."

Bridget's hard quickened its beat. "What, what do you mean? Why? Is he okay? What happened?"

Allyson leaned forward next to Bridget. Bridget found comfort in her nearness. "Where did she go?" Allyson demanded.

Hank's eyes widened. "I told you, I don't know."

Bridget pointed at him. "Let me in there. Let me in . . ." She rushed him, fury raging within her. He was thin and didn't look very steady on his feet. She was sure she could rush past him. Sure she could knock him down. She lowered her shoulder slightly, ready to plow him over.

Bridget tried to burst past him into the house.

"Let me in!" Hank was stronger than he looked, pushing her back with more force than she expected.

Allyson's grip pulled her back gently. Bridget stumbled back, and she practically ran into Cabbie. He strode up like a Knight from the Roundtable, but instead of wearing a suit of armor he wore a dark blue polo shirt and his brown fedora hat.

Cabbie moved past Bridget with a determination she didn't expect. "Let me handle this, girls. Let me handle this." He approached and looked Hank up and down.

"Ha, ha, ha. You . . ." Cabbie jutted out his chin and stretched out his hands toward him. "Look at you. You pathetic primitive. You leech on society. You, that represents everything that's wrong with the American economy." He wagged his finger, emphasizing each word.

Hank looked down at himself, as if trying to figure out what those words meant.

Sondra looked at Bridget and lifted her eyebrows, as if she was also trying to figure out what this had to do with anything. Bridget just stood there, thankful to have him—someone—sticking up for her. And waiting to see how it was all going to play out.

Cabbie motioned to Hank again, continuing. "Here's what you're going to do. Listen closely. In three seconds you're—"

Hank didn't let him finish. Instead the door slammed shut.

Cabbie's head jerked back in surprise.

Bridget didn't know what to think, what to do. Did that just happen? Did Hank just have the nerve to slam the door on them?

The cabbie stepped back up to the door, knocking on it again with his knuckles. From behind him she saw that the back of his neck was red, and she assumed that his face was the same color.

"Hey open the door!" Cabbie called out. "I don't like that." He pounded harder. "Would you please open the door?"

Would you please? She couldn't help but snicker. He had to be British for sure. This was no fake accent to get a better tip. She tried to imagine what Bones would be saying, would be doing. He wouldn't be saying, "Would you please."

The words barely rolled out of Cabbie's mouth when the door swung open and a punch came from nowhere. A sharp right hook, right to Cabbie's nose.

The sound of fist on face was loud, and Cabbie's head jerked back, and then he stumbled backward. All four of them rushed to him. Bridget grasped his back, trying to push him forward so he wouldn't tumble, and realizing he smelled of Old Spice and gasoline.

The door slammed shut again, and she heard a lock clicking shut. They had no choice. They weren't going to get any help from Hank. Bridget knew there was only one person who could help her now . . . Bones.

Hank had said Phoenix had been crying. He hardly ever cried. He was such a good baby. He was such a sweet baby . . . was he okay? Where had Caprice taken him? Did she have his car seat? Was he safe?

They turned and hurried to the taxi. "We need to go get Bones. We need to bring him here . . . he's the only one who can help. Can we hurry?" Bridget pleaded, turning to the taxi driver. That's when she saw it . . . blood on the hand that covered his nose.

The other women didn't argue with Bridget. They didn't offer any suggestions about what they should do. Fear furrowed their brows and tightened the muscles on their faces, and she was sure the same worry burdened their thoughts.

What had happened to baby Phoenix?

***

Allyson never thought she'd find herself here again, in the dark alley. Standing in something sticky and disgusting. Behind her she heard a man's voice crying out. It was the cabbie. He'd parked the taxi at the end of the alley in their full view. Seeing that gave her a small sense of peace . . . at least she knew where to run to if anything happened.

Izzy had come to the rescue with the baby wipes that she found in her purse. Allyson looked back and saw her trying to dab the cabbie's nose. She tried to pat his nose, but he jerked back.

"Ow!" he cried out. "Would you please stop?"

"Why are you being such a baby?" Izzy asked.

"I'm not!" Cabbie declared, whining.

Allyson turned back around to face the door.

Bridget approached the back door of the tattoo parlor, and Sondra stood just a few feet behind her. Allyson was a few steps behind Sondra, preparing herself not to jump when the mountain of muscle that was Bones swung open the back door again . . . at least she hoped that it was going to be Bones.

Bridget pounded on the door. "Bones help! Bones!"

The door swung open again. There was no shotgun in his hands this time, thank goodness. Allyson let out a sigh of relief. Instead, Bones wore a large scowl on his face.

"I thought I told y'all to stay out of the alleys." He looked to them, and his eyes widened.

Bones eyed Bridget. His face scrunched up in worry. "What's wrong, darlin'?"

Allyson rolled her eyes. The problem should be obvious—even to him. There was no baby in Bridget's arms.

Bridget brushed her hair out of her face. It had been soft ringlets earlier tonight, but now it hung limp. Bridget's shoulders, too, slumped in defeat. "Caprice isn't there. There's some guy named Hank. He said she took Phoenix and he won't tell us where."

Allyson waved a hand to the waiting taxi cab. "Then he assaulted our cab driver!" she said, still disbelieving it.

Sondra lifted a fist and mimicked the punch. "Right in the nose. Blood everywhere!"

Allyson turned to look at the cabbie, who was leaning back on his car where Izzy still dabbed his nose, then she turned back, waiting for Bone's response.

But instead of responding to Bridget, Bones turned to Sondra.

"Lollapalooza?" he asked.

Allyson assumed it was the location of some type of wild, Rockfest like the other places he'd mentioned.

Sondra shook her head, adamant. "No."

"Ozzfest?" He widened his eyes, as if hopeful.

"Never." Her voice was firm.

Allyson could see the gears in Bone's mind churning through his old memories.

"Live Aid?"

Sondra pushed out an open hand toward him. "Please stop."

Bridget stepped forward and yanked on Bone's jacket. "Can we PLEASE just pull the conversation back to my MISSING CHILD? I have no idea where he is. I'm so worried sick about it. I just don't know where else to turn, so . . ."

Bridget looked so small next to Bones. So young. Like a child who needed caring for, not a mother on a desperate search.

Bridget swallowed a heavy breath and looked up at him, her eyes wide. Tears filled Allyson's own gaze when she saw the tears welling up in Bridget's.

"Why did you leave him, Bones?" Bridget's words released in a shaky breath.

Allyson stood by Bridget's side, trying not to blame herself. If she wouldn't have scheduled this night, none of this would have happened. She'd be home with Sean, Phoenix, and her kids. Bridget would be making a paycheck to pay for her bills. And her friends . . . well, Izzy wouldn't be dabbing the nose of some stranger with baby wipes and Sondra—her pastor's wife—wouldn't be standing next to her in some dark, stinky alley trying to seek help from a questionable biker/tattoo artist/Rockfest enthusiast.

If she'd just left things as they were none of this would have happened.

Why did she ever think that things could have changed for the better? Was it foolish to hope for something that obviously wasn't within her grasp?

CHAPTER SIXTEEN

A knock sounded at the door, and Hank let his eyes drift open. His stomach growled, and he moaned. The television blared, but he didn't feel like moving. A banging came again, louder. First that stupid crying baby and now this . . . his second interruption of the night.

Can't a man have peace in his own home? Not that it was his home. It was Caprice's . . . but still.

He lifted his head and his jaw dropped open. His mouth was dry and he needed a drink . . . yeah, a drink.

The pounding was louder—echoing off the walls, shaking the house—and he jumped. Maybe it was Caprice and she lost her keys. It wouldn't be the first time.

"Alright. Fine. I'm coming." He tried to rouse himself and then moaned. He pushed himself up from the sofa that smelled like cigarettes and stumbled toward the door, stepping over junk that Caprice had left around. He didn't know why she'd brought a baby here in the first place. He had little brothers and sisters and he knew kids just made a bigger mess.

Hank unlocked the door and let it swing opened slowly. "Why do you have to be so loud?" he moaned.

The door opened fully and he wondered if it was the end of time and the death angel had come for him. A large jfigure stood in the door, and Hank let out a squeal.

Suddenly something grabbed the front of him and he was being jerked upward.

His shirt twisted tight, cutting off his oxygen. Hank dared to open his eyes and was staring into a scruffy mustache, beard, and the beady, dark eyes of . . . Bones!

Bones had pulled him eye level, and he held Hank's face only inches from his own.

"Hello, Hank." Bone's breath reeked of cigarettes and beef jerky.

"Ahhh!" Hank let out a shriek of terror. He was dead. It wasn't the death angel, but close . . . he'd never been on Bone's good side.

Hank pushed up on his toes, trying to get some balance and then stared into eyes of pure rage.

***

Bones took pleasure in tightening his grip on Hank's sweaty shirt, cutting off some of his oxygen. He didn't know what Caprice saw in this kid. She had a good soul, that was for certain, but she didn't like to be alone. Yet being alone had to fare better than living with a rat like Hank, didn't it?

Hank's breaths came short and quick, and he wiggled in Bone's hands like an ugly catfish on the end of a hook.

"Bones." Hank managed to squeeze words out of his clenched teeth. His eyes were gray, the color of sludge, rimmed with red.

He smelled of sweat and beer. Bones thought Caprice deserved better than this no-good, ungrateful jerk . . . not that she was on Bone's good side anymore either.

The color drained from Hank's face. Bones used to like that—like that people were afraid of him. It meant he could protect himself . . . and those he loved, but not this time. He'd failed Bridget. Deep down he knew it. Now it was up to him to get things right. And if he had to use his ferocity to do that, he would.

"Bones!" Hank went limp in his grasp, knowing it was useless to fight.

"Hank, where's the baby?" His words came out in a growl.

"Bones . . . I . . . I don't know."

Bones pulled him closer. "Don't lie to me."

Hank quivered in his grasp. "I'm not lying—"

Bones shook him, hoping to shake some sense into this worthless ingrate. Hank winced, and his head bobbed like one of that little dog bobbleheads that his Aunt Peggy had on her dashboard. Hank's teeth clattered. His arms flopped at his sides. But Bones didn't let up.

"Do you know what's going to happen to you?" Bones sneered. "Where did she say she was goin'?"

"I . . . um . . ."

Bones could read it in Hank's eyes. There was more that he knew . . . something he didn't want to say.

Hank swallowed hard, and Bones could feel Hank's Adam's apple scratching against his knuckles as Hank's swallowed down his fear. Hank's eyes widened.

"I think her exact words were, 'I need a drink,'" Hank finally squeaked out.

"A drink?" Bone's pulled him even closer so that their noses nearly touched. "You let Caprice, six month's sober, go drinkin' . . . with a baby?"

Phoenix's cute face flashed in Bone's mind. That little kid had trusted him. He hadn't even let out a peep as Bones had handed him over to Caprice. Pain jabbed in his heart and it hurt worse than the last time he'd wrecked his Harley and scraped up his arm. Hurt far more than that.

Hank nodded. Terrified. Bones could tell that he knew what was coming next . . . and Hank winced. "Yes." He lifted his eyebrows.

"Hank, you deserve this." The anger—at both Hank and himself—pulsed through him as Bone's jerked his head forward. Their heads connected in a head butt, and a loud cracking sound split the air. At the same time, Bone pushed back Hank from his grasp, and he tumbled back, falling behind him. Even seeing Hank on the floor did nothing to ease the pounding anger flowing through him.

A voice broke through, coming from the taxi cab behind him. "That's what I would have done!" the cabbie called out.

Bones turned back to all the women. He strode down the front porch stairs. Regret punctuated each step down the sidewalk. The cabbie stood there, too, as eyes as wide as theirs.

Bones cleared his throat. He spread his arms wide. "I'm sorry to be the one to tell you this, but it seems your baby is the drinking buddy of a relapsed alcoholic."

"Oh, no." A sob escaped Bridget's lips. He could see the strength that she'd been working so hard to maintain, drain from her. He reached a hand forward, she's sure she was going to crumble onto the floor.

Way to go, Bones . . . way to go.

He moved to his bike, ready to take action. Bones had to do something—anything—to fix this. Even if that meant hitting every bar in town in search of Caprice. In search of Phoenix.

***

Bridget didn't want to believe Bone's words.

A drinking buddy? Caprice's drinking buddy?

That's when it happened. Her legs refused to hold her up any longer. She'd worked so hard to be strong. She'd tried to keep herself on two feet . . . but it was no longer possible.

Her body shifted, and Bridget thought for sure she was going down. That's when she felt hands on her arms, holding her up. She glanced over her shoulder to see Sondra standing there.

Bridget sucked in her breath, surprised. Yet as she thought about it, Sondra had been the one who'd taken them down that alley. She'd led the charge first, fighting for justice.

Ally had invited Bridget to church before, but she'd made a thousand excuses. And after a while Bridget had just denied her outright. She thought the church ladies would look down on her—reject her and Phoenix. The pastor's wife, especially. Now Sondra was the one who was standing strong beside her, holding her up.

Sondra's breath was warm on her cheek. "Just breathe. Just breathe."

Bones motioned them toward the taxi cab. "We don't have much time. Let's go."

And that's when she knew, really knew that she wasn't in this alone. She saw the determined looks on everyone's faces. They weren't going to give up . . . let it go . . . until Phoenix was safe in her arms.

Bridget straightened and moved to the taxi. "Let's go, com'on!"

"We'll start on the East side," Bones called to them, moving to his motorcycle. "I know every bar in town."

***

Mary sat rocking in the chair by the front window. She'd looked out the same windows for the last forty years, and until lately she had no interest in living anywhere else. But in the last few months . . . sometimes she wondered if it was still safe here. She glanced at her husband Ronald. He lifted the edge of the curtain, peering out, and from the way his forehead folded in worry and his lips curved downward, she knew he was wondering the same thing.

Ronald had been watching that house across the street all night. Since that young woman had moved in, there had been all types of unsavory characters coming and going. Tonight was no exception. No, scratch that. Tonight seemed to be even worse than normal.

This was the second time the taxi had shown up. A taxi full of women, pounding on the door and asking to be let in. Even though she couldn't see too well in the dimness and in the distance, she wondered if they were ladies of the night looking for someone.

And then when they'd arrived a second time, the large biker on the motorcycle had been with them. Then she knew the people across the street were surely up to no good.

"What's all the ruckus over there anyway?" Ronald murmured, letting the curtain drop.

Mary let out a long sigh. "Honey, you know there is no telling. Lord have mercy, those people across the street." She continued rocking and then looked down at the baby in her lap. He was an adorable little thing with dark hair and eyes. He was as happy as he could be in her arms. "Your mama be here in a little bit, baby, I'm sure."

That young woman across the street hadn't said much when she'd come to the door. The baby had been crying, and the woman had seemed stressed. "Can you just watch him for a little bit," she'd asked. "His mama will be here later to get him."

Mary didn't know what "later" had meant, but she'd been pleased to see a very organized diaper bag with step-by-step instructions on what he liked, when he needed to eat, and even his favorite songs to calm him. Mary didn't know why his mama had trusted someone like Caprice to watch her son, but she trusted that this boy was loved very much and sooner or later someone would come.

Outside the engine of the motorcycle started with a roar. It was loud . . . so loud driving off, followed by the taxi.

But inside the baby snuggled to her chest. She hummed along the tune to "If You're Happy and You Know It," and watched as he sucked his fingers.

How long had Mary been praying for those young folks—ever since the new renters moved in six months ago? That young woman was hard at first. So much pain carried around on her small frame. So much worry on her face. Mary had worked to build up trust over time, and this was proof that her work—her prayers—had paid off.

Mary snuggled the baby boy closer. The Lord did seem to work in mysterious ways.

***

Sean meandered through the hallway of the hospital, holding Beck in one arm and trying to open the swinging door with the other arm that was in a sling.

They sent him to the emergency room, although he'd assure them it wasn't an emergency. He pushed against the door and the room blurred around him because of the pain his movement caused . . . but only for a second. He was fine . . . almost as good as new. He looked around and realized that every chair was filled. No problem, he could stand. Beck wasn't that heavy. And surely this wouldn't take that long, would it? Maybe he'd even be able to get home and have time to clean up before Allyson got there.

He stumbled in, and made his way to a line at the front desk.

It's then Sean heard a familiar voice behind him, and the shuffling of footsteps.

"Sean? What's going on?"

Sean snapped around. He saw his pastor there. Concern reflected in Ray's gaze.

"Ray? What are you doing here?" Sean took a step toward him.

"Ah, just visiting a church member." Ray reached for Beck, and Beck went to him.

Ray's eyebrow's furrowed. "You heard from the girls? I can't get a hold of Sondra." Overhead a doctor was being paged, but Sean tried to ignore it, focusing on Ray's words.

"Really? Ally too. Weird." Sean remembered that he'd told Ally to unplug. At first he liked the idea that she could just focus on her friends with no distractions, but he hadn't thought about how worried it would make everyone who tried to get a hold of them.

He opened his mouth to assure Ray that everything was fine, and the buzzing of his phone interrupted his words.

Sean held up a finger. "Hold on." He saw his sister's name on Caller ID. He pressed his cell phone to his ear. "Hello?" He heard a muffling voice. "Bridget?"

"No!" It was his wife's voice. "It's Ally." He didn't know why she was calling on his sister's phone, but that didn't matter. The thing that mattered most was the desperation in her voice.

People were talking around him, and he wished he could tell them to quiet. He waved a hand their direction and then closed his eyes, focusing on her words.

"We're in crazy trouble—" Her words cut in and out, and then there was static.

"I can't hear you. You're breaking up."

"—a Tattoo Parlor. It's on 5th Avenue." She was breathing hard. There was the sound of traffic. Was she riding with Izzy? Had they found the car? Sean didn't have time to ask because Allyson continued talking. "Bones. Bones."

Bones? Was she talking about her dinner . . . was someone choking on a bone? Or maybe Izzy was getting a tattoo of a bone?" He shook his head. Nothing was making sense. Then he realized . . . Bones was the name of someone . . . and his heart skipped a beat.

"Didn't want you to worry," Allyson continued. "—Use a little help. Our cab driver is bleeding everywhere. It's insane."

Cab driver? Maybe they hadn't found the car after all.

"Bleeding?" Sean's voice rose, filling the waiting area. "Someone's bleeding?"

Sean remembered that he was in a public place, and he knew that he shouldn't be shouting, but the last thing he worried about was proper etiquette. His wife was in trouble.

"Look out. Look out!" Allyson's voice rose in volume over the phone.

Ray moved toward him. "Did you say bleeding?"

Then the phone cut out. Just like that the phone was dead.

Sean turned to Ray. "She's in trouble, we got to go!"

Ray nodded and didn't hesitate.

Sean reached for Beck who was perched in Ray's arm, but forgot the pain that movement caused. He forgot his dislocated shoulder. With his reaching, pain shot into his shoulder and through his arm. It was intense, and it caused his stomach to clench up. He thought he'd be sick, but he swallowed it down.

Sean jerked away and staggered around the room. "AH! Darn it. It's. Wow. Searing pain." He reached up and touched his shoulder and then pulled his hand back again.

Ray followed him, still holding Beck. "We're in a hospital," he commented.

Sean sucked in a breath and then released it. He leaned over, his body folding in half. "It's just my shoulder. It's okay." He waved a hand toward Ray, trying to brush away his concern. "I have a plan."

Sean moved to the wall nearest to the registration desk and knelt down. "It's okay." The front desk receptionist eyed him, but he didn't have time to explain.

He sucked in three quick breaths and then gathered up all the courage he could muster. Before he could change his mind, Sean threw his body—his shoulder against the wall. In his mind's eye he pictured Mel Gibson in *Lethal Weapon*. It looked cool in the movie, but the pain that erupted in his shoulder overwhelmed him, nearly causing him to black out.

"Oh!" Ray called out behind him. "That can't be good."

"AH!" Sean cried out, sure that every pair of eyes on the room was focused on them.

He didn't have to explain, but he didn't have a choice but to do it again.

He slammed his shoulder against the wall, harder this time.

"Ahhhh . . . WORSE. Much worse!" he shouted.

The receptionist leaned over the desk, looking down where he knelt on the white tilted floor. "Sir, sir. I think you need to see a doctor for that. You really need to see a doctor."

He reached his hand up and grabbed the top of the receptionist's desk. Amazingly he now found himself at the front of the line—most likely because he'd scared everyone else away—but even if they could get him in this second, he didn't have time to be examined. Allyson was in trouble. He needed to figure out her coded message . . . and then he needed to find her.

The nurse tried to hand him a sign-in form but he shook his head.

"I know I need to see a doctor," Sean was panting now, "but my wife's in trouble. It can wait."

He allowed the room to stop spinning and then he moved toward the wall again. He gave the nurses a thumb's-up sign.

"Third time's a charm. Third time." He slammed into the wall again and then felt movement in his shoulder—the shifting of bone and muscle. That was it! His shoulder was jarred back into place. The pain subsided.

"Hey, it worked!" A smiled filled his face.

"Seriously?" The nurse stared at him with her mouth dropped open.

"It worked?" Ray asked, standing over him.

"Okay." Sean stumbled to his feet. A larger smile filled his face. "Okay. We're good. There it is."

Sean stretched and then he worked the sling off his arm. With a flip of his wrist he swung the sling onto the nurse's desk. He moved his arm in a wave, getting out all the kinks.

Ray patted him on his back. Ray still cradled Beck in the crook of his arm. "Won't you let me drive, okay?"

They rushed outside together. "Ally said something about a tattoo parlor on 5th and some guy named Bones." It was only as he said it altogether like that that it made sense.

All he knew was this wasn't the moms' night out that he'd expected to hear about from Allyson.

He just needed to get to her fast . . . real fast.

CHAPTER SEVENTEEN

Ally fixed her eyes on the biker leading the way. She was thankful that she'd gotten a hold of Sean on Bridget's phone; she didn't know how much he understood with her words cutting in and out like that, though. Would he be able to figure it out? Would help be coming?

Bridget's phone was a cheap model that had been dropped one too many times. To make things worse, the battery was almost dead. Now there was no way to get a hold of Sean if things didn't go as planned.

Bones was decked out in leather, and he wove his chopper in and out of traffic with the cab following.

"Okay, just try to follow him." Allyson sat in the passenger's seat of the taxi now. Bridget had climbed into the back, staying close to Sondra. It's as if she got strength from the older woman.

Allyson understood. She'd turned to Sondra time and time again. As they'd gotten into the cab Allyson had seen Sondra stop, close her eyes, and send up a silent prayer. Her lips had hardly moved, and not a sound had emerged, but Allyson knew what she was doing. Sondra was the one who people turned to because she knew Who to turn too. Allyson hadn't realized before tonight how draining it must be for the older woman to be the rock for everyone. Thankfully, Allyson knew that Sondra had a greater Rock—their Lord.

Even now Sondra was in the backseat, trying to comfort Bridget. Bridget was breathing into a brown paper lunch sack, which Izzy just happened to have in her purse.

Allyson said her own quick prayer in her mind, and she then placed a hand on Cabbie's shoulder. His hands were fixed at ten and two on the steering wheel.

"Sorry about this," Allyson mumbled.

Cabbie's eyes were fixed on the road, and he wore the intensity of an Indy 500 driver. "Don't worry. I'm a trained professional."

They swerved from lane to lane, following Bones. The distance between them, and the car in front of them decreased, but instead of slowing down, Cabbie gunned it and wove around the car—and the next—like a stunt driver.

"Learned this during a short stint in Germany!" he called, with an accent heavier than it had been earlier in the night. "The Autobahn is no place for the weak."

Cabbie pushed down on the gas again, and he blazed past a couple of cars. He jerked the wheel again, and Allyson's body was thrown against his. She understood it now—why he'd been so adamant about them buckling up when the first got in.

"We're going to die!" Sondra called from the backseat.

"I'm getting sick." Izzy's voice sounded weak, desperate. "Oh, I'm going to throw up."

Allyson sucked in another breath, and she told herself to keep breathing.

Allyson was about to suggest that the cabbie slow down just a little when she noticed something ahead. Her eyes widened and she blinks twice, wondering if she was imagining things, but no—just a few cars ahead . . .

"Wait! That's . . ." She gasped.

Allyson looked closer and then started banging her hand on the dashboard. A mix of excitement and anger surged through her. Excited that they found it, and angry again that someone stole her van—her minivan—from a very public spot. What a jerk!

"That's my van!" she shouted again, pointing. "That's my van!"

Ahead the gray minivan, covered with bumper stickers, drove down the road lit by streetlamps and stars.

They had to stop them. They had to get those thieves. They had to . . . get their cell phones! And they had to get out of this taxi. She didn't even want to know what the fare was going to add up to.

***

Marco liked Kevin's idea. Instead of heading back to Sean's place, they could drive around for a while. At least in the van the kids were buckled in. That's why he'd decided to take the long way back. Or rather, the long, long way back.

Instead of sitting in the passenger's seat, Kevin was crouched on the floor, between the front two seats, leaning in to mess with the radio. As Marco drove over unknown roads, Kevin tinkered under the dash, holding a bunch of wires, trying to fix the radio.

Elmo's voice blared the same song from the moment that they'd gotten in the car. "L M N O P Q R S . . . ," Elmo sang. Personally, Marco didn't mind it too much. After all, the twins did need to learn their ABCs, but each time Elmo's voice started the alphabet again Kevin started panting harder. If there had been room for Kevin to pace, Marco was sure that he would have done that.

Finally . . . the stereo turned off.

Kevin looked up at Marco. "I did it! I did it! No more noise—"

Marco looked down at the radio and smiled, but nearly as soon as the noise went out, the cries of the kids arose. One of the twins wailed, the second one started screaming, loudly. More shouts arose, until the whole van was filled . . . FILLED . . . with noise!

"Put it back!" Marco's voice rose above them as he wailed at Kevin. "Put it back on right now!"

Yes, Elmo was annoying but the kids, their cries, overwhelmed him. The hair on the back of his neck stood on end. Yes, that was far worse. Thankfully he only had two.

Marco looked to Kevin. Kevin rolled his eyes then disappeared again under the console. Marco sent up a prayer. He wasn't sure if anyone had ever prayed for loud, Elmo music. Maybe this was a first, but as the screams of the kids rose, his fervent prayers did too.

***

Allyson couldn't believe it. Out of all the cars in the parking lot she wondered why the thieves hadn't stolen another car. There had been sports cars and luxury vehicles. There had been cars that probably cost as much as her house. Out of all them, why hers?

Maybe because those other cars probably had alarms. Or maybe tracking devices. Yes, that had to be it. Also, her van had space, and they could fill it with all types of stuff. The thieves probably needed her van to haul other stolen goods. She pictured stolen televisions and stereos piled in the seats where her innocent children usually sat. The idea caused her skin to crawl.

No, sir. Not on her watch. She couldn't allow that to happen!

Allyson reached over and pounded on Cabbie's shoulder. "The van. The van. Get the van!"

She heard squeaks from the back, and maybe Sondra praying under her breath.

"The van! Get the van!" she repeated.

She didn't have to ask him again. Cabbie narrowed his gaze and pushed on the gas. They flew along over a bridge, and the cab bounced and rattled as if it wanted to be launched into outer space.

For a man who wasn't willing to go one mile an hour over the speed limit on his way to the tattoo parlor, Cabbie was fully into the chase now. His hands gripped the steering wheel, and his eyes fixed ahead. With the intensity of a race car driver, he sped up, pressing the gas pedal to the floor board.

The taxi cab moved faster than she thought it could—it should—and Allyson's heart pounded. Adrenaline surged through her. Even more adrenaline than when she saw raw eggs all over the kitchen and living room. She was scared, but excited. She felt as if she was in a roller coaster, by the way her body was being tossed around. She wanted to tell him to slow down, for their safety, but her sense of justice prevailed even more.

With a turn of the steering wheel, Cabbie jerked the taxi cab into the free lane next to him and swerved up alongside Bones.

Bones' motorcycle roared next to them. He glanced over, and Allyson read confusion on his face. Allyson motioned to the van ahead of them.

Ally rolled down the window, then she leaned out, waving to get Bone's attention. "That's my van!" she called to him. "That's my stolen van!"

It was then Bones understood. He nodded and then darted ahead, closing in fast.

A squeal sounded from Bridget, who was pressed in the backseat between Sondra and Izzy. "What about my baby?"

Allyson wanted to reassure Bridget, but her eyes were focused on Bones. Who knew what would happen if they lost sight of the van? Maybe it was being driven to a chop shop this very second. Maybe it was already filled with stolen goods.

Bones sped up, still trying to catch up with the van.

The bridge ended, and they moved into a business area, not too far from her house. The van turned, making a sharp right. The cab followed. The cabbie jerked a turn to the right, as wildly as if he were playing Grand Theft Auto . . . and not driving around four church ladies.

Ally squealed and slid against the cab driver. More cries erupted from the back, and Ally glanced back just in time to see the women behind her sliding into one side of the cab in a heap. Behind their heads she looked out the back window. There!

Instead of following him, almost as in slow motion he jerked on his handlebars, causing his bike to spin out in front of a state trooper.

Genius!

The trooper took the bait. The lights and sirens blared on. Bones roared down the road after them, and the trooper followed in hot pursuit. The siren wailed! Blue and white lights flashed in the night sky. What Allyson would give for Kevin to see them now. For Brandon to see them. His words echoed in her mind. *Triple Kill!*

Now both the state trooper and Bones followed the cab. Allyson's heart pounded and she gripped the dashboard.

"Yes, get him! Let's get him!" she cried out.

Yet her words were drowned out by the moans of the women in the backseat. Moans for a child, moans because someone felt sick. And, if she knew Sondra, moans and prayers for them to make it out of this mess in one piece.

The chase sped up, and the businesses on the side of the road blurred. The siren sounded from behind, and Allyson inwardly urging the cabbie to drive faster. To catch those thieves!

∗∗∗

Marco heard the siren first. Even over the sound of the screaming children, the siren's wail pierced the night air. He looked into the rear view and spotted a taxi, followed by a motorcycle, followed by a state trooper. His eyes widened.

Marco glanced from the commotion behind him to the road ahead. He realized he was drifting into the oncoming lane and jerked back into his own. Kevin, still not buckled up, tossed against him, like a rag doll in the hands of his twins.

"What are you doing?" Kevin cried.

Marco pointed a thumb behind him. "We're being chased by American choppers back there!"

"Go faster! Go faster!" Brandon yelled from the back.

"Go faster! Go faster!" Kevin echoed.

Marco's eyes grew wide. "The cop is following us too!"

The siren continued to blare, and it took all of Marco's self-control not to let go of the steering wheel and cover his ears.

He scanned the road, looking for a place to pull over to let them pass, but the streets were lined with parked cars. If he attempted to slow—to stop—there'd be a pile up behind him for sure.

His heart pounded. The kids screamed. The siren blared and Marco's breaths came quick and short.

"Get out of the way!" Kevin shouted.

"I've been trying to get out of the way but they keep following me!"

Kevin hit Marco's arm. He pointed to the stoplight. "Light red, light red, light red!" His shouts echoed off the interior.

Marco panicked. He pressed his back into his seat and slammed his foot down. Too late, he realized he hit the gas instead of the brakes.

What kind of van is this?

They flew through the red light, as if they were in one of those violent video games that Kevin liked to play. Kevin wasn't so brave in real life. He screamed louder, and from the corner of his eye Marco saw him throw his hands over his head.

Headlights bore down on them from both sides. They made it through, and then the motorcycle followed.

Marco glanced to the road and then back to the rearview mirror just in time to see a yellow cab also fly through the red light. His stomach leapt to his throat seeing a car barely missing the cab. Marco's heart pounded faster, faster. His hands locked to the steering wheel. His flight mechanism kicked in and he pressed on the gas harder. Still, they were unshakable.

Why do they keep following him?!

CHAPTER EIGHTEEN

Breathe, Marco, breathe. He told himself, trying to calm. *I have full confidence in myself and my abilities as a . . . driver.* The words play through his mind.

Then, as if something in a bad dream, the motorcycle blazed past the taxi and pulled up alongside the van. The motorcycle kept pace with them and the huge scary biker reached over and pounded on the door.

Did that just happen? That only happened in movies, didn't it? Not in real life!

"Open up!" The biker's voice roared as loud as his engine. "We need to talk!"

Fear made every inch of Marco's skin feel on fire. This was worse, far worse than Halloween!

Marco released the scream he held within. He always did have an unusual fear of bikers. The scream filled the space.

The kids started screaming next. "Ahh, ahh, ahh, ahh!"

And then a clarity came to him. A feeling that his actions would—could—change everything. This was his moment. This was his time to stand up to his fears. Nothing had gone as planned tonight, and maybe it was for a reason. Maybe he needed to show his boys what a real man looked like!

Marco rolled down the window and reached for something to throw. His hand landed on a sippy cup. A full sippy. A deadly weapon to be certain . . . or at least something to slow down the biker. With his jaw set, Marco held the steering wheel with one hand, and threw the sippy cup at the biker.

"You wanna piece a me?" he yelled. "You wanna piece a me! Say hello to my sippy cup, baby!"

The cup hit the biker. *Nailed him!*

The biker swerved.

Marco reached for another. Then another, from the cup holder on the center console. The biker swerved to miss them, and Marco was sure the bike was going down.

Kevin's scream echoed from his ears, and his own screams joined in. Hitting the gas harder, the van pulled ahead of the biker. And then, like a demon slipping into the night, the biker peeled away.

Marco felt . . . amazing! He couldn't help but smile. He waited, expecting the police car to follow the biker, but instead from the rearview window he spotted the form of a person hanging from the taxi's window waving. The cop pulled alongside the taxi, but instead of pulling it over, it continued around . . . after him!

"Get me off of this crazy train!" Kevin shouted right into Marco's ear.

"Everyone just hold on!" Marco shouted. Then, with every ounce of strength in him, he jerked the van, hard right. The van whipped around the corner, the backend fishtailing.

Behind him the chopper was still nowhere to be seen. And then he heard the sound of the cop car screeching through the intersection.

He'd done it! As he continued on down the road Marco realized he'd done it. He'd evaded them all!

Victory! The word pulsed through his mind. *Finally free!*

***

Allyson's body hung out the side window of the cab. The cold wind blasted her face, and she motioned to the trooper.

She waved her arm, pointing ahead of her. Her hair flew back behind her, and her words seemed to fly back and hit her too. "That's my van! That's my van!" she screamed.

If she ever was going to have a mommy moment, she was going to have it with the van thief. She knew her van. It had never had that much pep before. Whoever was behind the wheel had to be professionally trained. Her breaths came harder and faster. They had to get that van!

The cop motioned for her to get inside the cab, and then he zoomed ahead of them.

Allyson pulled her body into the cab. Ahead, the van screeched around the corner, trying to evade them, and the cop car slammed on his brakes. Smoke rose up from its back tires, yet the cab didn't slow. The cab was headed straight for the back of the police car!

"I don't want to DIE!" she screamed, the words ripped at her throat as they escaped. Sean's face flashed in her mind. Then the kids' faces—Brandon, Bailey, Beck. No, she didn't want to die like this.

She reached over for the steering wheel, trying to get the cabbie to swerve to the sidewalk on their side. He pulled against her, trying to swerve into ongoing traffic.

No!

His grip overpowered hers, and the cab jerked into the oncoming lane.

They slid past the cop car on their left and straight toward an oncoming car. She screamed again, and the screams of her friends filled her ears. They can't die either. What would happen to their kids? All of their kids.

The oncoming car slammed on its brakes and fishtailed, just missing them by inches. The children . . . all she could think about was their children who needed their mothers.

The cab swerved to the left, and cars flew by on their right, one, two, three. Their headlights strobed by like disco lights, and Allyson thought she was going to be sick. Then, seeing more cars ahead, the cab swerved onto the sidewalk.

Tires hit the sidewalk and a loud explosion erupted.

Their cab flew toward a trash pile and hit. Trash flew everywhere, like a piñata being split open. Cans, bottles, milk cartons, cereal boxes flew up and splattered over the top of the car.

Her body flew forward, and Allyson braced herself. From the corner of her eye she saw Cabbie's head jerking forward, and then it hit the steering wheel with a smash.

They were stuck . . . stuck here in this pile of trash.

Cabbie reached forward and turned off the engine.

Then, as if the world around them had just been muted, all the noise around them stopped. There was no roaring of motorcycle, blaring of siren, or screeching of tires.

Allyson looked to the cabbie, who now held his nose. And she was certain she saw more blood.

"That's gonna smart," he mumbled.

Her eyes darted to the women in the backseat, and thankfulness flooded her heart. They were alive, unhurt! Their hair was tousled, and they looked like they were in a waking coma, but no one appeared injured.

Sondra looked to Bridget and then to Izzy. Izzy checked them out too.

Their wide eyes displayed their fear, and Allyson didn't know whether to laugh or cry. They'd found her van. They'd found her van! She just hoped that the trooper was able to catch the thief . . . and make him pay for this night!

CHAPTER NINETEEN

Marco looked back over his shoulder. A huge grin filled his face, and then he felt it fall. He expected to be free of his pursuers. Instead, he spotted the police car once again following him. Gaining fast. Sirens still blaring.

"Why are you still following me? Why are you still following me? Why are you still following me?!" He did the only thing he knew to do and pulled over to the side.

Marco's heartbeat jumped as he watched in the side mirror. Slowly, tentatively the trooper stepped from his car and paused behind his door, as if for protection.

Marco rolled down his window and leaned out. "Good evening, officer."

"Put your hands out the window!"

Marco jumped in his seat, sure the trooper was mistaken. Wasn't it that motorcycle driver—or that cab—who the cop had been after?

Marco stretched both hands out, unable to hide their shaking.

"Now exit the vehicle slowly." The trooper's voice was low, firm through his loud speaker.

The trooper's spotlights were on him, and his lights continued to flash, yet the trooper didn't move from behind the door. Marco could see the man's hand on his gun and he told himself not to faint. This was all a misunderstanding.

Marco climbed from the van. "Did you get that biker back there?" He pointed down the road and moved toward the police officer.

"Stay where you are, sir," his voice was sharp. The officer's flashlight shone on him, and his hand was still on his gun. Surely, the man didn't understand; it was the other guys he was after. Marco knew he had to explain.

Marco took another step forward.

"Stop where you are!"

Marco froze in his steps. He stretched his hands out in front of him, straight out, putting his hands in full view.

"Back up three paces and turn around to face the light!"

Marco turned forward, and then realized that there were more red lights behind him. He turned back around.

"Turn around, toward the light!" the officer shouted.

Marco pointed to the streetlight. "That light?"

"To the other light. Turn and face the light!" The trooper's tone was sharp, direct. "Now get down on your knees now! Put your hands behind your head."

Marco did what he was told. He sunk to the ground. The gravel on the road poked through his jeans, biting at his skin, sinking in.

The trooper approached. His flashlight cast a spotlight around Marco. The cold of the night bit at his skin, but the goose bumps that rose were from fear. Fear!

The trooper cleared his throat. "Sir, is this your vehicle?"

"No sir." Marco didn't understand. What was happening? He glanced over his shoulder.

"Stay right there!" the trooper barked.

"Okay!" Marco turned back around, and put his hands back on his head.

"Have you been drinking?"

"No sir," he answered flabbergasted.

"Is there someone else in this vehicle?"

"Yes!"

"Stay where you are."

Marco didn't move. He heard the door open, and then the screeching of the kids. "Ah! Hi! Hello!"

Marco followed the officer's gaze, into the van. Some of the kids had gotten out of their car seats and were piled on top of Kevin.

"Sir, is this your vehicle?" the trooper asked Kevin.

"No, sir!" Bailey answered for him.

"Thank you, my dear."

"Is this your Daddy?" He pointed the flashlight to Marco.

"No, sir!" Brandon called.

He shined the flashlight onto Kevin. "Is that your daddy?"

"No!" Sean's kids called again, with Bailey being the loudest.

"Who's your daddy?" the officer asked.

"He's in the hospital!" one of the kids answered.

"What's going on here?" the officer asked.

"He's taking us to his house where we don't want to go," Bailey piped up.

"Where you don't want to go." The officer jumped back slightly. "That's very bad. What else should I know?"

"He killed their Mama!" Bailey called out.

"He what?" The officer's voice raised an octave.

Marco knew how bad this sounded. He couldn't just sit there and listen. "I can explain!"

Marco jumped to his feet and turned. "You see, Mama's the name of the bird."

It's then he saw it. The trooper's gun drawn and pointed at him—right toward his heart.

Marco reached his hands toward the man. Why wasn't he listening? Why wasn't he trying to understand?

"Down on your knees now. Face down. Face down!" the trooper's words split the air.

"No, don't shoot!" Marco dropped to his knees. His hands stretched out as if they could shield him. He felt light-headed all of a sudden. Dizzy. "Don't shoot!" he cried again.

The trooper's shouts intensified. "Dispatch, I need backup now!" The trooper called over his radio. "Ten units now."

Marco hit the ground, splaying his arms and legs out as far as he could reach them. The road smelled of asphalt and gasoline, and he thought he was going to be sick. "I'm down. I'm down. I'm down!"

Even without seeing it, Marco could feel the trooper's gun pointed at the back of his head.

And then a single voice broke through the drama, as clear and controlled as can be. Kevin's voice. "Guess what, kids? We're all going to jail."

"Oh man, I hate jail!" Bailey called out.

"Me too." Marco wept into the asphalt. "Me too . . ."

"We got a felon!" the trooper shouted, and Marco wondered if he'd ever be able to survive the big house.

***

Allyson stood beside the taxi with trash strewn by her feet. This is what her night felt like. Like a crash. Like a dump heap. She still had no way to get a hold of Sean. They still hadn't found Phoenix. Surely things couldn't get worse, right?

On the other side of the cab, Sondra did her best to bandage up the cabbie's nose. After hitting the steering wheel it was bleeding even more, and she wondered if it was possible to add a "pain and suffering" tax to a cab fare. Izzy tried to help Sondra, dabbing Cabbie's face with her baby wipes.

Bridget stood beside her, quivering in her tennis shoes. Allyson wanted to reassure her, but no words came. Every time she'd thought they were close to finding Phoenix they'd come to a dead end. Or in this case, a trash pile.

Then, in the distance, she heard the roaring noise of a motorcycle's engine breaking through the night. She jumped slightly, not with fear, but expectation. Sure enough a few seconds later Bones pulled up, parking his motorcycle beside them.

"What happened?" Allyson called to him. She hoped he had good news. What she needed—really needed—was good news.

Bones glanced over to them. "Sorry for the flight mechanism, ladies. I lose control when I see them flashin' lights." He offered a sheepish smile. "I have a checkered past."

Allyson spread her arms wide and took a step forward, "Okay, what—what about my van?"

"Quite a mess up there." Bones turned and looked over his shoulder. "Got as close as I could. Hauling the criminals off now." He removed his helmet and placed it on the handlebars. "It seems it was stolen by a mentally unstable man with some kids, and some other dude. The first dude was Hispanic . . . I think . . . I'm sorry if that sounded racist."

"Marco!" Izzy's voice split the air. She raced around the cab toward Bones.

She looked from Bones to Allyson.

Allyson was trying to process it all. Could that really have been Marco, driving like a wild man . . . with their kids in the car? Tension tightened her gut.

Allyson looked to Izzy. "Why is Marco driving my van?"

Instead of answering, Izzy's eyes grew wide. "Where are my kids?" Izzy looked from Allyson to Sondra, and back to Ally again. "What if they're in jail?

Bones stretched out a hand toward her, trying to reassure her. "I don't think they can book a baby," Bones said calmly. "I could be wrong, but I don't think they can."

Their British cab driver dipped his head, as if in defeat. And Allyson approached him.

"To the police station?"

He didn't answer for a few seconds, and then he slowly lifted his head, looking at her.

He pointed to the cab. "Get in, ladies. The next stop on our Tour of Destruction is about to embark!"

CHAPTER TWENTY

Ten minutes later the cab pulled up at the police station, and the women jumped out.

A gasp escaped Sondra's lips, and Allyson followed her gaze. There, parked in the parking lot, was Ray's vintage mustang parked under a streetlamp. Allyson chuckled under her breath. Did he really think it would be safe . . . even there?

"She took her daddy's car!" the words exploded from Sondra's lips, talking to no one in particular. "I told Zoe that if she went to that rave that she was going to learn the hard way. Her daddy is going to kill her when he finds out she's in the clink." She threw up her hands. Then she slammed her hands against her legs and leaned back against the door.

Bridget was still inside the car. She was trying to get out, but Sondra was leaning against the door.

"Clink? Really?" Bridget pushed on the door harder. "Can you please move?"

Izzy waited by the front door. "Come on!" Allyson could read the worry on Izzy's face. She had to get her babies out of prison . . . now!

Allyson leaned down to talk to the cabbie. "I think you can just leave now," she told him.

He smiled up at her. "Oh no, darling. I'm totally committed to this. I want to see how it ends."

If that's what you want.

She personally wanted to see how it was all going to turn out too. Not only did they still not have Phoenix, but now she was also worried about her own children. Who had them? Were they safe?

Allyson followed the other women into the police station. They quickly hurried through the metal detector in a single-file line. They rushed up to the front desk officer.

"Are you taking my children?" Izzy asked, rushing forward.

"Do you have my daughter?" Sondra called frantically. Her hair was tousled all over her head and her clothes now looked as if she'd slept in them . . . or as if she'd been in a high-speed chase and crashed in them.

"We need to file a missing person's report," Bridget called out.

Allyson rushed ahead, and then she looked back to see Bones entering. Instead of walking through the metal detector, he turned and walked around the side of it. The security guard didn't seem to notice. She was too distracted by the commotion of the women, all talking at once.

"Do you have my van?" she asked the police. Allyson's voice joined in with the rest.

The young handsome officer eyed them, trying to figure out what had just happened. Trying to make sense of their words.

"Can you tell me which foster care home you took my children too?" Izzy asked.

"She's just going through a phase," Sondra explained.

"I'll find whatever foster home you took them too . . ." Izzy's voice grew louder.

"Wait, wait, wait!" The young officer held up his hands, trying to calm them. "Just hold on. Hold on."

Bridget leaned forward, the mama bear emerging. "What do you mean HOLD ON? I have a MISSING child!"

Ally nudged past her. "Look. What's she's trying to say is—"

Instead of letting Allyson talk, explain everything to the officer, Bridget pushed Ally out of the way. Ally staggered backward, and then caught herself, steadying herself.

"NO, ALLY! Stop. Okay, nothing you've tried to do tonight has helped in any way. So just stop trying to fix things." She waved a hand in Allyson's face.

Bridget's face was beet red. Anger flashed in her eyes. Allyson sucked in a breath, not remembering the last time someone had ever treated her this way. At least she was trying . . .

Emotion filled in her throat. Trying to help.

Before Allyson had a chance to catch her breath from Bridget's words, Sondra leaned forward. Anger flashed in her eyes too, causing Allyson to pull back.

"This is what happens when you take away people's cell phones!" Sondra seethed. Then rolling her eyes she directed her attention back to the front desk officer and started in, trying to find out information about Zoe.

"I want to talk to your boss!" Bridget's voice rose to near shouting as she tried to talk over Sondra and Izzy. "If you're not going to help me then I want to talk to your boss!"

Sondra placed a hand to her forehead. "Where's my daughter? Do you have my daughter?" She turned her back to the others. "I knew this would happen," she mumbled under her breath. "This is God punishing me for the Woodstock Reunion."

"Woodstock Reunion!" Bones called out, pointing. "You were in the caravan. I never forget a face. Sarah? Hmmm." He scrunched up his face. "Sandy?"

Izzy turned to her. Her face registered shock, horror. "Sondra?" Izzy cried out.

"Sondra!" Bone's face broke into a smile, and he seemed pleased with himself. "I love your tattoo."

Tattoo? Allyson scrunched up her face and looked to her pastor's wife. She waited for Sondra to laugh. She waited for Sondra to deny what Bones was saying, but from the look on Sondra's face Allyson saw it was true. True!

Sondra gasped. And then a small cry escaped her lips.

Izzy's jaw dropped, and Allyson could see that she already looked at Sondra differently.

Ally tried to take it all in. Not only had everything else failed tonight, but now Sondra's reputation was ruined. She was called out—found out—by some tattooed biker. This was even worse than the Dance Cam incident and that was bad. Real bad.

Allyson felt like running, escaping. Her stomach ached and it had no relation to her hunger.

They were right. It was all her fault. All of this. If it wasn't for her . . . none of this would have happened. She had wanted her way. She had pushed and pushed . . . and look what it had done to all of them. There was nothing peaceful about this night. She'd drug her best friends into this ordeal only to have Izzy starving to death, and to have Sondra humiliated.

The color drained from Sondra's face. She looked around as if she'd just lost her best friend in the world. As long as Allyson had known Sondra, she'd done her best to always take care of others and now everything she'd worked for had come to this.

The door next to the front desk opened, as an officer led a criminal out.

Seeing her chance to break free from their gazes, Sondra turned to the door that was slowly closing.

"Com'on, ladies." Sondra rushed toward it, opening it farther. Then Sondra hurried inside, as if trying to escape their knowledge of her past. But she hadn't moved fast enough. Allyson had spotted the plea in Sondra's eyes. The one that had said, *Please don't tell anyone.*

"Wait! You can't go back there!" the man at the front desk called. Izzy and Bridget followed Sondra. The officer at the desk picked up the phone, and Allyson knew it would take a lot of backup to wrangle those mama bears out.

Allyson tried to hold back her tears. She'd done it again. She'd tried to do her best but she'd fallen short. She'd ruined everything. She doubted that after tonight they'd want to be her friends anymore.

She forced back the tears and glanced up at Bones. He was the only still one standing by her.

"I—I don't think they want me back there right now, Bones." She turned and leaned against the wall and stared up at the ceiling. She'd tried to do something right, but things had gone so, so wrong.

"All I really want to do right now is call Sean and the kids," she confessed.

Bones pointed. "There's a phone right over there by the metal detector."

Of course he knew that. Allyson glanced up at him, wondering how many times he'd been in this place. Lots, she'd assumed. And she thought about her own Brandon and Beck. Bones had been a little boy once. Had his mama had dreams for him?

She didn't have time to think about that for very long. She hurried to the phone. She wanted to hear Sean's voice. She needed his strength. She needed his help. She needed his optimism.

More than anything, Allyson needed Sean to tell her that things were going to be okay.

✱✱✱

Sondra did the only thing she knew to do. She ran. She ran from their stares, and she ran from the truth as she'd been doing for many years.

Sondra rushed into the back area, where the criminals were held and the officers worked, with Izzy and Bridget trailing behind her.

"Sir, we have a situation up here," he could hear the front desk officer saying into his radio.

Still that didn't stop her steps. She needed to—had to—find Zoe. This was her fault. She'd made the mistakes, and now her daughter was going to be the one who suffered. No, she couldn't let that happen.

"It's a maze back here," Izzy called, weaving through rows of desks.

Finally they found their way back around to where the desk officer was. She had to talk to him face-to-face. She had to get information about Zoe!

Sondra raced up to the officer, noting the terrified look in his expression, as if it were Bones, not her who rushed him.

Maybe he'd overheard about her tattoo. A shiver raced down her spine.

***

Sean leaned over the desk. Around him the walls were plastered with . . . art, he supposed. He looked at the guy with the Afro and the large aviator glasses.

Ray had driven them up and down 5th, and this was the only tattoo parlor. He winced thinking of Allyson being in here without him. Why had she come? Had Izzy wanted a tattoo? It was the only thing he could think of. Or maybe they'd brought Bridget. After all, Ally had been on Bridget's phone. But why had Ray's wife agreed to that? Sean shook his head. Nothing made sense.

"Did anyone come in here tonight that wasn't supposed to be in here?" Sean asked the front desk guy.

"Oh, man, I don't know." The man with the large Afro spoke in a slow, easy tone and the words just rolled off his tongue. "I don't think of asking them those kinds of questions, but I think you're on to something, 'cause I should inquire more of our patrons." He straightened in his chair.

"What about this?" Sean covered his face with his hand, trying not to let his frustration build. "Does the word Bones mean anything to you?"

The man nodded. "It does."

Sean forced a smile, and his eyebrows lifted. "What does it mean?"

Ray leaned forward. "Is it a person?" He tapped on Sean's shoulder, urging him to ask that question.

"Is it a person?"

The man nodded, as if Sean's words were finally filtering in. "It is."

"Is it a manager?" Ray asked, tapping Sean's shoulder, urging him to ask.

Sean stood on his toes so he could lean in a little farther. "Is it a manager here?"

"You are correct. Correct." The desk guy pointed to Ray, as if he'd just answered the Question of the Day on *Jeopardy*. "You're good at this one." Then he waved from Sean to Ray. "Keep him."

"Did you see any women with Bones?" asked Sean.

"I did . . . you guys are good at this!"

Ray's voice rose, and he motioned to the desk guy. "Do you know where they went? Which direction they went?"

"No, but I did see them leave," the man offered.

"Where did they go?" Ray asked. Sean could tell his patience was wearing thin.

"To the right." He pointed to the right with two fingers.

Both men turned to see where he was pointing.

"Out and to the right," the man said.

They turned back to him.

"No destination?" Ray looked puzzled. "They didn't say where they were going?"

"Well, I think the right is east." The man smiled, pleased he'd come up with that on his own.

"Okay." Ray lowered his head, and Sean could see his mind racing, trying to figure out what questions he needed to ask in order to get what he needed.

Sean was also trying to figure where to go from here when his phone chimed, telling him he had a call.

"Hello?"

"Sean?" It was Allyson's voice.

"Hon?" Relief flooded over him. He tilted his head back and closed his eyes. He stumbled forward slightly and placed a hand over his racing heart. Just hearing her voice took away a ton of burdens that he'd been carrying.

"Where are you?" she asked.

He wanted to ask her the same question, but he could hear worry on her voice. Most likely worry about the kids.

"We're fine, we're fine. We're at the tattoo parlor."

"What?" shock registered in her tone.

"Yeah, at the tattoo parlor," he said. It should be obvious why, shouldn't it? Since that's where she told him to go.

***

Sondra hurried toward the officer, and his face registered shock. All she needed was one minute . . . why didn't he just calm down and listen to her—to them? Somewhere in his jail Zoe sat behind bars. The idea of it made Sondra unable to stop pushing forward. Unable to be still.

"Whoa, whoa, whoa." The officer lifted a hand toward them. "Calm down. Just wait a second!" the officer called out to them.

"Do you know where my daughter is?" Sondra pleaded. "She's not a hard criminal."

"Hold on." The officer waved his hands, and then he moved behind his rolling chair, as if using it as a shield.

Izzy lunged forward. "Please NO!" her voice erupted with emotion. She reached a hand toward the officer. "Don't put them back there. Take me! Take me instead! Just arrest me!"

Sondra also reached for him. "Do you know how much it scars a teenager to be in here!"

Then, as if by a miracle Bridget's phone rang, interrupting the commotion. She whipped it out of her pocked to answer it.

Sondra barely paused, and then she started in again, seeking answers. Izzy's voice joined hers.

"Calm down for a second." Then he leaned down and spoke into his radio. "We have a situation here!"

"Quiet! SHUT UP!" Bridget's voice broke through, over-powering theirs. "It's Caprice!"

***

On the other end of the line, Allyson let out a heavy sigh. "It's just been the worst night ever, Sean. I don't know how it could get any worse."

"Alright, hon. Don't move."

A group of officers rushed past Allyson, toward the back rooms of the police station. She pressed the phone tighter to her ear and shuddered thinking of what type of hardened criminals they had back there. They surely had to be really bad to need backup like that.

"Alright, yeah, alright," Sean repeated. "Where are you?"

"Don't freak out. I'm at some police station."

"With the police?!" He nearly shouted into the phone. At his words a group of bearded men, sitting in chairs in the waiting area, raised their hands and then rushed toward the back area of the tattoo parlor. The front desk clerk sat straighter and lifted his hands, too, looking around.

Weird.

Sean listened as Allyson gave him directions to the police station. "Okay, okay we're coming." Then he hung up and hurried to Ray. "We've got to go. We've got to go."

"You found them?" Ray's eyes brightened.

"Yeah, yeah." Sean still had more questions than answers, but at least this was a start.

Ray rushed toward the door. "Let's do this." Sean tucked his cell phone into his back pocket.

Sean moved to follow Ray, and then remembered he was empty-handed. He turned to where one of the tattoo artists was doodling with Beck.

Sean rushed over and swooped him up. He didn't know why Beck seemed to stress Allyson out so much. Tonight he seemed game for anything.

"Uh, thanks very much," Sean told the guy who'd been drawing with Beck.

The guy smiled and waved and Sean hurried to the door.

"Wait, so are the police coming or not?" the front desk clerk called after them as they exited, his arms still raised high in the air.

Sean decided not to answer. He chuckled, wondering how long it would take him to figure out that answer.

Then Sean followed Ray into the night, wondering why they hadn't swung by Ray's house for his vintage Mustang. Maybe they'd do it next time they came down to this part of town . . .

CHAPTER TWENTY-ONE

Bridget pressed her cell phone to her ear, trying to hear Caprice. "Phoenix is WHERE?" Bridget shouted into the phone. Sondra and Izzy were still talking, pleading with the officer, arguing with him . . . making it hard for her to hear.

Caprice started to answer and then . . . nothing. Only silence from the other end. Bridget looked to the phone and then realized it was dead.

"No. No. NO! I HATE YOU!" she shouted into the phone. She shook it and hit it and considered throwing it to the floor, but she didn't have money for another phone. Like it or not, she had to deal with this one.

Rage surged within her. "I'm so angry I could kill somebody!"

Why did this have to happen? Just when she was getting close to an answer . . . Ugh!

She growled under her breath, and then she looked up, focusing on the officer who wore a strange expression on his face. He was holding something. It wasn't a gun, but he was holding it that way. It was a small black device with a handle and trigger. Bridget lowered her hand that held her cell phone to the side.

"Is that a taser gun?"

The desk officer pointed it Bridget's direction. "I will tase you. STAND DOWN!"

Sondra stepped in front of Bridget. Again Bridget felt cared for, protected by this pastor's wife.

"I will tase you, woman!" the officer shouted again.

"How dare you!" Sondra shouted back at him. She spread her arms wide, as if putting up a shield for Bridget.

Bridget sucked in a breath, hoping he wasn't serious. Then she heard footsteps behind her.

"Sir, they just came in here and—" the officer was spouting off to someone behind them. Bridget didn't turn to see who it was. Her eyes were locked on that device.

"My husband is the Pastor of First Ba—"

Before Bridget could understand what was happening, there was a small popping sound. Then Sondra stiffened, standing erect and straight as a plank. Bridget's hands jerked up, and she jumped back, just in time to see Sondra fall straight back to the floor with a thud.

A soft buzzing filled Bridget's ears and she looked to the officer in disbelief. He held the taser, and he looked as shocked as her. Wires protruded out of it, stuck to Sondra's chest.

Sondra lay on the floor still, unmoving.

Bridget gasped. Izzy's eyes were as large as mini-pizzas. She swayed, as if she was going to faint, and with frantic motions the office reached up and turned off the taser.

Everything was silent then. Bridget's blood turned to ice water within her, still not believing this was possible. She looked to Izzy, who wore a shocked expression.

"That was an accident." The wide-eyed officer pointed to Sondra. And behind him, through the front desk glass, Bridget could see Allyson rushing to the front counter, disbelief clear on her face.

Bridget noticed something else on Allyson's face too. Guilt . . . as if she'd been the one who'd pulled the trigger.

***

Sondra leaned against the wall of the cell, not even caring if the grime of the walls got on her suit jacket. After getting tased, she supposed she didn't need to worry about things like that anymore.

On either side of her sat Izzy and Bridget. Both of them had forlorn looks on their faces. Sondra's own face felt as if it had been frozen and hadn't yet thawed. It was numb . . . like how her lips got when she got a filling at the dentist. Only this time it was from forehead to chin.

She pressed on her cheek with her hand.

"I can't feel my face," Sondra mumbled. Or at least that's what she tried to say. It sounded more like, "I fant ell my fawce."

"Is this a nightmare?" Izzy's voice was barely above a whisper.

Sondra turned toward Bridget. "My fawc has no feewling."

Bridget didn't respond. Instead she stared straight ahead, no doubt thinking about—worrying about—her son.

Despair filled the young woman's face. Bridget was slumped down, leaning against the wall. Slowly, slowly Bridget tapped the back of her head against the cinder-block wall.

Sondra's heart raced . . . most likely from being tased. But it also ached for Bridget. She couldn't imagine being in the young woman's shoes. At least Sondra knew that Zoe was in a jail cell somewhere near them. But Bridget . . . she still had no idea where baby Phoenix was.

Sondra reached over and took her hand.

"Bi-get. We ah gonna fine ya ba-be. He is saff. He is in the alm of Gah's hand." Sondra nodded. Even as she spoke the words they spoke to her heart too. It was as if she was preaching to herself. She was in God's hands. Zoe too.

No matter what had happened tonight. No matter how crazy things had gotten, God was watching over them, holding them up. She'd been numb to that, she realized now. For most of the night she'd tried—they'd tried—to handle this night herself, forgotten that God had it all in His hands.

She wished Bridget could see that. Sondra wished she understood that she didn't have to face this alone.

"And you know wat?" Sondra continued. "I wuv you. I wuv you . . . and you know wat. Gah wuvs you."

Bridget glanced over at Sondra, and wrinkled up her nose. She tried to smile, but it came across more like a wince.

"Sondra, you know what?" Bridget's eyes widened. "Why don't you just rest?"

Sondra quieted . . . wanting to say more, wanting to speak truth to Bridget's heart, but she knew this wasn't the time. She believed in the Scripture that said God would give you the right words when you needed them . . . but now she understood that sometimes you needed the right pronunciation and clarity too.

As Sondra watched, Bridget rose and paced, and then she sat again, looking at the two women. "All I heard Caprice say was that Phoenix was fine, but she didn't say where he was . . . my phone died." She released a heavy breath.

Izzy was still staring ahead, as if in a trance. Sondra glanced over to Izzy and offered her a lopsided smile. She told herself not to say anything. Not to offer any encouragement. For Sondra's pride it was better that she just keep quiet for a while.

Not that she had much pride left. Not after tonight.

***

Allyson stood at the front counter of the police station. She hadn't thought this night could get any worse, but she was wrong. Forever—as long as she lived—she'd never forget that sight of Sondra going rigid and falling backward like a tree being downed in the forest. Never forget her pastor's wife lying there, unmoving as if she was dead.

Ally took a deep breath. "Please—"

"Ma'am." The desk agent held up his hands. His fingers trembled. He was clearly shaken. "Ma'am, the kids are fine." He pointed one finger, asking her for one minute—one minute of her time.

"Just wait," he said in a near whisper. He backed away from the window with tentative steps.

Allyson turned back from the window. She stared into the nearly empty waiting room and let out a long, heavy sigh.

"Tonight played out differently in my mind," she whispered. But there was no one to hear her. No one by her side.

The only person who she knew sitting in the waiting area was Bones. He sat reclined back on a metal row of chairs with his arms stretched out over the backs of those closest to him, and his feet kicked up on the tile wall.

The lights of the waiting room dimmed, and she wondered how late it was. Way past her children's bedtime, she was sure. Allyson was certain they were worried. Terrified. Were they crying for her right now?

***

Kevin leaned back in the chair, his feet kicked up on the questioning table. He looked to Marco. Marco looked stressed. Marco leaned against the table, obviously wondering what had gone so terribly wrong. It was the same look that Marco always had when Kevin saw him.

A box of donuts sat before them—a gift from the officers for the kids. Sugar. Just what they needed. At least Krispy Kremes didn't have any red food dye. He'd heard that was really bad on kids.

"I'm calling my lawyer," Kevin mumbled to the officer who waited with them.

"Have a donut." Bailey stretched a half-eaten one out to him.

Kevin leaned forward and took a bite.

He couldn't wait to see Allyson's face. He couldn't wait until Sean explained what had happened tonight. Beck getting stuck. The bird—the dead bird. The car chase.

The kids had quite an adventure, that was certain. They'd probably be scarred for life.

Kevin let a smile lift his lips. The best part was, he had nothing to do with it. He hadn't lost Beck. He hadn't killed the bird. He hadn't even been driving the van.

He'd even fixed the radio.

Yes, as much as Allyson would hate it, he was the hero tonight.

And that just made everything a whole lot better.

Kevin took another bite of the donut that Bailey held out and grinned even wider.

Being a real hero was better than a triple kill.

***

An officer slowly approached the see-through door of their jail cell, and Sondra perked up. They'd been sitting motionless for the last ten minutes, and Sondra felt as if all the energy had been sapped from her. It most likely had.

Now there was hope.

The officer stood before the glass-fronted door. "You ladies, front and center."

Without a sound they rose and walked to the door.

"Hello ladies. I'm Sergeant Murphy. We've been filling out a lot of paperwork trying to figure out this mess. But for now . . . stay calm. Can you do that for me?"

Sondra looked to the other two women. Both Izzy and Bridget looked to her. She'd seen that look a hundred times, no make that a thousand. They needed her to be the strong one. To be the example.

"I'm—I'm calm." The sergeant breathed in a slow breath. He clutched a powered donut in his hand, as if clinging to a lifeline. "I feel very calm. Can we all stay calm?"

Sondra nodded and the other two followed suit.

"Good then." He looked to Sondra and then took a bite from his donut. "You have a visitor."

He took one step back, and motioned to someone with one finger. Within a second a blur moved forward. The blur was Zoe, rushing into the place where he'd just stood.

Zoe pressed her hands, her face, to the glass. "Mom!" she cried out.

Zoe's warm breath fogged on the glass of the jail cell door. It reminded Sondra of when Zoe was five and she used to fog up the windows in the back seat of the car of cold winter days and then draw on it. Where had time gone? Where did that little girl go?

Sondra rushed forward. She placed her hands on the glass so her hands matched up with her daughters. "Zoe! Why are you in jail?"

Zoe's head jerked back slightly and she shook her head. Her eyes widened even more. "I'm not in jail. You are!"

Sondra's mouth dropped open, and she realized Zoe was right. Zoe was on the outside of the jail cell, and she was on the inside . . . how had this happened?

"I've been in the back filling out a missing person's report," Zoe said. "But you're alive. I'm so glad you're alive!" Tears came to her eyes. "I . . . I called the restaurant and they said your car had been stolen. And I called dad—he's with Sean—and he said you were in trouble and . . . I got so freaked out that I drove over here in his car, which was . . . AWESOME." Zoe's face transfixed to one of pure pleasure, and then realizing her mistake it turned sorrowful again. "I'm so sorry."

"So you . . . didn't go out with Steve?" Sondra's words were clearer, and her mind was too. It was starting to make sense now. She'd been worried—freaked out—about Zoe for no reason.

"What? Him? No! Ew." Zoe's face scrunched up as if she'd just stepped in dog poop. "He's a total player. You were right. I looked on Facebook. I'm his #3."

"Ahh." Sondra released a happy, contented breath. "Ahh, Zoe."

"Go ahead and say it." The emotion came back to her daughter's face, only this time it was a mix of worry and resolve. "You were right, I know. I'm a pastor's daughter. I should be perfect."

"No, Zoe." The words shot from Sondra's lips. "That's not it at all. I love you, and I am proud of you." Warmth filled her chest as she said those words, and Sondra realized how very true they were.

Why had she been so hard on her daughter? Why had she worked so hard to tame her and control her? Teenage Zoe was not teenage Sondra. Zoe loved God. Zoe had standards. Yes, she needed advice, but as Sondra was discovering, Zoe knew how to discover truth—the truth about people and God's truth—on her own. And isn't that what any mother wanted for a daughter? Someone who could stand on her own two feet and who could make a wise choice when push came to shove, not because someone directed her, but because of the wisdom she'd stored up deep inside?

"I just . . . don't want you to go through the pain of making the same mistakes . . . that I did," Sondra confessed. "I was wild, Zoe." Her tone grew serious. "I was a wild child, and there's something you should know about me."

Sondra placed her hands behind her back, and tugged at her white blouse, pulling it out from her skirt. Then she turned with her back to her daughter. "I have a tattoo."

Emotion caught in her throat like a T-bone steak, and she couldn't swallow it away. She lifted up her blouse a little higher, making sure that Zoe could get a full view.

Sondra pinched her lips together. She blinked her eyes slowly, trying to hold back her tears. Sondra held her breath, waiting for Zoe's response.

She couldn't see the horror on her daughter's face, but she could imagine it. She saw Izzy's reaction though. Her eyes were wide, so wide they nearly filled her large glasses. And Izzy's mouth was open so big that Bones could drive into it and park his chopper inside. Even Bridget seemed surprised, and she turned and looked at Izzy.

Sondra wasn't surprised by their reaction. They'd seen the worst of her tonight, and she didn't know if they'd ever look at her the same. But in a strange way it was also freeing. Burdens were heavy and hard to carry around. Her heart had been carrying this one around for a very long time, and just knowing that this was no longer a secret made her feel lighter, as if it was only her shoes that held her to the ground.

Finally Zoe spoke. "Is—is that a . . . face?" Her voice seemed both shocked and horrified.

"It's Donny Osmond," Sondra blurted out, and then she held back a sniffle. "Mad crush. I was gonna have it removed but . . ." She shrugged. "It's kinda starting to look like your dad."

"Ick . . ." Zoe spat the word. "I'm never getting a tattoo!"

"Thank You, Jesus," Sondra muttered to herself. She lifted her eyes heavenward and then added, "Thank you, Donny."

Sondra turned around and looked at her daughter, realizing her daughter knew her secret too, and still loved her. Sharing her past hadn't pulled them apart, rather it had brought them together. Sondra vowed then that she'd stop all her hiding. She'd stopping keeping everyone at bay with fears they wouldn't like who she really was, or they judge her.

And she'd start right away . . . well, right after she got out of this jail cell.

CHAPTER TWENTY-TWO

Allyson stared up at the ceiling of the police station waiting room, wondering what to do now. But the more she thought about it, the more she realized there was nothing she could do. Bridget was right. Sondra was right. She'd done too much already. There was no way to fix this—to redeem it. So with slumped shoulders she headed over toward Bones.

Allyson slowly sank down into the metal chair beside him. She set her small purse next to her in the empty seat.

"All my friends are in jail, Bones."

"I know how that feels," he said.

Allyson fixed her eyes on the wall straight in front of her. "I'm a failure. I have failed again. It's all I do."

Bones said nothing. He gave no answer. Instead, he just half-turned to listen and to take it all in.

"I had a plan." She splayed her fingers for emphasis and pressed her lips together. "I was going to help myself, and help my friends unplug and have fun," Allyson confessed. "And then Bridget . . . *happened*, and I thought I could fix that too."

A disheartened laugh split from her lips. "Instead . . . I can't."

She held her words in, trying to find the right ones. She turned away from him, hoping he didn't notice the tears pooling in her eyes. "I can't get in front of it. No matter how much I try." She sucked in a long breath and then released it. "No matter how much I give, I just . . . I'm not enough."

Finally Bones turned to her. She expected a lecture, or a really good pep talk, but instead only two words slipped out.

"For who?"

"What?" she asked.

"Not enough for who?"

"I mean, Sean. My kids." Her eyelids fluttered. "My mother. God. Everybody . . . I don't know."

"You?" Bones's voice was gentle.

She finally turned to him, fixing her eyes on his.

"You're not enough for *you*?"

She understood and nodded, letting his words sink in. Yes, that was exactly right. All her life she thought she knew what type of wife she'd be, what type of mom she'd be, but she'd fallen so painfully short. A heaviness overwhelmed her, and she felt the size of an ant. Her expectations were like big shoes stomping around her, squishing her again and again and again.

Bones sucked in a deep breath, and then he released it slowly. He laced his fingers together and then set them on his lap. "I was raised in church," he finally said.

Allyson raised her eyebrows and then lowered them, trying not to be surprised.

"This might come as a surprise, but I've since . . . drifted from the faith." He made a swooshing motion with his hand, as if being washed away by a wave.

"Ah . . ." She nodded, again looking at him, fixing her eyes on his. "Shocker."

He tilted his head back slightly, as if looking for the right words. Or maybe trying to be brave enough to speak them.

"My mama worked three jobs. Never met my daddy. I had to get up early and walk to school but I'd wait up for her coming home from the diner. I'd wait up every night."

Memories flickered in his eyes, and from what Allyson could tell they were sweet ones.

"'Cause she'd come home and she'd put me to bed and tell me something. She'd tell me the same thing every night. 'He loves you, Charles. No matter who you are, what you do, how far you run. Jesus will always be lovin' you with His arms open wide. Just for bein' you.' Then I'd smile and go off to sleep."

Tears came then, and she couldn't stop them. Allyson thought of her own sweet boys. She didn't work three jobs, and she was with them all day, but did she take enough time to tell them that? Did she remind them about Jesus' love? Or did she spend so much time on all the good things that she did for them that she forgot to point out all the best things?

Bones sucked in a deep breath and she turned to him. He was blurry through her tears. His face looked softer too. Talking about his mama he'd lost his hard edge.

"You know, I saw something on Pinterest the other day," Bones said.

Had she heard him right? Ally's eyes grew wide.

"It was an eagle just caring for its young."

Her lower lip quivered, and she knew where he was going with this. Or at least she thought she did, because that same image had drawn her—drawn Sondra—too.

"It's a beautiful thing to watch one of God's creations just doing what it was made to do," Bones continued, waving his hand. "Just being an eagle, and that's enough."

He turned to her. "Ya'll spend so much time beating yourselves up, it must be exhausting."

Her hand covered her mouth, and she tried to hold in her emotion.

"Lemme tell you something, girl. I doubt the Good Lord made a mistake giving your kiddos the mama He did. So just be . . . you. He'll take care of the rest."

If Allyson hadn't seen those words coming out of Bones's mouth she wouldn't have believed them. She'd expect something like that from Pastor Ray, but hearing it from Bones tugged at her heart even more. He was an unlikely prophet, sent to speak to her at an unlikely time. Only God could do something like that.

Allyson wiped away a tear, sniffling as she did. "That was really. . . profound, Bones."

"What? What'd I say? What did I say? Was it good?" He straightened in his seat.

A giggle erupted then, breaking free the dam of emotion welling up in her. She laughed and then wiped away a tear.

"Pinterest? Really?"

Bones laughed along with her. "Yeah, I don't go on Pinterest much anymore." He sighed and shook his head. "Everybody's tats are better than mine."

She laughed harder and doing so caused a soothing balm to flow over her soul.

It wasn't just Bone's humor that made the laughter come. There was something else inside. A splash of joy.

Were they true, Bone's words? Was she enough? Had God made her enough just as she was? Was she enough just in being who she was . . . no matter how well she performed?

Allyson had never expected such wisdom from this old hardened biker, but she'd take it. She could also see something in his eyes too: Hope. It was as if words had stirred a memory, and that memory had stirred a longing for something lost. Something he could regain . . .

Allyson hoped she wasn't reading something into his gaze that wasn't there. Could this moment, this shared wisdom, be as much for Bones as it was for her?

An officer approached, and Allyson quickly wiped her tears away.

"Ma'am, can you come with me?" he asked. And so she did. Allyson rose and walked with a lightness to her step. She knew she'd walk away from this night being different than she'd gone into it . . . and one of the main reasons was unexpected. It was because of Bones, and his willingness to tell her what he saw. To hold up a mirror and let her gaze at her reflection. And as Allyson did, she realized that things—many things—were different than how she'd been looking at them. Mainly her life. Mostly herself.

***

Allyson hurried over to the jail cell door. Izzy stood in the window of the door, looking forlorn. Lost. Like the time when she was ten and her little puppy had run away from home. Izzy's puppy never had come back, but thankfully tonight things had been cleared up.

The officer opened the door. "Another visitor," he said with a stern voice . . . yet even as he said those words Allyson noted a twinkle in his eyes.

Allyson stepped forward into Izzy's view.

Izzy stepped out into the hall. "Ally, get me out of here!"

Allyson nodded. "Yes, I just cleared up the misunderstanding with the van. Just saw Marco and all our kids."

"Your kids too?" Izzy's jaw dropped.

"Yep. Don't ask. Everyone is fine." Allyson handed her a small, clear plastic bag. "And here's your stuff."

Relief flooded Izzy's face. "Where—where are they?"

"They're waiting in an interrogation room," Allyson explained.

Izzy flipped her head around and glared at the officer. "Interrogation room?"

The police captain lifted his hands in a defensive gesture. "Only because the kids wouldn't stop playing with the finger print equipment!"

Allyson put her hand on Izzy's shoulder, regaining her attention, and then she extended her van keys to her. "So can you take my van and watch my kids for a couple of hours?"

"Sure . . . why?" Izzy leaned in closer.

Allyson glanced into the jail cell. She focused on Bridget who is still sitting there. Bridget's head was lowered and her hands were folded. Her forehead is resting on her hands, and she looked as if she'd lost everything. Allyson knew that feeling wouldn't go away until Bridget held little Phoenix in her arms again.

Izzy nodded to Bridget, understanding.

"Follow me," the officer said to Izzy. She obediently followed.

Ally hurried into the cell. She paused. Bridget didn't even look up, and Allyson's heart went out to her.

The young woman had faced so much in her growing-up years. She was the youngest, the baby, and had always tried to act more mature than she was. She'd tried to find love, and she'd found heartbreak instead. She'd tried to do her best to care for her son while going to school and working, and now this . . .

Allyson sat down next to her.

"Hey, Bridg."

Bridget didn't look her in the eye. Instead, she fiddled with her watch. "I bet you think I'm an awful person, right? Worst mother ever." She picked up her plaid shirt and turned in over in her hands.

Mindless movement, Allyson supposed, to get Bridget's mind off the burdens of her heart.

Allyson gritted her teeth. "I know how that feels." Did all mothers feel like this? Feel like they were the only ones who didn't have their act together. She was starting to think so.

"But you have it all figured out, right?" Bridget's tone was solemn.

Allyson pressed her back harder against the concrete wall. She shook her head and blinked her eyes, unable to hold back her humored smile. "Not even one little bit."

She glanced over at Bridget and saw that the tough girl, the rude girl, the bossy girl personas that she'd always tried to portray was gone. One could only wear those masks for so long.

There always came a time—no matter how one tried—when one felt too helpless, too weak to keep them up. Bridget had come to this place. Tears rimmed her eyes, and her lower lip trembled.

"I'm sorry I dragged you into this." Bridget's voice was hardly above a whisper. "I'm sorry I ruined your night." She looked over at Allyson with sadness in her gaze, and Allyson took Bridget's hand. Holding it tightly.

Allyson leaned her face closer to Bridget's, emphasizing her words. "Okay, first of all, you did not ruin anything." She raised her eyebrows and focused deep into Bridget's eyes. Bridget let her. She didn't look away. She soaked up Allyson's words like a sponge. No—more than that—she soaked up Allyson's acceptance like a sponge. "And second, Bridge, this mom thing is crazy hard. But you're doing an amazing job."

Bridget looked a way for the briefest second, and then looked back, daring to believe those words. A smile broke through. "Really?"

"Yes, yes." Allyson nodded for emphasis. "So com'on . . . We got a baby to find. Let's go, girl." She took Bridget's hand and pulled. Allyson rose, and Bridget followed her. Deep down she had optimism that things would turn out right. They didn't know where Phoenix was—not yet—but God did. Allyson trusted that

God would lead them to him, and somehow she and Bridget would grow closer in the process.

Allyson glanced back. A smile crossed Bridget's face as she followed.

"Com'on." Allyson urged again.

They exited the cell, and Ally paused. Sondra sat just outside the jail cell door with Zoe. Both looked wrung out. Zoe's hair hung limp around her face, and Sondra's once perfectly combed short haircut was a mess. It stuck up in back as if she'd just woken up. Or had been tased. Allyson bit her lip. Allyson guessed that Sondra never saw that coming tonight when she'd accepted Allyson's invitation.

There was something more to Sondra and Zoe too. Sondra's arm was around her daughter and there was a closeness to them that Allyson hadn't seen before. Weary, but together.

Allyson rushed forward and placed her hand on Sondra's hand that was on Zoe's shoulder. Zoe glanced up looking exhausted. Whatever fight had been in her earlier was gone.

"Ah, Sondra. Are you okay?" Allyson asked.

"Yeah, I'm fine. Now where are we going?" Sondra attempted to stand, but then plopped down again.

"We're going back to Caprice's, but don't worry. I've got this." Allyson felt energy surging through her. They'd gone through so much together, yet they'd come out of it in one piece. She saw herself differently thanks to Bones. She saw Bridget differently too. Now they just had to finish this.

"Yeah, I'm going to come." Sondra lifted her weary face and the florescent lights of the police station were especially harsh, making wrinkles appear where there hadn't been any before. Or maybe it was the taser that has done that. "I want to move, but I'm a little stress paralyzed," Sondra admitted.

Allyson turned to leave. "I knew that was a thing," she mumbled.

Bridget walked by her side. They both moved with determination. With focus.

Sondra waved them on. "Yeah, I'm right behind you, just give me a few minutes and Ray and I will join you," she mumbled as they left.

"Sounds good, and if you see Sean, please tell him where we have gone," said Allyson.

Allyson rushed to the front waiting area, and she saw that Bones was gone. The warmth of his words was still with her, though, and that's what mattered. They strode through the doors of the police station and Bridget stayed right beside her.

They walked out into the night, and she realized she had no idea what time it was. The stars were high, and the lights outside the police station highlighted one vehicle still parked right out front. Cabbie still waited for them, patiently.

Allyson jogged up to the side of the cab and realized that maybe he wasn't being so patient after all. Cabbie was asleep. He was using his fedora for a pillow as he leaned against the window. Through the open window on the passenger's side Allyson could hear his gentle snore. She leaned inside the open window and pounded on the inside of the door.

Cabbie jumped awake. His head popped up and eyes widened. "Yeah, sorry, referee!" he shouted, and he then realized that whatever he was shouting at was just a dream.

He looked around, startled, and then he fixed his eyes on Allyson. Cabbie smiled at her as if she was an old friend, and after tonight she guessed she was.

"Back to Caprice's, yeah?" she asked.

He nodded, understanding.

Allyson opened the door and settled in the front seat. It was only as she sat that she'd realized she'd forgotten to get her cell phone from the console in her van before Izzy had left. No matter. Her guess was that Caprice should be back by now. Surely someone wouldn't stay out this late with a baby.

CHAPTER TWENTY-THREE

The cab parked outside of Caprice's house, and Allyson and Bridget climbed out of the cab and raced up to the door. Allyson knocked on the wooden door with both of her fists. There was no answer, and they banged harder. Still no answer. They listened close for moment, but there was nothing.

"I know that you're in there! Is Phoenix with you?" Bridget called out.

They moved to look through the windows but the curtains were too thick. They could see light, but nothing else. Surely if Phoenix was in there, and he heard Bridget's voice, he'd cry out for her. Little babies loved their mamas, Allyson knew. Bridget was the one person who cared for him, who loved him most. What she succeeded at or failed at in life was no concern to him, as long as he was loved.

Bridget leaned closer, placing her ear against the window. "Is that a wrestling show?"

"All I hear is anger and rage. I don't know." Allyson hit the thick glass of the window again with her hand, harder.

They continued on for five more minutes, shouting, banging, calling out, but there was nothing. Finally, they both came to the realization that it was no use.

They pressed their backs against the cool door, defeated. Allyson didn't know what to do next. Where to go.

"Got any other ideas?" Allyson asked, looking to Bridget out of the corner of her eye.

"Nope."

It was a long moment of agonizing defeat. Then Allyson tilted her head. It sounded like a vehicle had stopped just beyond her line of view.

"Thanks for the ride!" a voice called. It sounded like Joey's voice but she had to be mistaken.

Then, from the opposite direction of where the voice was, she spotted movement down the street.

"Wait, there's the deadbeat!" Cabbie called out. Then he gunned it, taking off in the taxi.

Allyson tapped on Bridget's shoulder, getting her attention. She pointed to Hank.

"Hey!" Bridget called, and before she could change her mind, Allyson raced his direction.

Hank's eyes grew wide, and he panicked. Fear filled his face as if it was Big Foot that waited for him, not two women. "Lady, I don't know! I told you I *don't* know." Hank tossed up his grocery bag, and then turned and ran. He cried out in squeaks as he darted.

Allyson ran down the steps, down the sidewalk, and across the lawn. Her dress pulled and tugged against her legs with her movement, but she gave it no mind. She carried her small purse like a runner carried a baton.

"Hank, get back here!" Allyson called after him. Feeling her speed—speed she didn't realize she had—Allyson turned back to see if Bridget was following. Bridget had just rounded the corner of the house and was also in pursuit.

"Bridget, come on!"

Allyson turned back around just in time to see that someone stood directly in her path—an older man walking a dog. She flung her arms, and tried to put on the brakes, but her momentum was too strong. She braced herself and plowed into him. Thankfully he stood as firm as a rock. His dog danced around her, and she tried to pull free from the leash, still motioning after Hank, calling to him—as if it would do any good.

"I'm sure your baby's fine!" Hank called back at them as he continued to run.

"I'm so sorry," she murmured to the older man.

Bridget raced up, holding her hand out, pointing something at the older man. "I have pepper spray, and I'm not afraid to use it!" Bridget called out.

The man lifted his hands. "Just calm down."

"No, no, no!" Allyson called out to Bridget.

"I'm so sorry," Allyson muttered to him. Then she spun around to Bridget. "It's okay. It's my fault . . ."

She opened her mouth to explain when another voice called out.

"No, no, no, Bridget!"

From the corner of her eye, Allyson saw someone else approaching—Joey!

"Bridget!" he said again, touching her arm.

Panicked, Bridget whipped around and sprayed the pepper spray at her attacker. Allyson gasped as she saw the spray hit Joey in the face.

He fell to the ground as if knocked off his feet.

"It burns! It burns!" His cries were so loud Allyson was sure they'd wake everyone in the neighborhood.

Bridget hurried over to Joey. He lay on his back, kicking his feet up in the air and then turned, pressing his face into his hands, and resting it on the ground, crying out.

"Wait. Joey?" Bridget cried, realizing what she'd done. "What are you doing here?" Bridget reached down to try to help him up.

Allyson didn't have time to worry about them. She jumped up and down and pointed to Hank. "He's getting away. He's getting away!"

"You're crazy." Hank called over his shoulder, his greasy hair flapping as he ran. "You're crazy!"

And just when Allyson thought there was no hope for catching up with Hank, Cabbie rounded the corner in the taxi, driving like a mad man. The cab fishtailed and headed straight toward Hank, to block him off. The cab started to brake, but not soon enough. Hank smacked into the hood.

As if in slow motion, his body somersaulted up the front of the hood, hitting the windshield. He slammed into the light on top that read Taxi, before sliding down again.

Allyson covered her mouth with her hand. It looked like something from a James Bond film.

Allyson winced, and she expected Hank to get up, but he just lay there as still as a statue. Then there was the slightest movement and moan. Allyson released the breath she'd been holding. The smell of burning rubber from the taxi's tires filled the air.

Cabbie climbed out of the driver's seat of his taxi and looked down at Hank. "That's going to bring tears to his eyes."

"Does he know where Phoenix is?" Allyson called to the cabbie, throwing up her hands.

"Well, he's not exactly conscious," the cabbie answered, wincing. The cabbie rubbed his chin. "If you know what I mean."

"What?" She felt like sinking down to the ground in desperation. Couldn't they get a break at all tonight?

Bridget wasn't concerned about Hank. Her eyes were still shooting flaming arrows at her baby's daddy.

Another moan filled the night, this time from Joey. Allyson looked back at him.

Joey stood, moaning again. He wiped his eyes. "I'm trying to find Phoenix," he explained.

"So, after your big date you decided to come and help me?" Bridget cried out. With an open palm she swatted at Joey's shoulder for emphasis.

Allyson could hear the pain in Bridget's voice. Not only had Joey neglected their son, he was with someone else. No matter how much Joey had hurt Bridget, there was still a bond there. There would always be a bond.

Joey flinched and pulled away. He no longer wore his fedora. His dress shirt sleeves had been rolled up. His tie was loose and awkward. His hair was a tumbled mess, and tears ran down his face. There was nothing cool and suave about him now. Allyson just hoped that part of those tears were because of his missing son, not just the pepper spray. From the desperation in Joey's voice, she guessed that they were.

"After my big date?" Joey shook his head. "What? No. After my interview. I was trying to get a job, man!" He rubbed at his eyes with two balled-up fists.

The anger on Bridget's face softened. She brushed a strand of hair from her face. "You're trying . . . a job?"

Then in the distance, Allyson heard something . . . the roar of motorcycle engines. Many engines.

"What is that?" She ran toward the road.

A mass of headlights moved up the street, casting a warm glow over the dark night. She recognized the person leading the way—Bones. If this had happened just one day ago she would have freaked out, would have run, maybe would have peed her pants. But even though Bones looked as big and tough as a WWF wrestler, she saw him differently now. He was Charles. He was on his own faith journey. Allyson smiled softly thinking that maybe her and Sean, Izzy, and Sondra would be there to help him with that. Bones had helped her see God differently. Maybe she'd been a little scared of him before too. Mostly because of Bones she saw herself differently too.

As the motorcycles neared, the dark street brightened around Allyson and Bridget like the morning sun. The ground began to shake and rumble. Allyson chuckled, and even though they had no idea where Phoenix was, they'd crossed a lot of miles tonight, and the sight of these motorcycle headlights stirred a glimmer of hope inside that they'd finish their journey with Phoenix in Bridget's arms.

The motorcycles pulled up and parked one by one, smelling of oil, exhaust, hot metal, leather, and heat. Following them was a police car with lights strobing and behind that a vintage Mustang with Pastor Ray at the wheel. Allyson placed her hands on her hips. If she hadn't seen this for herself, she never would have believed it.

With hurried movements, Pastor Ray climbed out of the driver's seat, and then Allyson realized who his passenger was. Sondra! She climbed out, slammed the door, and rushed to them.

Sondra's hair was no longer perfectly in place. Her white blouse was no longer tucked in, and from the awkward way she ran Allyson wondered if her limbs were still a little numb from the tasing. Yet Allyson had never seen her friend look so . . . real. Yes, that was the word.

Allyson reached out her hands. Sondra took them in her own. "Ally. I told Ray everything and he made some calls."

Pastor Ray approached Bridget. It was only then that Allyson saw that the young mom's eyes were larger than an Anime character—those Japanese cartoons that man-boy Kevin sometimes watched.

"Don't freak out," Pastor Ray's voice was soothing, despite the production happening around them. "Half of these guys are from the First Baptist Church. The other half are from the bike gang known as the Skulls—" He paused and glanced up at Bones as if still trying to believe this was happening. "And we're all here for the same reason."

Sondra stepped closer to Bridget. "We love you, Bridget. We love your family. We always have," Sondra cooed.

"That's right," Bones said.

It was then that Allyson saw someone else who'd shown up. Sean dismounted the coolest Harley of all. Where he got it from she had no idea, but her heart doubled in her chest and quickened its beat at the sight of him. He pulled off his helmet and approached, his lip curled up in that wonderful crooked smile of his. "Hi, honey."

She wrapped her arms around herself, knowing that things would be better now.

"You okay?"

She swallowed. Yes, she was now. She hoped he saw that in her eyes. And from the reflection in his own she knew he did.

"We got a baby to find!" Bones called out. A cheer rose up, and she recognized two more voices. She turned to the side and noticed Izzy and Marco were there too. They were all here. They'd all come . . . for Bridget. For Phoenix.

Many of the bikers shifted from side to side and their shoulders straightened. They looked ready to take action. They were here for a purpose.

The police captain had brought a few other cops as well, and they approached the small huddle. Looking around and seeing the anxiousness of the bikers, the police captain held up his hands.

"Whoa, whoa, whoa. First things first. We need to establish a twelve block grid."

It was then that the older man stepped forward. He was the one who Allyson had run into earlier. Literally ran into.

His dog hunkered behind him and looked up and down the street, wondering who all these people were on his turf.

Allyson watched as the man took another step forward, scanning the faces of those circled up. "Ya'll here looking for a baby?"

Hearing him, Bridget rushed forward. Her usually primped hair hung tangled around her face. "Yes. My son. He's ten months old."

"And dressed like Bono," Allyson added.

"What?" Bridget turned to her, a puzzled expression on her face.

Allyson circled up her mouth, feigning innocence. "What?"

The man shifted from side to side. He still seemed unsure. "Name Caprice mean anything to you?"

Bridget's eyebrows flattened out. Yes, that name meant a lot to the young mom, but tonight that name meant the key to finding her son.

"That—" She looked to Ally and held her gaze. "That's the person who was supposed to be keeping my baby."

"Yes!" A half-dozen people answered at once, finally catching on to what was happening here.

Hearing that, a big smile crossed the man's face. Then he motioned toward a small, neat-kept house across the street. "Ya'll come with me. I have something to show you."

CHAPTER TWENTY-FOUR

Bridget had finally done it. Seeing Pastor Ray—and all those bikers showing up—she'd done the one thing she'd been holding back on. She'd prayed. She'd told God that if He'd help her find Phoenix that she'd stop being offended with Sean and Ally when they brought up God. And maybe He'd listened. After all, if all these people—especially Pastor Ray and Sondra—cared about her and Phoenix, then maybe God did too.

She followed the man into the small house. The scent of apple pie greeted her, and she wondered what it would be like to live in such a place. It was neat, clean, and she felt a special peace here . . . then she saw the most important thing. Across the room there was a rocking chair. And in the rocking chair was a beautiful, older woman. And on her lap was . . . Phoenix!

Bridget rushed in, feeling Ally right by her side, right where she'd been all night.

Noticing Bridget's smile, her excitement, the older woman cast her a grin. "You must be Momma. He's just woke up." She lifted the handsome baby with sleepy eyes and handed him over.

Bridget took Phoenix from the woman's arms, and the woman released a contented sigh. "It's been so long since I've held a baby. So precious."

Bridget kissed his cheeks, taking in their softness. She pressed her face into his neck, breathing in his baby scent. *He's okay. He's okay!*

The sound of the screen door slamming caught her attention. She looked up to see Joey rushing in. He froze when he spotted Phoenix on her lap. "Oh, that's him!" Relief flooded his face. "Oh thank God." And, as if using every ounce of energy he had, Joey slumped to the floor, grasping the La-Z-Boy for support.

Giving them some time to themselves, Allyson returned outside. She looked across the manicured lawn to the street. Circled up around a map that was spread upon the top of one of the cop cars was Cabbie, the police chief, and Bones. And just outside the door were her friends—Izzy, Zoe, Sondra, waiting for the news. Pressing her mouth into a smile, she nodded to them.

Then she lifted her chin to call to the others. "We found him!"

A cheer rose, and if there was anyone in the neighborhood still asleep they were awake now.

The police captain nodded, and then he lowered his chin and spoke into his radio. "Call off the helicopter."

The mood immediately changed, and the men started booing, disappointed that their adventure was over.

"Guys," Sean called out to them. "We just found a baby!"

The cheers rose again.

"Alright, wrap this puppy up," Bones said. "Let's get out of here."

Allyson turned to Izzy. "Wait, where are my babies?"

Izzy waved a hand, as if that wasn't a worry. "They're at your house. With Kevin. Sean said it was okay."

"With Kevin?" Allyson snapped. She sucked in a deep breath, and it was all she could manage not to have a panic attack. She could see it now. Her nightmare—Kevin sitting in the middle of her barricaded living room. The children circled up around him. He lifted a knife into the air. "This is a knife," he was saying. "Who wants to hold it?" All the hands shot up.

"Sean!" she yelled. He looked up at her, and he no doubt could see what was coming. The "moment" was now focused on him. Sean turned and began running. Allyson sprinted down the porch steps and across the lawn. She couldn't help but smile as she ran.

She was just about to leave when she remembered Cabbie.

Allyson hurried over to him. "Okay, sorry. I know tonight has been—"

"Profound," Cabbie interrupted. "You owe me all kinds of money."

"Yes, I do." Her eyes widened. "I—uh . . ."

Seeing her dilemma, and her need to get home, Pastor Ray stepped forward. "No, no, no . . . you go. I got this."

Allyson didn't wait for him to offer twice. All she could think about was Kevin, home with her children.

Pastor Ray looked to the cabbie. "What are we talking about here?"

"Uh, right, what are we talking about? Let's see. A tire, actually two tires. The police station, and then there and there." He looked up from his notepad. "Nine hundred and eighty-four, fifty."

"Is that dollars?" Pastor Ray gasped.

"No, Chinese yen. Of course it's dollars!"

***

Ten minutes later Allyson's van sped down their road and parked in their driveway.

Before the van even stopped fully, Allyson rushed out of it and raced to the house with Izzy right behind her. Sean and Marco followed slowly, most likely believing the nuclear fallout wouldn't be that bad from a distance.

"I still don't know what the problem is," Izzy said, rushing across Allyson's front porch after her.

"It's because he's a man-boy, Izzy!"

They barged in, and Allyson rushed forward. Then halfway across the living room she halted her steps.

Kevin was sitting on the couch with all of her kids curled up around him . . . asleep.

"Shh . . ." Kevin motioned for them to be quiet.

The place was clean, and Kevin was intently reading a children's book. Allyson winced when she read the title, *Peter Pan.*

Kevin glanced up at her. He cocked an eyebrow. "Allyson."

She leveled her gaze. "Kevin."

"This is such a great book," he said, and she forced back a smile, realizing maybe there were many more things that weren't as they seemed.

***

Last Saturday seemed like a dream. After the big adventure, Allyson had slept well, knowing that all her kids were in their nest—that Sean was at her side—and that Phoenix was at home with Bridget. And she'd slept well every day since.

It was Saturday again. *This* Saturday. The sun filtered in through the curtains, and Sean's side of the bed was empty. She reached her hand over, smoothing the place where he'd slept, and then she rose. Maybe *next* Saturday she'd sleep in, but today . . . today she had a mission on her heart.

Allyson meandered downstairs. Yawning. Still waking up. Her hair was everywhere, and she brushed it out of her face.

When she got to the bottom of the stairs, Allyson paused. The house was clean—scrubbed down clean. And her computer was opened on the dining room table. A cup of coffee was waiting for her. She walked over to it, a smile filling her face. Sean had left a note.

"You DO have something to say." She pulled off the sticky note and smiled, sitting down.

She typed . . .

> When at first you don't succeed . . .

Allyson paused, and then she tucked a strand of her hair behind her ears. The sun streaming through the dining room windows felt warm, but she felt even brighter inside.

> When at first you don't succeed . . . just sit
> down and eat cake! Then try again ;)

She breathed in a breath and then let it out.

So here goes . . .

> My life needs to change for me to be happy.
> That would be FALSE.

She looked to the calendar, and where she circled last Saturday she'd written: "I Survived!!!" Yes, she'd survived. That was an understatement. It was that day she'd learned to *thrive*.

> In truth, my life hasn't changed much at all. *I have.*

Allyson continued typing, and she thought about Brandon's second attempt at breakfast for her. The eggs had been cooked this time, and flaked with white shells. The toast had been the color of the night sky . . . but she'd smiled and accepted it.

"Breakfast in bed, boom!" he'd said with a smile, and she realized she loved him immensely . . . not for what Brandon had done for her. Though his attempt had been noble, it hadn't been successful. Not at all.

Her love, instead, had stemmed from who he was. Her child. And that was enough.

"Wow, thank you." It was the only answer she could muster.

And, as she kept typing, she thought of Bailey. Bailey had painted Allyson's toes and had gotten more on her toes than on her nails. Yet it was their time together—not the perfection of Bailey's skills—that had mattered.

> True. I'm not smiling all the time, but I'm smiling more, at my crazy, stressful, over-the-top kind of beautiful life.
>
> FALSE. I am a failure. Yes, very, very false. I'm not perfect. I make plenty of mistakes, but I'm right where God wants me to be, and He's given me everything I need to be a mom.

Allyson paused her typing, and she looked over at Bailey's marker drawings on the wall. They were just scribbles, but she loved them. She saw them as art . . . just as God saw her. Tears filled her eyes.

> I'm a mess, but I'm a beautiful mess. I'm His masterpiece. And that's enough.

She read over her words she'd written, and a happy sob escaped her lips. Would it be strange to dedicate this post to Bones, her unlikely muse who God brought to her at just the right time? The one person who dared to speak just the right words that she needed to hear?

And to think God would go to all those lengths just to put Bones in her path. And He'd created such an incredible series of "moments" so she'd be willing to listen. Allyson's heart was full just at the thought of it.

***

The next time she went to the bowling alley, Allyson had a few more people in tow. When the man at the counter handed her a pair of saddle shoes, he'd given her three pairs of small ones too.

Ugly bowling shoes. But little ones, for the little ones who belonged to her. And that made them beautiful.

Sean took the boys, wrangling one under each arm, and she moved to help Bailey.

Allyson kneeled down and slid the bowling shoes on Bailey's feet, tying them tight.

When she lifted her head, Bailey grabbed her cheeks. "Mommy!" She cupped Ally's face and smiled. "I love you the most out of everybody!" Bailey squealed.

"And I love you." Allyson leaned forward and kissed Bailey's nose. Then Ally wrinkled up her nose, taking in the sweetness of her.

Then, content with the moment—with the love—Bailey jumped to her feet. "Gotta go bowl!"

"Okay, honey," Allyson said as she watched Bailey scurry away.

Bailey raced out to join her brothers. They pranced around the lane, excited about their shoes. Excited to just be there together.

Allyson stood and approached Sean with a smile, holding out her phone. "Hon, you've got 235 followers!"

Her eyes widened, and she noticed she'd had more comments on her blog lately . . . but 235 followers. She tried to picture that many women in one room, and the thought overwhelmed her. Joy filled her heart.

He sat down at the small table, and she sat across from him.

She took her phone from his hand and looked at the stats. Sure enough the widget read 235.

"I have a blog." Allyson grinned at him. "I am a mommy blogger."

"Yes, you are." Her husband looked at her with adoration in his gaze, and she knew she could never get enough of that.

Sean leaned forward, his gaze fixing on hers. "Wow, Ally, your job—"

"Is hard. I know," she interrupted.

But instead of answering, Sean's gaze narrowed, as if he still held words bottled up inside.

"That's what you were gonna say, right?"

He cocked an eyebrow.

"Or not. Easy maybe? Or unnecessary?" Finally, she leaned forward, giving him her full attention. "Sorry for interrupting." She softly tapped his arm. "What?"

He continued to fix his gaze on her, giving her one of those special looks that happened now and again when spouses truly appreciated each other.

"Important," the word slipped off of Sean's lips. "That's what I was gonna say. Your job is important."

Around him the sound of bowling pins crashed. Music picked up, growing louder. Children's laughter joined in the noise, and the place smelled of French fries, but this was exactly where Allyson wanted to be. There was no place better than being here with him, with them.

She focused on that look in his eyes, and tears filled her own. Allyson told herself to remember that look. On days when she was exhausted and overwhelmed she'd remember this moment.

"And I know it's hard," Sean said, "but look at them."

Allyson glanced over her shoulder, following Sean's gaze. Beck was rolling a ball down the lane. Bailey stood next to him, dancing and twirling. And Brandon cheered on his siblings with a smile that flashed brighter than the disco light above.

She wiped a tear and then turned back to Sean. He had a knowing look on his face. "So worth it . . ." The words slipped from her lips, and emotion filled her throat. She tried to swallow it away, but she realized that was part of it too. These crazy feelings of love.

She turned back to Sean, and he met her gaze. "The hand that rocks the cradle," he said, "is the hand that rules the world."

"Where did you read that?" she asked him, surprised.

Sean shrugged. "On some blog somewhere."

He put his hand on the table, halfway across the space that divided them. She smiled, and placed her hand in his. They lean toward each other and kissed.

The kiss was both charged and sweet, just like her husband. Just like her life.

Then, just when Allyson was sure the moment is perfect another voice broke through.

"Guys," Bridget said. "No, hey, guys, that's gross."

Allyson didn't have to open her eyes and look up to know that Bridget stood over her, wearing a bowling shirt, and carrying a tray of drinks in her hand.

"Ew," Bridget continued. "Don't do that in here. You're really way too old."

Allyson pulled back from Sean's kiss, but just slightly. She allowed him to embrace her with his gaze.

As they sat at the table, cuddled up and watching their kids, Izzy and Marco walked by.

Marco had more confidence than Allyson had seen in a while. He carried a boy on each arm.

"You know." He turned to Izzy, balancing his load. "I totally feel I'm made for this . . . I'm made for two."

"Marco," Izzy's voice squeaked out, just barely louder than the crashing of pins . . . "I'm pregnant."

Sean jumped to his feet and grabbed the boys from Marco's arms. Marco swayed and Allyson was sure he was going to topple, just like one of the bowling pins.

Allyson looked up at Izzy, surprise on her gaze. "Another one?"

Izzy's eyes widened, and she shook her head. "I just went to the doctor today and . . ." She let her voice trail off, and she lifted up her hand, putting down all her fingers but TWO.

"Two?" Laughter spilled from Allyson's lips. Wonderful laughter.

And, just when Allyson thought things couldn't get any better the black lights flashed on and the DJ called out, "Dance Cam!"

Sean put down the twins and stretched out a hand to her. It was a night to celebrate—to dance with family and friends. To celebrate life . . . together!

Their wonderful, multiplying with goodness, life.

EPILOGUE

The house was quiet, too quiet. Allyson was up early again. She hurried downstairs and thought she heard someone in the kitchen. Was it one of the kids—getting into something? Allyson stepped over, and that's when she saw him . . . Sean down on all fours, trying to clean under the refrigerator. He was sweaty. He was gross. He was . . . gorgeous.

She paused at the threshold of the kitchen, placed her hands on the countertop and peered down.

Sensing her gaze, Sean looked up. "Oh, hey." He sat up, cleaning rags in hand.

Allyson's heart started to pound wildly, and she couldn't help but smile. She bit her lower lip and started to feel warm all over. "You are so hot right now . . ." she told him.

"I know it's disgusting. I need to take a shower."

She shook her head and narrowed her gaze on him. "That's not what I'm talking about," she whispered.

"Oh." Sean's mouth curled into a circle, and then his eyes flashed, understanding.

She rushed toward him, and fell into his arms. He wrapped them around her, but just as he bent out to kiss her he let out a moan . . . a moan of pain.

"Oh, no. What did I do? What did I do, honey?" She tried to pull back from where she was laying against him.

"It's just the shoulder. Just the shoulder."

"Sorry."

Sean didn't seem to mind, and he pulled her closer to him, kissing her again. "Don't move."

"Okay," she said, snuggling closer and kissing him again.

"What are you doing?" It was Bailey's voice, interrupting. They looked up, frozen in each other's arms.

There Bailey sat on the kitchen counter, looking down at them.

"Uh, just giving Daddy a little cuddle. A little cuddle." Allyson patted Sean's cheek. Sean leaned down and kissed Allyson's temple.

"Mornin', baby," Allyson said. Then she pulled back from his embrace, and Sean sat straighter, holding himself awkwardly.

"Just give me a minute." He moaned, louder.

"Okay," she said.

He got onto his knees and moved to the kitchen counter. "Don't be scared."

Then, before her eyes, he slammed into the cabinet.

"Ah!" he cried out in pain. Then he pulled back and straightened. "Whoo!" he said. "Then he spread out his arms. "But then it's good."

"It's all good."

DISCUSSION QUESTIONS

1. Allyson is a mom who loves her kids and loves her life, yet she wonders why she's not happy. Why do you think Allyson feels this way? When have you felt this way?

2. Sondra is a pastor's wife who does her best to "hold everything together" at church and home. Why do you think Sondra works so hard to put on a good show? In what ways have you struggled to put on a "good show" for others?

3. Bridget is a young mom who has many challenges as she tries to balance her roles. What are some of Bridget's biggest challenges? What things do young women like Bridget need most?

4. Both Allyson and Sondra find themselves "addicted" to watching the Ustream of a mama eagle caring for her baby. Why do you think they were both drawn to the eagle and her baby? How can you relate?

5. Izzy is faced with an unplanned pregnancy, and her thoughts bounce between denial, worry, and feigned excitement. What stood out to you the most about how Izzy handled the news? Does anything have you anxious or worried in your season of life?

6. Who was your favorite character in the book? What did you like most about this character?

7. Allyson's plans go crashing down when she arrives at the restaurant and discovers she'd made reservations for *next* Saturday, instead of *this* Saturday. Why did Allyson take this so hard? Was there ever a time in your life when your response to a "little inconvenience" highlighted a deeper issue within your heart?

8. While the moms are handling their challenges the dads are having their own adventures with the kids. How did the fathers handle their challenges differently than their wives? What differences do you see in the way you and your spouse handle your children?

9. How do you think *Moms' Night Out* shared the importance of the roles of both parents?

10. Allyson sees Kevin—Sean's best friend—as someone who never grew up. How do you see Kevin? Have you ever judged someone and later discovered he or she was different than you thought?

11. When Bridget and Allyson discover that baby Phoenix is in the care of Bones—at the tattoo parlor—everyone's plans change. What worried you most during their search for baby Phoenix? Why?

12. Bones becomes an unlikely advisor and hero in the book. Out of all the things he told Allyson at the police station what stood out to you the most? How did his words resonate within you?

13. All of us have things we try to hide from others. What type of freedom did Sondra experience after the truth of her tattoo came out? Was there ever a time in your life when a hidden truth, that you dared to share, set you free?

14. Sitting in the jail cell Bridget asked Ally, "You must think I'm a horrible mom, don't you?" How did these two women's worries about "not measuring up" change throughout the book? Do you ever find yourself comparing yourself to other moms? What has God said to you about this?

15. At the end of the book unlikely forces gather to help find baby Phoenix. How do you imagine things playing out within the community after this night? What changes would you like to see happen in your own church and community?

16. Have you seen the movie too? What things did you like about the movie? What things did you like about the book?

17. Who would you like to share this story with? How do you think this story will impact him or her?

FOR MOMENTS OF ENCOURAGEMENT...

and when you need to laugh.